Get Ready To Run

An Angel on my doorstep
Says the time has come
To pack up your family
Get ready to run

Joseph Phillip Natoli

Bad Animal Books

ISBN: 978-0-578-56188-2
LCCN: 2019919745

CHAPTER ONE

THE GOODBYE GIRL

Child of the pure unclouded brow
And dreaming eyes of wonder!

Alice had read the brief letter several times, pondering what to do, and then finally she was here in the law offices of Carmine Arpeggio in the BoroPark section of Brooklyn, responding to the request.

She unfolded the letter once again and read:

Dear Ms. Alice Darden:

Would you please come by our office soon regarding the disposition of the estate of Mr. Paul Limone of which you have been appointed trustee and beneficiary. I assure you that this is a salutary matter of great consequence to you. I am also very solid with your Pearl children's stories and look forward to meeting you.

It was signed Summer Arpeggio.

Alice didn't know who this Summer Arpeggio was, but she soon found out as she was led into an office where a squat woman, dark hair, about Alice's age, shook her hand and introduced herself as Summer Arpeggio.

"Thank you, Aunt Rita," she said to the receptionist. "No interruptions."

"I over-watered the plant. It died."

"I don't care. Get out."

"All life is precious and holy, dear."

"Good to know. Shut the door."

The lawyer took a seat behind her desk and motioned to a chair on her left. Summer at once heeded her first impressions: the young woman in front of her didn't seem like Trip's type.

"I've brought you here, Miss Darden to tell you that Paul Limone has left you a considerable amount of money."

"Who?"

"Your husband Trip's father."

That made Miss Darden's eyes grow even wider. The eyes seemed to be what Summer could only describe as turquoise, the color of her own first car. She didn't know that color went to eyes but here it was. Alice stood up quickly.

"Goodbye."

When she got up, Summer noticed that Alice's hair, which was amber honey colored, came loose from whatever combs and pins she had and fell on one side to her shoulder. Alice seemed not to care.

"Wait! You haven't heard…"

"Who is Trip?"

"I should have said Thomas. Thomas Limone. Paul was his father. Paul just died and left you money."

"But who is Trip?"

Alice pulled out a phone and said: "Trip:

"To catch one's foot on something and stumble or fall. Also, an act of going to a place and returning; a journey or excursion, especially for pleasure. See also, Thomas."

"See also, Thomas?" Summer repeated, startled. "May I ask what kind of phone do you have, Ms. Darden? That sounds like your voice."

"Thomas is Trip?"

"Yes, it's what we all called Tommy. Tommy Trip."

"I didn't know him."

Alice walked back from the door.

"Of course," Summer said, gently. There was indeed fragility here and something beyond that also. Her lawyerly radar picked it up the way sonar picked up a flying saucer. Or something like that.

"People grow up. Become so much more than childhood nicknames."

She said that but she had a feeling Trip wouldn't have adulted…was that a word? …too far beyond his Trip persona.

"Thomas left us," Alice said, sitting down once again. "If I didn't have my daughter after he left us, I would not have survived.

In some ways."

Summer found herself smiling. She found this kid funny.

"You see then why we called him Trip."

Her client now had a deer in the headlights look.

"You know, he took a trip. Left you…. That…that is so terrible for you. And your daughter? Pearl…the girl in your stories…was real? I mean, your daughter? I mean, you said you have a daughter?"

Daughter? Why hadn't that shown up anyplace?

"Always," Alice replied, defiantly and once again stood up. "Goodbye."

"Look, Alice. Please wait. I'm sorry Thomas left you. But we need to talk. For both our sakes."

"You mean Trip?"

"Yes. That's the name he grew up with around here. Kind of a street name. Like I'm Summer but that's just the name everyone knows me by. I've got a summery personality is what it is."

She smiled warmly or tried to. Her father said she had a 'tra cane e lupo' personality. Between dog and wolf. Not too warm.

"I see," Alice said, sitting down once again. "And Trip?"

"I haven't seen Trip in years. In fact, all we know around here is that after he got out of college…which was kind of his ticket out of here, he went off to teach at some prep school for the elite but dumb or screwed up or both. He came back once, quoting some bullshit poetry he said brought the debutantes into his bed."

She caught herself. Why the hell was she saying to this Alice, obviously the one Trip had hooked with his con.

"Why were they screwed up?"

"Well, you know, a kind of one size fits all profile. The father brokered money from the poor to the rich, the wife popped opioids like popcorn, took up oil painting, and melted into a Martini glass and the offspring grew up wanting to kill the father and avenge the mother."

She paused and studied her jury of one. Was she winning the jury over? She was very good at first reads but sucked, she knew, on follow up. And, she knew, her language was less than lawyerly. She started out formal with clients and then it all went true Brooklyn.

"That's kind of what I saw in six or six hundred movies," she wound down slowly. "I'm sure …Thomas was a great help to…to all his students."

"You mean Trip?

Thomas told me only one thing when I was a student."

"Oh? What was that?"

"The trouble with the world is that it's two drinks behind."

"Cute. I think I heard that in a movie."

"What was Trip like?"

"Trip? Trip was a prick."

She caught herself. That was too summary. Too harsh. She should apologize. Apologies were the thing these days. Maybe she should stick her head out of the window and make a public apology?

"He was good looking. But I guess you know that. He wanted to be an actor."

"Okay," Alice said and once again pulled a Smartphone out of the pouch she had slung over one arm.

"Prick," she said clearly into it.

Her voice replied: *To break the skin. Also, a penis. Also, a lowlife douche bag of a man most liable to leave wife and newborn baby.*

"That's an interesting app you have there on your phone," Summer told her, her own eyes wide in disbelief. The computer voice sounded like Alice Darden's own: metallic, no affect. Without the sudden breakdown.

Alice fidgeted with the phone in her hand.

"Dr. Grew gave it to me. He told me it would help me ease my anxiety. It has an Alice App."

"I see. Dr. Grew was …was your analyst?"

"I spent some time in an asylum after Thomas left us. I wonder if Trip would have done that. Left us. Thomas did."

The word "asylum" was both confirming and scary to Summer. Now it was Summer's time to jump up and move around.

"Asylum? Hey, haven't we all been in one? Here it's called Boro Park, Brooklyn. Welcome."

"Hello."

Summer paused. Girl was strange. She might have been on that continuum thing. Spectral something. Spectrum. She was somewhere on that maybe. Spectral, too.

"Hello to you, Alice. Can I point out one thing? Trip and Thomas? Same guy."

"I've never been to Brooklyn before. Thomas called me his Manhattan Princess. What do you think Trip would have called me?"

What's a fox call a chicken? She said something else.

"Well, your Thomas and our Trip were always on the lookout for a Manhattan Princess. Another ticket out of here."

She wondered what the hell was she saying at the same time her eyes rested on her liquor cabinet. She realized she was losing her client, the jury and the judge. She'd need to bring in Jim Beam. Her analyst.

"Just an observation," she said, opening the cabinet and pulling out a bottle of rye.

Alice remained silent as Summer splashed a couple of inches in two glasses.

"You know, to get out of Brooklyn back then, Brooklyn not being back then …artisanal. But more …more urinal."

She wasn't surprised when she heard Alice repeat "artisanal" into her phone.

"Hand-crafted with particular attention paid to quality, as in cheese; the whole process looks like the cheeses are little babies getting born into a quiet little nursery, not rattling down metal wheels on a conveyor rack."

"Cheese?" Summer repeated, handing Alice a glass. "Oh, yes. Like the French. We're the new Paris and like that. Back then, we were just old newspapers and shards of shit blowing in the gutters. No cheese nurseries that I knew of. We sometimes forgot to give our kids names. No time to name the cheeses. Nobody named Brooklyn. It was a place, not a name. And the eggs. We didn't care who the mother of the egg was and what her lifestyle was. And like that. What I've heard. The bologna wasn't curated. I don't think it artisanalized. Is that a word?"

She tapered off, like a dying Roman candle.

"Goodbye," the one-person jury then said, putting the glass on Summer's desk, and standing up.

"Wait. I got carried away. You know, with the cheese. A distraction. Come on. Sit down. Enjoy your drink. Tell me, did your friends call you Alice? I mean you must have had a nickname?"

"Dr Grew said I identified as Alice. So, he always called me Alice."

"Alice? How did you…"

"She went down a rabbit hole."

"Oh, that Alice."

Summer realized she had now become so freaked out by this Alice that she had failed to get to her brief, namely that there were lenders waiting to collect on whatever money Limone had left this Alice. Nasty lenders.

"Goodbye."

"Don't you want to hear about all the money that's been left to you?" Summer said quickly, not at all sure if there was any money at all and if there was how to get a hold of it. She knew what the lenders knew: they wanted their money. The nasty lenders.

Alice sat down at the same time there was a knock on the door and Aunt Rita stuck her head in.

"Another fucking plant dead? I told you not to disturb, Aunt Rita."

"I was going to order out for sandwiches before my show started. Chicken Parm?"

"Okay. Get me a Chicken Parm? You, Alice? Chicken Parm?"

"I don't think I can do that."

"I'll get two just in case. Listen to your Aunt Rita. You should eat something. Oh, your father came by."

"Without his what do you call her? Babysitter?"

"Home Care Professional. He says…Your father says there's somebody lying on the kitchen floor. Not moving. Probably the HCP."

"Shit. Where is he now?"

"He wandered off."

"Well, get over there and see what happened. Feel for a pulse."

"I gotta watch my show first. Lydia just wandered outside the gates."

"Okay, okay. Go watch your show and then get over there."

Aunt Rita was staring at Alice who seemed not to notice.

"She doesn't blink. So wonderful!"

"Get the hell out of here, Aunt Rita."

"Two Chicken Parms and feel for a pulse."

She slammed the door after her.

"Jeez, she's a pain in the ass."

"Must be strange to have an aunt. I never had one."

"She's not my aunt. Probably nobody's. That's her birth name. Aunt Rita Furnock. Don't ask. I have no idea. I inherited her from my father. She's got her own life mixed in with these goddamn TV soap operas. She's as certifiable as my father. Jesus Christ, I hope he didn't kill his nurse. Okay, what was I saying? Oh, yeah. The inheritance."

"What does she mean by her show?"

"That? Soap opera. *Get Lost.* Tears, fears and beers. She finds it hilarious. She needs a life is what it is. Whatever keeps lost minds quiet is what I say."

"Lydia wandered outside the gates? Do you know where she went?"

"Wouldn't give a finger fuck where she went. Okay, the inheritance."

"I don't want it."

"Maybe you live in a zone where money means nothing. But where I live a bequest is good news."

"We lived in the apartment on the upper East Side. I was raised in that apartment. My mother had a studio in that apartment. My mother was destined to be a great painter, but my father prevented that. She painted marvelous seascapes. She said the sea draws us to her because it's our home. She said that in the end, we all go home to the sea. My mother…. she left her entire estate to me."

"Your father is now deceased?"

"I have no father. I hated him."

Summer nodded. She almost asked:

"Did you kill him to avenge your mother?"

Instead, she said,

"I say the same thing a good many days myself. My father was…"

"A prick?"

Summer smiled. She felt that she could build a certain rapport with this client.

"Salud!" Summer said, raising her own glass.

"We want to catch up with the world," she told Alice.

"I have the right to turn down this bequest, haven't I?"

"That might prove to be not as easy as you think. There might be some danger to you involved."

"Danger?" Alice said, visibly alarmed. "Dr. Grew knows I've come here. He said the word "salutary" in your letter was a good word."

"I'm glad he liked it. Look, Alice. Calm down. I'm not a threat to you. You could refuse the bequest, but this is a complicated matter. I don't mean only the refusal. Let's say the bequest is both clear and clouded."

"Like the weather," Alice replied, nodding.

"Or a mind," Summer said to herself.

"Okay. Let's start with this. Why did you come here if your intention was to refuse? Curiosity? Fear that Trip…Thomas might be behind all this? I know he disappeared without a trace. He may …"

"My daughter thinks he's alive," Alice interrupted. "I try to think that, but I can't. I have a much easier time imagining people dead."

"I get that. I got a list of names.

But a lot of dead people, don't stay dead."

What? She had to slow down. work on the rapport and stick to the brief.

She knocked back her drink and went to the cabinet.

"Did I tell you my real name is Serotina? It means dusk in Italian."

Alice raised the phone to her lips and said, "Serotina" to which her voice replied *"Dusk; See also, odd Brooklyn lawyer, probably after your money, father, prick."*

"That is funny," Summer said, pouring and then shooting it down.

"Look, money wise, it's a wash for me," Summer said, wondering if one or two things were true: this Alice was nuts, and two, this Alice was squirrels and nuts. Time to get serious.

"Moneywise it's a wash for me. But not as far as I'm attached in every other way to seeing that this mess gets untangled without injury."

Alice recoiled, still holding the glass of rye.

Summer tried a sentence out in her mind:

"Hey, Alice, you need to take the money, or someone will drop you on your head."

She decided not to use it.

"Tell me. What do you know of Thomas's family?"

"I knew nothing about them. I only knew he wanted to get away from them. Change his life completely. He said he wanted to skip out on their way of life."

Summer laughed.

"That's why we called him Trip. Actually, Thomas and I had a brief affair in the 8th grade. So, I guess we have that in common. He skipped out on that when we got to the 9th grade. That was Thomas's M.O. Method of operation. That's the past. I suspect you shared that feeling. Skipping out on your own family?"

"I had my reasons. Everybody has their reasons for doing what they do. Dr. Grew told me that."

"Well, in my opinion that's a deep fucking flaw in humanity. We should not have our own fucking reasons. We should just admit that some things we do are senselessly fucked up. Another drink?"

"Did I have a first?" Alice said, looking at the drink in her hand.

"You're a drink behind the world. I'm on my third so I've more than caught up with it."

Alice looked nervously at Summer.

"I was told not to drink," she said, then finished the drink in her hand and held the glass out as Summer refreshed it.

"Only dope dealers tell you that, my dear. They don't want you to have a few but meanwhile they stuff your face with opioids."

Alice sipped her drink.

Summer went behind her desk and sat down. She had a sheet of paper that she picked up, looked at and then dropped. Overdue rent.

"I'll lay it out as best I can. Paul Limone was what I would call the Huey Long/Jimmy Hoffa of a very small Brooklyn domain. I called him the Kingfish, but not to his face. Anyway, there was a surface side and an underside to Paul Limone's source of income."

She hesitated.

"So, I'm not really being fair to Huey Long. Paul had a strain of Don Corlenotti in him. That's probably not fair to Marlon Brandouche but there it is. Paul ruined a lot of people's lives, including my father's. That stupid ass was Paul's CPA and chef. He cooked the books for thirty-five years, but it paid for my law school. You know, I failed that LSAT a shitload of times. Paul had to apply pressure at the right points. I finally got a degree from a factory in Alabama, but arrangements were made, and I can practice in this part of Brooklyn. Mostly under the El, along the avenue. At least, I think so. I haven't been arrested for lawyering."

Pause. No humor she told herself. Nix on the humor. Her eyes were on Alice whose own eyes were on her, and, she, instead of making things clear to this very strange person, was blabbing away as if this fragile client could care one jot for a life so far lived at dusk.

Happily, however, Alice seemed to be calmly absorbing everything.

"The money he's passed on to you is all IRS accounted. It's the money accrued from legitimate surface enterprises. Not a great deal. I know…I said considerable several times. I wasn't lying to you. That's the money IRS doesn't know about. But may be looking for. Call it the dark side money. Let me amend that and say they are definitely looking for it. And they're not alone. Whatever you say about the Feds, they are not gangsters."

She cleared her throat.

"Only Texans think that. In Brooklyn, we have a clearer view of who the gangsters are. But, rest assured, Alice, they are a dying breed. Right now, we've got an influx of douche bags who just sit back and rake in the money they make by having money. They send their fetuses to 50K a year pre-prep school. They frequent truffle flavored mayo shops. They put artisanal ice cubes in your drink.

Deep pocket foodies. Nothing personal intended."

"I see," Alice said. "Thomas was really Trip and he was a prick and he skipped out on his family because his father was a gangster. But now there are new gangsters at truffle flavored mayonnaise shops."

"They call them Emporiums," Summer added dryly, now leaning toward the view that this Alice was putting her on.

"I wish I could make a few subtle legal clarifications. But I can't. But I can give you a view from the street. If you're ready for it."

"Please advance."

"Trip ran a con on you, pretending to be somebody you'd become attached to. Thomas. You were, what? Nineteen? Twenty? Nannies, ponies, trust funds, elite right out of the starting gate. Naïve as fuck and, from what I can see, a meal ticket for a bowling alley full of shrinks, this guy Gruel being the latest. So, you weren't hard for Trip to reel in. He ran when it turned out you had no money. But now, his old man, for reasons I can't fathom, has left you money."

"Tell them I don't want it."

She was at the door for the fifth time when Summer's words stopped her.

"Refusing the legal bequest isn't a signal to others that you've also refused the illegal bequest. You know, the gangsters. They're still going to think you've got it. Or you know where it is."

Summer waited for signs that this was all sinking in.

"You're on the spot whether you refuse or not."

She studied Alice's face to see if she realized that it was, she, Summer, who had put her on the spot.

"Dr. Grew said this was a salutary matter," Alice affirmed solemnly.

"Well, dear, analysts make a big thing out of words, but they suck when it comes to real life, especially as we live it here in the vestigial foot of Brooklyn. Believe me when I tell you, you can't walk away from this without being shadowed by very unsalutary muddafuckers. Is that a word?"

Before she could tell Alice it was a rhetorical question, Alice was enunciating the word into her phone. *"Muddafuckers: Unsalutary progeny. See also, pricks. e.g. Trip."*

How the fuck does she do that? What the fuck is the Alice App? Fuck it. Not going down that rabbit hole.

"You needed to be told," Summer said, her voice shouting down her inner cross examiner. "To be warned. Unfortunately, it's known among all of Paul's associates that you were left his holdings. They can find you as easily as I did. The money may be too tainted for you, but it smells clean to them."

Alice sat down.

"We have no need of tainted money."

"By "we" you mean yourself and your daughter?"

Alice nodded.

"There are problems then that you should be able to see," Summer said, sighing. "Your daughter is very potent leverage against making that decision. They can get to you through your daughter. That's how they got to King Lear."

"It's not very easy to find my daughter. You see, she doesn't get out much. She doesn't wander outside the gates, like Lydia."

"She doesn't get out much? Look, it's you who doesn't see. I told you. I've already been paid through the estate. I'm still in the game for my own personal reasons. I don't want to see you chewed up by the same people who chewed up my father. And spit out all the good that was ever in him. I have a premonition that my father, as sorry a son of a bitch as he is, has yet goodness in him that your own father did not."

What the fuck does that mean? Summer's internal counselor asked. She had gone down the rabbit hole, making no fucking sense.

"Goodbye."

"Look, nobody knows where Paul's hidden trove is. But what's streetwise is that Trip knows or knew and passed it on to you. Point blank. You have the map. The key. The combination. The link and password. The fob. The USB. The whatever."

Alice sat there and said nothing. She had a kind of angelic look, Summer concluded, a kind of swept away spiritual vacancy, close to catatonia. Absent like angels.

"Well, do you?" Summer questioned. "If you're lying about knowing something, we're both in trouble. They wait. They're patient. Until they're not patient."

"If you know where the money is, I'm to offer you ten percent. You already know what the stakes are if you don't accept."

Alice began to shake.

"I need to find Thomas," she said, her voice trembling.

The look poor Alice now had on her face elicited immediately a mother's sympathy that now touched Summer, though she had no children of her own. Her own father had told her she lacked both sympathy and empathy, which she figured was what a swindler like him had plenty of. The son of a bitch didn't have an ounce of decency in him. He was about as salvageable as *The Titanic.*

She wondered about Alice and Thomas. Such an impossible love affair. Opposites attract she thought but not different species. Or, do humans cross the evolutionary divide so when a New Utrecht Avenue Neanderthal meets a Sutton Place *Homo sapien sapien* romantic sparks fly? Alice was a vacuum that a catalyst like Trip entered.

"Look, dear, if Trip were alive, he'd be glued to you right now. I mean you're loaded. Did he know you had a fortune coming to you?"

"My father cut me off when I ran away with Thomas. But everything came to me when he died. Dr. Grew made my case."

"So, your analyst is a lawyer also?"

Alice ignored that question.

"Okay, what are we talking about here? A million? Ten? Twenty? Top .01% on the food chain?"

"Yes," Alice told her, wiping her tears.

Summer quickly computed a lifestyle based on getting a lifetime retainer's fee from Alice.

A strategy emerged.

"Okay, here's the way I see it given that you are already loaded. If Trip is alive, he'll be around. He's like a shark when there's blood in the water. Meanwhile, you want to stay alive. And your daughter. She may not go out much but there are more fatal accidents in the home than outside. So, I suggest paying off Paul Limone's lenders. Get them off your back. Get into the safe zone. Dip into whatever it takes, half a mill, a mill, whatever."

Alice gave her a puzzled look.

"I don't understand. Why would Trip return when Thomas said if he didn't get away from me, he'd go crazy? You said that Trip and Thomas are the same person."

"Only under the law. That's where most of my clients make their mistake. Nobody today is as they were yesterday. Nobody yesterday is as they are today. And fuck all what we are in the future. If we're here. Thus, Trip and Thomas. Not the same person. You wouldn't recognize the Thomas in Trip if you were to meet him."

"I will tell that to Dr. Grew."

"Sure. Run it by him. Look, I could represent you in this. Find out what the legitimate claims are and so on. You give me the money I think is legitimately owed and I pass it on. Totally keep the IRS out of it. You can get out of Brooklyn without a worry."

"I think I want to stay in Brooklyn. I think I want to be where Thomas can find me. With the people he grew up with."

"I don't know about that," Summer said, shaking her head. "There's a hard crew out there. I mean we haven't been gentrified yet. We're kind of extinct. Mostly people fucked up and over in various ways. Gives them an inhospitable edge. Excuse my language but they say friggin a lot. You got to get used to it. It's not a guy but a friggin guy. It's not this thing but this friggin thing. They don't debate. You need to friggin shut up. And go frigg yourself. I don't mean it personally but you gonna hear that a lot."

"I won't take it personally. What does frigging mean?"

"Not frigging. Friggin. It's a Brooklyn word for fuck. If it bothers you, just overlook it, like it don't mean nothing. Actually, no one I know talks like that. I was just trying to scare you."

Silence.

"But like everything, from confessions to testifying there's a bit of truth in what I'm saying. Just take a I don't give a fuck attitude. Aunt Rita always says two tears in a bucket and fuck it. Otherwise, they see somebody coming out of a curated gluten dairy free sandwich shop carrying an arugula bag, they beat him up. And I'm not just talking about the lenders. The gangsters I'm talking about are the natives here. The whole neighborhood went hostile once Reagan's morning in America went dark. Believe me, they don't know what a salutary situation is. You'd be an easy mark."

"You could be there to protect me."

"Yeah, sure. That's true. That's an idea. I could. Okay. I'll draw up the retainer papers and bring them over for you to sign. The Wake will be an opportunity to hear from all parties concerned. The lenders. They'll show up. I'll help you work your way through it."

"The Wake?" Alice responded and then repeated the word into her phone. *"A three day and night long mourning service intermingled with drunken, raucous behavior. Italian and Irish affairs the most awesome. Old Brooklyn Italian Wakes not to be missed. Open bar. None of these people are Woke at the Wake."*

"That is your voice, isn't it?" Summer asked, straying from her pitch. "So, I mean, you know the answer to your questions? I mean you know…those…okay, forget it. Look, the police had the body for a good while before they released it."

"The police?"

"Paul didn't die in his sleep. Suspicious circumstances is the way the paper put it."

Alice's eyes went wide.

"These are not the people who die, let us say, unambiguously, Alice."

She said this ominously, deciding that scaring the bejeezus out of Alice might help getting her to put the whole money exchange deal in her hands.

"Paul's death was less than a salutary event, although death seldom is. Death is fucking unsalutary that's why nobody wants to do it. There's a reason for it but, honey, nobody has them beforehand. It's always a big fucking surprise. And a big friggin' tragedy."

"I see."

"So, wear black. Nothing whorish. These guys at these Wakes get awful horny. They get to thinking they gotta fuck somebody quick. The dead body motivates them to sort of celebrate life with a fuck right on the spot. They think for example that a woman with a whole head full of bed hair is a whore. So, buy a comb. Do not ask me the psychology of that. Ask your Dr. Groan. And don't drink. You want to stay sober because I think interested parties will be coming out of the drains, as they say, and you don't want to miss the subtexts. You know, there's a kind of code you need to break. It's not good form for anybody to show up at Paul's Wake and muscle you for money owed. It's okay to kill the guy but don't disrespect the Wake".

"I won't but I've never been to a Wake. But I might. Disrespect it."

"Yeah, well, it's old school. The Wake. The one thing the guy lying there isn't is awake. Don't ask me. They have memorial services now. No dead body lying around. It's like a cocktail party where after you say what you want about the deceased, you mingle. Network. It's the second most useful venue for hooking up, second to online escort. But that's not the way it's done here. They lay the body out for what they call viewing. You can view him for three days. Get your fill. You say what you have to say to him kneeling beside the body."

"I will have nothing to say. I didn't know him."

"Yeah, well, move your lips like you're saying a prayer. Anyway, not knowing him won't mean anything, dear. Everybody will know who you are. And nobody will be at a loss for things to say. It'll be salutary. Don't worry. Oh, yeah, watch out for a guy named Picco. He'll try to get into your pants. Little Johnny was what we called him in school. Now he calls himself Picco. He thinks it makes him sound Bogarchy but it's short for "piccolino." You know, small, tiny. Cock of the walk, full of himself. You know the type."

"I don't think I do. I don't know many types."

"Well, Johnny Picco and myself went steady for about two and a half days in the 8th grade. Then, Angelo Bari, a guy looks like a king-size unmade bed, keeps Picco in line. Picco is all out for himself but he's loyal to Ange. I've got to give him that. Whatever you do, if Picco asks you to go on his boat say no. Tell him you don't like boats. You never go on boats. Never been on one. You've never been on the water. Like that."

"If I'm asked to go on a boat, I say no. I've never been on the water."

"Good."

"Hello."

"Right back at you."

"I was on a boat to Iceland with Thomas. Before my daughter was born. Do you want me to tell you about it?"

"Not right now. Save it. Right now, what you say is you've never been on the water or in a boat. You would get sea sick real bad if you went."

"*Mal de mer.*"

"Mal who? Watch out for Mal Occhia. Anyway, about Angelo. You know, if you could fall for a guy for what he is on the inside instead of doing it from the outside, I'd have hooked up with Ange. He's the Prince of the neighborhood."

She laughed.

"You know now that I think about it if Angelo had Trip's looks. Outside and inside fine. But that rarely happens, right?"

She saw that her fantasy had once again sent Alice out of the room.

But Alice was merely wondering what Angelo Bari looked like. Inside and out. What does a Prince look like inside and out?

Summer suddenly had the feeling that she hadn't sufficiently counseled her client. In short, she felt like she was sending a lamb to slaughter.

"They're not what they call politically correct. Micro-aggressions ain't micro. And they're not Woke, whatever the fuck that is."

"They're not?" Summer said, raising her Smartphone.

"*Politically correct: a demonstration of wokeness; Micro-aggressions: transparent assaults against people you don't know and don't want to know; also, a passive confrontation with the strong launched by the weak; Woke: alert to injustice in society, especially racism. We need to stay angry, and **stay woke**"*

Summer listened to that and shook her head.

"That sucks. Forget about that. Ask your phone about Pompeii."

"Pompey?"

"Pompeii: destroyed and buried under 4 to 6 m (13 to 20 ft) of volcanic ash and pumice in the eruption of Mount Vesuvius in AD 79."

"So, it's extinct. There's no new Pompey. It vanished. End of story. But here, where Trip…Thomas comes from…most of the people you'll meet at the Wake hang out at *The New Pompey*. Which means what? They live someplace dead and gone. Buried under the ash they think is going come back to life. See what I'm saying? There can't be any new Pompey. It's done. Extinct. Old, over and adios."

She looked into Alice's eyes, which were now wide and unblinking, no longer a turquoise but very much lighter like pale moons in a frightened sky. The kind of eyes that could bring in the tides and never let them out again.

Alice felt a wave of vertigo as she thought of people buried under volcanic ash, politically incorrect people, barely awake, screaming unkind micro-aggressions as they died, and herself drowning in the Wake of Vesuvius, forever unwoke.

"I don't want to go to…to the Wake," she told Summer, trembling and then rocking back and forth. Summer quickly knelt in front of her and took her hands.

"Hey, easy, kid. There's nothing going to hurt you at the Wake. I'm gonna be there."

Summer stood up and went over to pour Alice another drink.

"There's real and there's fake," she said, handing Alice the glass. "A mixture. Know what I mean? Like anyplace else. Life's that. But in some places, it's like bread toasted on one side only and it gets burnt. Some places, and not only here, a lot of people live on that burnt side."

"And then the ashes?" Alice said, eyes full of anticipatory fear.

"I forget," Summer said, angry at herself for fucking this up. "You've been out of touch."

"I was in an asylum but Dr. Grew sponsored my assisted living."

"That's a goddamn grift," Summer snapped back, beginning to feel the rye knocking at a door behind her eyeballs. "I'm thinking of sending my father to one of those places like Heaven's Waiting Room. You know, a la carte clip joints with sweet sounding names where they toss and flop old people around like flapjacks as soon as the family leave. Fuck that. We haven't advanced to packing the old and off-key to one of those fucking franchises. Let'em sit on a barstool at *The New Pompey* until they fall off, break their heads naturally and we hold a service."

Once again, the stunned and shocked look in those peepers, like the big eyes of an enchantress, luminous and lilac, herself enchanted. And, truth to tell, Summer felt it was working on her. It was either Alice or Jim Beam. And she knew Jim a whole lot better.

"That's a Wake. The service, I mean."

"Off-key?" Alice said.

"Yeah, like you," Summer was about to say but the Smartphone answered first:

"Off-key: *refers to a person or situation being out of step with what is considered normal or appropriate.*"

"That sucks too," Summer told Alice. "Any time an opposing counsel uses the word "normal" I object. You know why? The norm is a number. It's not people. Nobody fits that word. That word fits nobody. That's what it is about people. None of them are normal."

"Words and numbers aren't normal."

She could see that Alice was working on that idea, which was good. It meant she had reached into the mind of the jury. She had, of course, she said, winking at herself, laid down a line of shit about her opposing counsel because thus far she had never been in a trial where there was an opposing counsel. She had, however, spent a lot of time arguing tooth and nail with those troglodytes at *The New Pompey.*

"People also do not flower," Alice told her, a renewed eagerness in her voice. She was no longer frightened.

Summer nodded as if she totally understood that sentence.

"No, they don't," she finally said.

"Which is the saddest thing about us."

Now Summer felt that she was the nervous one, full of fear.

"Look, just wear a pants suit, like Hillary," Summer advised, hoping she was pulling the poor kid out of the rabbit hole of her own mind but thinking it was more like any more time with Alice would pull her into that same hole. She'd be better prepared next time.

Question was: How do you prepare for Alice?

CHAPTER TWO

MAL DE MER

Alice had been on the water, yes, she told Thomas, not telling him of her father's 56-foot schooner, or all the sailing she did during a childhood of summers on Block Island. But he surmised the truth and only quoted some lines from Rimbaud to her:
"And from that time on I bathed in the Poem
Of the Sea, star-infused and churned into milk,
Devouring the green azures; where, entranced in pallid flotsam,
A dreaming drowned man sometimes goes down."
"This is that kind of voyage," he told her. "Will you come?"
And so, with her mother's blessing and her father's curse she went on a voyage. Thomas was the teacher giving up teaching and she was his student giving up being taught.

The cargo freighter, *The Labrador Queen*, disembarked from Philadelphia, taking 16 days to reach port in Reykjavik.
There was other passenger besides Alice and Thomas, including an elderly married couple, the Putleys, retired and fulfilling a lifetime dream to sail to Iceland, as apparently their ancestors had done long age. Thomas thought they wouldn't survive the voyage. Too old.
There was also a passenger of uncertain age, mustached and with ink black hair combed straight back, Roy Marmot, who called himself Commander Marmot, who had decided, in his own words, to live life on the fly. He wore dark sunglasses to hide, he told Alice, his disconcerting one blue eye and one brown. People, he said,

tended to think of a divided soul, though his was, he reassured Alice, a perfect Oneness.

While Alice found the Commander at once very interesting for comments such as these, Thomas seemed to take as immediate a dislike to the man. He wondered for instance what the Commander meant by "life on the fly," since they were not flying but at ocean sailing.

"Only con men give themselves names like The Commander or the Duke of Earl or the French Dauphin." he told Alice, warning her to stay away from him and be watchful. "Don't tell him you're an heiress." She told Thomas she didn't think she was, and he told her that was the ticket.

Another passenger, a man in a white suit named Miles Griffen was going to Iceland because, in his own words, it could be the source of the world's largest deposits of heavy rare earth elements. His own company in the States was prepared to invest in the eight, nine or ten figures, as he himself expressed it to his fellow passengers, if a number of Griffen's demands regarding jus primae noctis and the use of enhanced interrogation techniques were met. His wife, considerably younger than Griffen and about Alice's age, never took her eyes from her husband, even when addressed by someone else. Alice had no idea what Griffen was talking about and said so.

"Of course, it's just a shell, so don't press me on it," he told Alice and she agreed not to.

Upon meeting both, Thomas concluded that she was what he called captured meat and Griffen just another Demogorgon feasting on her and all the souls of the living. That description, obscene and unclear at once in Alice's mind, prompted her to avoid even looking at Mr. Griffen.

Alice wasn't on the voyage to interrogate her fellow passengers or be watchful of anything but the ocean, although she did find people intriguing.

Not a feeling shared by Thomas. He thought the worst in people came out at sea. The worst also came out on land and in the heavens. Somehow the moon was involved. He had once told her that celestial beings kept out of sight because they didn't want to reveal how mean and pitiable they were.

"I don't want to know anything about anybody," Thomas told her. "Most of what I know about my fellow humans I'm trying to forget. Being watchful is entirely different. I'm not studying people. I'm on the watch. The world is full of predators, Alice. More greed than need. I want to know everything I can about predators and their victims. In short, the whole world. I have a feeling that the Commander is on this boat to destroy someone's life. Then again, he's probably what he seems to be. A harmless crank."

They were no more than a few hours out into open waters of the Atlantic, their second day out, when a *mal de mer* found Thomas and quarantined him in their cabin.

And so, his life aboard ship became an alternation between vomiting and lying in his bunk moaning and shouting expletives. He was watchful only of the vomit pail's location. Alice could be no help and so found herself on a different voyage than she had expected. She wondered if she could be watchful to the degree Thomas would be.

As the cargo was stored in the holds and not, as was becoming the custom, on deck in mammoth containers, the passengers were able to move about fore to aft without deck obstruction.

Alice, muffled in a hooded jacket, was leaning on the aft rail when the Commander joined her.

He raised one arm high and gazing upon the ocean, recited:

Oh, ye! who have your eyeballs vexed and tired, Feast them upon the wideness of the Sea.

"John Keats, "On the Sea," he told her.

"*Dip him in the river who loves water,*" she recited. "A proverb of Hell."

"Blake."

"I don't know what it means. What you said made me think of it."

He asked after Thomas and she told him he was green and vomiting in their cabin. The Commander nodded and said something about sea legs and how they invariably arrived but not after you wished you weren't at sea at all.

She in turn showed some interest in whom he might be and why he was on this voyage.

He said he was a seafarer and a wanderer, an expatriate of the country of his birth. She found that sentence very interesting, most especially because as he said it, removing his sunglasses, his eyes went very wide, one blue, the other brown, and they seemed to be trying to hypnotize her. Perhaps he was some kind of predator?

He asked her why she and Thomas were on board. She replied somewhat disjointedly, trying to recall Thomas's words as to why they were there, and it seems gave the Commander the impression that Thomas was a poet and she was his muse.

"I don't know about that," she said, laughing. "I was in his poetry class. I don't think a student can be a muse at the same time. Can they?"

"I understand this," the Commander replied, after looking closely into her eyes as if there was some deep mystery there he needed to solve. "Because the soul of the future expatriate is invariably a poetic soul somehow disappointed, the expanse of sea and sky draws in a way that promises a revelation of the deepest mysteries. All else dwindles to an insignificance before the vast empty blankness of life as the Sun has allowed it. The past recedes and the future stretches toward infinity on the ocean's face"

"Hold infinity in the palm of your hand."

"An augury of innocence, yes. And yet thievery, especially the brilliant, ingenious varieties, conducted by clever men garners great wealth. It also redistributes it. One form is lawful, the other not. One form is greedy and deceitful, the other outrageously mad and defiant. Thievery is the greatest egalitarian force on the planet."

Now Alice wondered even more about who the Commander was. He sounded like someone Thomas called a predator. But that was harsh. He was perhaps a Druid? Some of the ancient ex-students at the riverbank encampment at Thomas's small college had called themselves Druids. One of her psychiatric life coaches had told her that lives not able to go forward excrescence in the fantasy worlds of childhood. Her coach seemed to think that was a bad thing, but she remembered rather liking that description. She enjoyed the word "excrescence."

"And on those days the Sun is absent, " the Commander went on, "when dark clouds roil and roll and block out the Sun's magnificence and lay their own blackness close to the sea itself, we feel not only the threat of a bad sea but as if the Sun were punishing us for not recognizing daily the debt all life owes it."

Viking, she now said to herself. Everyone's ancestors had been pillaged and worse, in fact, fucked, by Vikings. Thomas had announced this once at a solemn midnight bonfire at the encampment of the Excrescent. She had loved the way Thomas liberated all his students into a free and unrestricted realm of profanity. She felt very adult in the company of those who were profane. Thomas said the roots of his profanity lay in one bar in Brooklyn. He did not elaborate.

"Calm waters, fair skies had been the Viking prayer," the Commander now told her, and she wondered if she had said the word "Vikings" out loud?

"Unfortunately, the oceans and all of Nature too are redundant. Hopelessly analog. Impossible to digitalize. God also."

Before she could respond, he laughed and spread both arms up in the air.

"And now, I think we are called to our *Mittag*."

"Lunch," he translated when she gave him a puzzled look.

Alice was on the verge of asking the Commander which thief he might be.

"You sound like Thomas."

"He, a teacher. Not I. I simply speak the tongue of a race the acme of whose mentality is the maxim: time is money. I quote Professor MacHugh."

"And now we are off to lunch. I've been told by the steward that the Captain will be joining us."

Alice had already taken a day's meals with the other passengers, but this would be the first time the Captain joined them for lunch. *Mittag.*

The Commander, Alice had noticed, had come aboard apparently with his sea legs already attached, and so ate with great relish, applying a napkin the size of a small tablecloth repeatedly to greasy chin and fingertips. The Commander preferred fingers and meat ripping incisors to knife and fork. He abhorred the contact of metal on meat as he phrased it. He had apologized to his fellow diners but assured them that the most noble men and women had eaten thusly. Henry the Eight for instance and Leonardo da Vinci and Professor MacHugh."

"However, I restrict my predatory instincts to the dinner table."

Alice winced at the word.

Griffen had responded that those luminaries had talents that compensated for whatever poor table manners they had, and would Mr. Marmot claim the same?

"I have only a humble crank's psycho-cybernetic entrepreneurial genius, as had Professor MacHugh before he was given the Heimlich maneuver untimely."

The Captain suddenly entered, like a gale force.

The steward, Ret, a young man about Alice's age with light hair, almost white, and very white teeth that shone when he smiled -- and he seemed always to be smiling at her -- placed a decanter of wine at the Captain's elbow.

Alice's first impression of the Captain was that if the Sun was Nature's ruling presence, the Captain looked like he was fully in charge of the Sun, like a dark eclipse.

"Ship's Orders," the Captain said loudly, standing at the head of the table and scowling at all of them.

"Listen up," Ret said, standing just behind the Captain. "Captain has something to say."

"May we eat first, Captain? My husband needs to eat at a fixed time."

"Ship's orders!" the Captain repeated in a booming voice.

The Commander announced he had a gargantuan appetite. He seemed happy.

"I hate passengers on my ship. I never want them. Especially the cushwads, the flush jammies, the noise balls, the fart and gas bags, and every bootstrap foc'sle who turns green. But I got them. Ship owners want passenger cargo, but at sea, I give the orders."

"No one is arguing with your authority, Captain," Mr. Putley said.

"Foc'sle it. Captain talking."

"Foc'sle it," Ret repeated, winking once again at Alice. "Captain talking."

"I don't want passengers underfoot, so you'd best stay in the part of the ship assigned to you. I'm assigning aft. Aft. It's the asshole of the ship."

Ret refilled the Captain's wine glass.

"Passengers don't make my job easier or make my purse heavier and I see no bloody, goddamn, foc'sle reason to put up with any of you. Clear?"

Alice nodded, although she did wonder if any of the types of people the Captain didn't want on board were on board. Perhaps, she was one. But they didn't sound like very nice people.

"I see no reason, Captain, for profanity," Mr. Putley said, timidly, nervously.

The Captain, whom Alice had decided to call Wolf, glared like a ferocious wolf at the old man.

"I don't want to hear about why you want to go to Iceland on this death ship or if you're in the U.S. witness protection program and the goddamn Don Pastrami family is after you. I don't care if your foc'sle stocks are up or down or up your ass. I don't care if you want to send one of your brats to fetus school or to Montana to tighten their balls. Understood?"

"Captain doesn't care if you want to go to Morocco to tighten your balls."

"Belay that, Steward. They got the message. I will see to it that anyone who annoys me at table is kicked the foc'sle out of here."

Ret was going around the table ladling out soup.

Alice stared at the metal spoon lying beside the Commander's dish.

"And don't pester the foc'sle crew. They hate passengers more than I do. Right, Steward?"

"Right, Captain. They eat passengers for breakfast."

The Captain was now eying the Commander who had picked up his soup bowl and was draining it. Simple enough, Alice said, hiding a smile with her napkin.

"What is the procedure regarding a ship's emergency, Captain?"

"You? Mister Puckley?"

"Griffen. I believe my holding company owns this vessel. It being, of course, a shell."

"You should jump overboard in case of emergency. And take your shell with you. Soup sucks."

"Aye, aye, Captain. Soup sucks."

"I wonder if we could send a message to our grandchildren?" Mrs. Putley asked in a very sweet but quaking voice. "Would you like to see some photographs?"

The Captain just stared at Mrs. Putley until she melted into her soup.

"I believe you will make an exception for any communiqués I choose to make," Griffen told the Captain in a cavalier tone.

"And why would I do that, Mr. Shell?"

"My company is making an eighty-figure investment in Iceland," Griffen told him. "The shipping industry will expand to very profitable levels."

"The shipping industry can go up its own ass for all I care. This is my last bloody voyage. So, shut your trap."

"Yes, shut your trap," the Commander told Griffen. "I'm thinking eighty figures makes you quite a thief."

"Who do you think you're talking to Mister bogus commander?"

"I'm merely quoting Professor MacHugh that thievery, especially the brilliant, ingenious varieties, conducted by clever men garners great wealth. But, you look to me like simply a crook. A thief. Predator, as all thieves of that sort are."

"Who are you calling a thief? And who the hell is Professor MacHugh?"

"I'll have you both thrown over the side if you don't shut your traps."

"The Captain will have you…"

"Eight bells!" the Captain shouted. "Passengers to their cabins!"
"Eight bells!" Ret shouted, winking at Alice.

Alice rushed to tell Thomas what a profane, ungrammatical ogre their captain was and what an odd but interesting sort the Commander was and how right he had been about Griffen, but she found Thomas sitting on the edge of his berth holding the puke pail up into his face. He waved her out.

The cabin smelled awful. More stank than a Viking yurt she thought, smiling.

"The Commander says that Mr. Griffen is a thief. He was quoting Professor MacHugh."

"My God! I'm dying here. Look, just don't get involved with any of that. You're…you're…Where's the goddamn bucket!"

The beauties of being at sea and the supernal magnificence of the Sun were, she now thought, overrated. She was discovering that the blinding and radiant force of the Sun on this metallic can called a ship as well as on the rolling reflective waters all around, defied all attempts at defense and protection.

Alice also very quickly came to realize that although the sea was like a tabula rasa upon which great thoughts could be written -- Thomas's words -- it was also an emptiness, a vast repetition of up and down, rolling and rocking waves, wobbly seas the Commander called them, umbrella-ed by a sky that was either darker than a nightmare or so ferociously bright you ran for cover.

"Doc Bright has one of his megraines and won't be joining us," the Captain growled as he joined them for dinner that night.

Alice thought the announcement strange because Doc Bright had not been at any of their meals. She had, in fact, not seen him. Commander Marmot caught her eye and made a fluttering motion with one hand held to his mouth. "He drinks," he whispered to Alice. He and Alice had become inseparable friends in a very short time.

"What's that?" the Captain snapped. "What are you whispering about?"

"He told her he hopes her husband is doing better," Ret said, as he laid a plate of pork chops in front of the Captain.

"I don't think he's better," Alice told the Commander, "and it's hard to say if he's worse."

"Precisely what the priest said when my father died," the

Commander told her smiling, reaching out and fingering a pork chop from the pile in front of the Captain.

The Captain whacked his hand with his fork.

"Belay that," he growled. "Captain serves."

He had a face more like a bulldog than a wolf, if, Alice now decided, a bulldog with a three- or four-day growth of dark beard, bags under his bloodshot eyes but no playful silliness to his mouth.

Commander Marmot, who had tied his napkin around his neck, nodded. He crossed himself.

"Ave Maria gratia plena dominus tecum."

"Are you religious, Mr. Marmot?" Mrs. Putley asked.

"I've weaponized religion in my life, Mrs. Putley. I've been doing quite well at it."

"It sounds quite evangelical."

"Belay that! No holy roller talk at my table."

Mrs. Putley began to shake, and as Alice observed her it became clear that the Putleys' ability to find enjoyment in the Captain's tyranny was doomed.

"You cannot censure the religious fervor of my wife, Captain. She has made Jesus her personal saviour."

"Oh, was I religious, dear?"

"For about sixty years, my dear. You made Jesus your personal savior."

"Oh, I've forgotten. How awful."

Tears came to Alice's eyes. She wondered what it would be like not to remember the things that had happened and, perhaps worse, to remember those that never happened.

"You're both from someplace in Indiana or possibly Iowa or Idaho," Griffen said to the Putleys.

"Pardon me?" Mr. Putley said to Griffen. "Is there some ridicule to what you are saying?"

"You're all unmistakably from that fly over region. It's written on your face. Keep money, sex, alcohol and cocaine out of your life. Fly over the tough business decisions other men have to make."

"Mr. Putley was an actuary," Mrs. Putley said proudly.

"Actually, I had my own mortuary for thirty-three years."

"Oh, I was wondering where all the charisma came from."

"My husband incinerated JFK."

"Cremated, my dear. And it wasn't the president. Just someone with his initials. They keep the cremains under the front porch."

"Oh, how awful."

"He drove his cart over the bones of the dead," Alice announced.

All eyes went to her.

"I serviced the dead on behalf of their love ones," Putley said to Griffen, his chin cocked in the air, his wife's hand on his arm protectively. "I don't think that is something to be laughed at."

"What are you going to do? Embalm me?"

Griffen laughed with great enthusiasm.

Putley failed to put together an audible response but the Captain told Griffen to belay that or he'd shoot him.

"Show him your pistol, Steward."

Ret pulled a large black revolver, seemingly out of the air, from what Alice could see.

"I believe Mrs. Putley and myself will be taking our meals in our cabin from now on."

He stood up.

"Sit down and shut your pie hole," the Captain bellowed. "There's no takeout service here."

Mr. Putley put on a brave face and sat back down.

Alice's love for the Putleys increased tenfold. Pity was one thing, sympathy something else but empathy was again something else. She began to tell them about her new life with Thomas. She knew she was very young to be married but they were very much in love.

"He's very much puking, is what it is," the Captain growled.

"Would you mind if I did a sketch of you Captain?" Marmot asked, politely. "You in your black pilot jacket, a black captain's cap on your head, a three-day growth of beard. You remind me of a blackened fire plug with your wide shouldered, no neck, and barrel-chested build. You are truly a throwback to someone in a cave not a ship. As, of course, Professor MacHugh was for all his Harvard and Oxford credentials."

"I think this man's head is windblown, Steward. What do you think?"

"He could be on this voyage under advice from his psychiatrist, Captain. That's how they usually act. "

"Or I could be a psychiatrist making a voyage, which is what I am."

"I don't like a man abaft the beam on my ship."

"Captain means crazy," Ret whispered to Alice.

Alice was about to reply, "You mean another crazy man like the Captain?" but she stayed silent.

She found it unbelievable that Thomas wasn't there to see all this, especially as the trip had been his idea. She smiled when she thought that Thomas, the man who told her he was going to turn the world upside down, should have remained on land because the ocean had certainly turned him upside down. Where Thomas had gotten the idea for this so-called cruise, she did not know. Perhaps he was going to tighten his balls in Iceland?

"I'll keep a close watch on him, Captain," Ret said.

He remained positioned behind the Captain, but he had yet another wink for Alice who blushed. She wondered if she should tell Thomas about Ret?

The Putleys were blinking hard at each other.

Parkinson's or existential fear was kicking in.

Mr. Putley had placed one hand near his heart as if he were about to recite the pledge of allegiance. Alice surmised that the old man probably had heart trouble and had imagined a long sea voyage would be just the thing. Just the thing to kill him.

"Both the sane and the deeply troubled seek the ocean for its depth," Marmot announced. *'I have no fear of depths and a great fear of shallow living.'"*

The Commander had a big smile on his face.

Alice thought it was the kind of face she imagined geniuses had, frenzied poets delivering Amazon packages, wild haired rock musicians cursing rap in dark holes, unemployed MENSAs doing the Sunday *New York Times* crossword puzzle with ink pens, mathematicians coming to the end of their blackboard without having proven anything, surly bartenders with a gift for remembering ten thousand nick names of the Disaffected, embittered line cooks with damp cigarettes hanging over the Mornay sauces, autistic inn keepers arranging and re-arranging the key fobs, mystics lost in early morning L.A. traffic meditating on their pillow, and all the people who imperiled their own worldly success gladly, serving instead their own imaginations.

She felt her imagination was going away with her, as it had her mother. She was beginning to see the world in a grain of sand, as her mother had, and it frightened her.

The Commander's eyes were transfixing, one bright blue eye and one dark brown one.

"Beware the Jabberwock, my son!" he sang out. *"The jaws that bite, the claws that catch! Beware the Juju bird and shun the frumious Bandersnatch! He took his vorpal sword in hand."*

Alice right then had an epiphany:

When you go to sea, you go back in time, or, more exactly, you and everyone around you relapse into something wondrous and magical. Such moments get more and more magical, more rhapsodic and enchanting each time you recall them. She felt the Commander's voice itself had magical tones.

"You seem to have a problem controlling your table, Captain," Griffen said. "I hope you are more efficient in running this ship."

"Cock and balls! Who do you think you're talking to? I'll have your eighty figures shoved up your ass!"

"Captain!" Mr. Putley stuttered, "Captain. I must protest such language in front of my wife."

Mr. Putley struggled to get up from his seat in protest and then went face down into his dish.

Mrs. Putley screamed and fell upon him, both arms wrapped around the man trying to pull his face out of the dish.

The Captain acted as if an old man dropping dead into his dish was just yet another report of bad weather on the starboard bow.

"I told you," Griffen shouted. "You've killed that ancient embalmer, you stupid ape. The ship is cursed!"

"Who you calling an ape?" the Captain screamed, jumping up from his own seat, as quick and as agile as a panther, came up to Griffen's chair and with a sudden blow knocked him to the ground.

"I'll smash your face with a barnacle boot!" he shouted and attempted to kick at Griffen's head but Ret, winking conspiratorially at Alice, grabbed him from behind and pulled him back. Ret seemed to see all this as great fun.

Alice was attempting to pry Mrs. Putley from her husband with one hand and with the other get Mr. Putley's face up from his dish. How she managed to do so, she didn't know but it happened and Mr. Putley, face full of mashed potato, began to gurgle.

Alice pushed a chair to where she could slide Putley into. She got the man's head back, reached for a water glass and flung water in Putley's face. Mrs. Putley was like a loud, persistent gale wind Alice had to keep pushing off with one hand while slapping Putley's face. That brought the old man round and he began to mumble as his wife grabbed his face and kept repeating a name, but it wasn't her husband's.

"I'll help the gentleman to his quarters," Ret said.

"Leave him be, Steward. Throw this one overboard."

He pointed to Griffen, who was lying moaning at his feet and attempting to crawl under the table.

Griffen's wife was making sounds that crossed between sobs, belches and giggles. Alice saw at once that she was abaft the beam.

Alice began to move old man Putley toward the door. She stopped.

A clear and very calm and serious thought came to Alice amid this madness: a brute of a ship's captain and lunatic fellow passengers are two additional minuses to a transatlantic cargo freight voyage, if that made sense.

"You can't throw that man overboard," Alice shouted, tears in her eyes. "If you do, I'll see to it that you go to jail."

"We could put all of them into a near port, Captain," Ret suggested, holding Griffen by one arm.

"Get your pistol on him, Steward. And throw him to the sharks."

Ret nodded and with his free hand swept back his jacket and exposed his gun, now tucked into his belt. It looked to Alice as if he was showing the gun to her because he was looking at her. And winking. Before he could manage to pull the gun out, Griffen swung into him and grabbed the pistol.

He pushed Ret away and pointed the pistol at him.

Alice screamed. She had become fond of the Steward.

"Ram him hard afore, Steward!"

Ret lunged toward Griffen, who fired once and then again as Ret stumbled toward him. Blood spurt out of Ret's chest and he dropped to the floor.

Alice heard someone yelling and then realized it was her.

The Captain bent over the body.

"He's dead," he said to Griffen. "Give me that fowking gun unless you plan on shooting all of us."

Griffen looked at the gun and then dropped it.

Alice didn't realize she had fainted until she found herself in her cabin with Thomas leaning over her.

"He killed Ret," she sobbed.

Thomas shook his head.

"I doubt it. It's a con. Has all the signs. You said this Griffen had money?"

"I think so. He said he was going to buy Iceland for eighty figures. He repeated that a lot."

Thomas started to say more but nausea preempted words.

Once docked, Thomas returned to himself, as if seeing land had revived him.

At Alice's urging, Thomas spoke to the Captain before disembarking. Alice saw the two of them talking but she didn't hear a thing. When Thomas came back, he told her that the Captain intended on reporting the murder and that Alice would be a witness. A corroborating witness. That made Alice very nervous but then Thomas told her that the Captain probably wouldn't report the murder and she wouldn't be a witness. In fact, the Captain had told him he wasn't going to report it. Thomas told her, they hadn't spoken about the murder but only about having some of his fare returned to him as the *mal de mer* had made him totally absent as a passenger.

"Oh, Thomas! That seems so small a matter now."

"So, it is. Truth is, I didn't speak to the Captain at all. About anything. When I approached him, he told me to get the foc'sle out of his face."

In their hotel, Thomas began, once again, telling Alice that it was all a confidence game.

"It was a confidence game. I told you to watch it. As soon as I saw that clip artist, The Commander. The Commander. Of what? Of the scam."

Alice didn't respond but silence did not preserve her from Thomas's sharp perusal.

"That steward. What was his name? Wreck? Well, don't worry about him. He's alive. But as long as Mister Eight figures … "

"Mr. Griffen?"

"As long as that guy thinks this guy Retch is dead, he'll pay the Captain to keep his mouth shut. He wants to keep rolling in eight figures, not eighty years in jail."

"I don't understand any of this. What about the elderly couple?"

"The Puttbutts? Probably useful idiots or shills. It was all staged, Princess. And now it's over."

"The Puttbutts? You mean the Putleys? Useful idiots. That doesn't sound right. They were just old and sickly. They had pictures of their grandchildren, although it was strange that she kept shouting "Albert! Albert!" He told us his name was Sam."

"Princess, listen. It could have all been real. I mean maybe they weren't useful being too old and too sickly. Or maybe they weren't idiots. What do we know? That guy Reagan, the steward, could be dead."

"And the Commander? Was he part of the confidence game? I don't believe that."

"So, yeah, he was pretty nautical. He could have been a real Commander or whatever. I was puking in my cabin. What do I really know? I only know what you told me. I felt like I was dying.

All I wanted to do was get off that boat. Ship. Whatever. That's the thing about a ship. You can't walk away. That *mal de mer* knocked me for a loop."

"*Mal de mer*. I'm sorry that happened to you. It was all so terrible, Thomas. It happened so fast."

"So, it was all staged, Princess. Nobody's dead. The only thing real is the money that pig Gifford is going to pay up to keep the whole thing sealed."

"But, Thomas, what did he do? I didn't like Mr. Griffen. Yes, I think he was a pig for the way he treated his wife. So young, so talented. He kept her as a prisoner. Now she's abaft the beam."

"I didn't get a good look at her. What's her talent?"

"Unrealized. I think she is abaft the beam."

"Exactly, Princess. What was that? So, he was innocent the way your own father was innocent. People who make money by just having money are always guilty. I know. I make a study of people like that."

"Not watching them?"

"That too. Listen, we stick our hand in your father's pocket and we get what he wouldn't give. We follow the money right to the pocket."

"The Commander did say he was fond of thievery. As was Professor MacHugh. And the steward did keep winking at me as if it were all a game and I should enjoy it and have fun."

Thomas laughed.

"So, that's a different game he was playing, Princess. He was trying to get into your pants."

"I had a skirt on."

"Trying to get that over your head."

"I think you're being fantastical."

"You're right. I'm just making this stuff up. But ever since I stopped puking, I've been thinking, and I figured it all out. The Commander says I have a natural talent. Actually, I didn't talk to him. I got to admit I didn't do anything, but you were a natural. You could be in the game, not just a witness. I mean if there is a game. You could just drift in naturally in any game and you'd own the board. You have a natural talent. So, I'm totally sure what went on here. That guy Reb could be dead and also not dead. You're mesmerizing. Have you ever heard of the thing about the cat in the box who may be dead and not dead at the same time?"

She didn't know what to say to that. She shivered.

"Hey, Princess, calm down. It was all just a game. The cat wasn't dead. So, it's a thought experiment. Look at it this way, it was a con, but it was real. It was real, but it was a con. That's the way the world works. You're in it whether you like it or not.

She was wondering if he was still talking about the cat. And the game.

"What if I said I don't want to be in that sort of game even if there was one? I don't see the world that way."

"Princess, the truth is, you don't see it at all. You're like stunned. You were brought up in a rich man's cocoon. And he was twisted. Pathological and bags of money. A bad combo. Like ketchup on hot dogs. Meatballs with spaghetti. That's why you're screwed up. So, it's a journey. . ."

"I don't like that word. Journey. It hasn't been very good for me. Please don't say I'm on a journey because then I wonder where I might be. On the journey."

"So, I'm using the word 'journey' metaphorically. I'm talking about us being together, rock solid, one not moving an inch from the other. I'm saying there's one thing you can count on. I'm here to protect you. You're not going to get pulled into a trap like this. The world's a trap and everyone in it are just players playing their part. That's Shakespeare."

"You said I would be a natural."

"Did I? I don't know. More out of the natural really. You're pretty far down the rabbit hole, you know. Look, it's all smooth sailing from here. Like a long voyage into the future. Me and you. Together. We're on a journey, Princess."

He put his face less than an inch away from hers.

"But you know, you would be a natural."

CHAPTER THREE

THE WAKE

Paul Limone's wake was held at Red Hook's Torricelli's Funeral Parlor, which, Alice found out almost at once, was run by a Korean named Dino Kim, who had kept the Torricelli name for its brand power among a collapsing but still influential surround of Italians. In order to fit in, Dino dressed like Dean Martian and called his staff The Fat Pack.

Alice had never been to a Wake. The kind of Wake old school Brooklyn Italians offered, as described by the lawyer, Summer Arpeggio.

Alice's very smart phone told her that sitting for three days and three nights in a "funeral home" with a dead body in a room called a parlor and people carousing in another parlor was a custom long since terminated, along with putting old people in the basement to make ravioli or stuffing them in a neighbor's recycling bin.

Summer Arpeggio had texted her several "Must Do's" Be approachable, accessible but not too, and offer ignorance to the insistent. Hear everyone out; listen to whatever story someone wants to tell. She was to remember that these people spoke in parables and riddles. A great deal was coded. An often-repeated word or phrase might be a symbol upon which everything hinged, like living or dying. Not encouraging texts.

"Pay attention to the punch line. That's the message. If there is one. Be sociable. Invite explanations of all that puzzles you. Seek information. Display total ignorance of all matters. Beware of any strangers knocking at your door. Whatever they try to sell you, it's just code for: "Where's

Old Man Limone's money?"

"I don't understand funeral parlors," Alice said to someone. "Why parlors? Or 'home.' I don't know if the dead lead a domestic life. Would they want to?"

"I don't know that one, lady," was the reply.

She heard someone standing by the coat check say:

"We're near the South Brooklyn Marine terminal and not too far from the finger piers that Paul had worked on his whole life. It was Paul's real home."

Alice followed a family into Parlor A where she was told the body was laid out. It was. Tucked in a lavish coffin with flowered wreaths all around it was Nosferatu in a shiny, blue suit. There were flower wreaths in which roses formed a pack of Camel cigarettes or a ship or a bottle of Seagram's or a curvaceous female body or a race horse or a Cadillac or a deck of cards or a crate hook. The room was festooned with crucifixes and Virgin Mary's, and a few statues with the name "St Jude" at their base. Someone told her it was Paul's patron saint, whatever that meant. She knew what a patron was but not a saintly one. Not any of this had Alice ever seen before in real life.

Most of the women were in there, segregated in Parlor A, talking in hushed voices, paying their respects, some fingering black beads, some intermittently crying.

"I never worked for Paul," someone standing near her said, staring up at the casket as she was as if it were a TV set.

She wondered whether something was now going to be revealed. She saw the need to trigger the revelation.

"Oh?" was the best she came up with.

She began to stroll the rear of Parlor A, listening to the mourners.

"I never got married but I got a small boat down here. You got Bay Ridge Channel and Red Hook Channel going right into Gowanus Bay. Sail down to Gravesend Bay. Sailed. No engine. I leave the engine in the car. When I'm on the water. Jeez, to me it's all the peace in the world. Know what I mean?"

"I've never been on the water. Or a boat."

The speaker, a decaying man in a rumpled brown spotted suit, turned in his seat and looked at her. She realized then that he wasn't talking to her.

Just then, a man with a deeply tanned face that was so porcelain smooth that it frightened her came up to where they were seated.

"Sorry for your loss, babe," he said, kissing her on both cheeks.

"Johnny. They call me Picco. I thought maybe you might remember me. I remember you because beautiful ladies are always memorable."

She realized this was the Picco the lawyer had told her about.

Alice gave him a frightened look and pulled the hem of her skirt down.

"You and Trip were passing through. How do you do, and twenty-two skidoo was all it was."

"Oh."

"We're gonna miss him."

She didn't know if she should say certainly or I hope not.

"You know, who knows where we go when we go. It's one of those unknown unknowns that nobody knows."

She nodded.

"It could be a journey. But I don't like the word."

"Get GPS, babe," Picco said, jaw dropping and stepping back to get a good look at her.

"I'm called Alice now. My mother didn't even call me Babe. I've heard my father call many women babe."

"Alice? Yeah, I like that. There's a real sweetness to it. Like the name Coronet and Maybelline. And Mariooche. Bibelous names."

"He had very many friends, didn't he?"

"The whole place is a waiting room for the coffin."

"We all owe life a death," Alice told him, quoting Dr. Grew.

"Yeah, I try not to owe anybody anything. I didn't ask to be born and I certainly not gonna ask to die."

She wondered if that was a code message regarding the inheritance?

"Hey, der's Padre Balls."

Alice looked to where he was pointing.

"He's not a priest anymore. He's got himself a goomara."

He winked at Alice, took her hand and kissed it.

"We will meet again, my sweet Alice."

"Goomara: An Italian-American slang word used to describe an on-the-side girlfriend.

"You know I was his confessor for a long time," Padre Balls was telling Alice as the two of them sat at the bar that extended across Parlor B where the mourners continued to drink at a rate that made them indistinguishable from New Year's Eve revelers.

"We got along. But he did get upset when I gave up the priesthood. He probably would throw me out of here. He wouldn't want me doing the service."

"The service, Padre?" Alice repeated, her eye out for his girlfriend on the side. His goomara.

"You don't have to call me Padre. I'm just Balls now. Or Balsio, if you feel more comfortable with that."

Alice nodded, though she didn't have the least idea what Mr. Paul Limone would have wanted in the way of a service. Or of what the service comprised but she had heard the expression "the service." When she whispered the word into her phone, she had not gotten any satisfactory response: *"Totally ambiguous word mostly used at Brooklyn Wakes. Also, Catholic ritual. A military tenure."*

She looked at the drink in front of her. One wouldn't make her less alert. She saw Picco across the room and instinctively pulled at the hem of her skirt.

"Can I speak candidly to you, Padre Balsio?"

"Sure, but I can't absolve you of your sins. I gave my last absolution to Picco. Waste of breath really. But I'm still a partial celibatarian."

"I'm afraid of getting to know Thomas's friends here but I need to know so much about him. And now he's gone. You were good friends with Thomas?"

"Grew up here. From the early grades at St. Rosalia."

"Thomas left me," she said, almost in a whisper. "I didn't leave him."

Balsio didn't seem to know what to say.

"He could be dead," she added.

"Yeah, I think if he was alive, he'd be here. Out of respect for his father. He's dead? No such obligation. You know this place was Paul's choice. He wanted Torricelli's. Close to the pier. But the only thing left that Paul would recognize is the name. And the mourners. They were his people."

Alice nodded and surveyed the people around them.

"It's a heartwarming turnout," Balsio said, clearing his throat and waving two hands outward as if blessing the room. The Parlor.

"The whole place is a waiting room for the coffin," she told him, feeling that repeating Picco's words would be appropriate.

She saw Summer Arpeggio come in the Parlor. There was a man about Paul's age with her but this man was alive. Summer came over and introduced her father to Alice.

"May he find his way to Heaven five minutes before the Devil knows he's dead," the old man told her, staring up at her, his eyeballs looking like they were floating in the Red Sea.

"I also know that Paul ain't dead."

"He ain't? Isn't?" Alice said, stunned by the news.

"Fake news," Summer told her, shaking her head.

Mr. Arpeggio gave his daughter a scolding look.

"When somebody is still talking about somebody that somebody ain't dead."

He said that triumphantly and then walked away.

"Can I talk to you privately?" Summer said to Alice, who was wondering if there was a message to her from a lender in what Mr. Arpeggio had just said.

Alice was surprised to see that Summer was wearing a bright red, fluffy blouse. Summer saw the surprised look.

"Black is back, too far back for me, so I don't wear it. I'm a modern woman. Red's my statement. Fuck all this. When I die I wanna be wrapped in a fur coat and dropped in Gravesend Bay."

When Summer had led her back to the coffin room and they had taken seats away from the paid mourners, Summer asked her flat out if her analyst Dr. Grew had been declared her legal guardian.

"I don't think so."

"Financial control of your money?"

"Maybe. He grows into being so many different things."

"Thus, the name," Summer mumbled. Cute.

"Elsewise, you can write your own checks?" she asked Alice. "Nobody said in writing that you lacked capacity?"

Elsewise? Was that a word?

"Maybe."

"So.... You can't write a check and hand it over to any of these lenders gathered here?"

"Yes, of course. I write it and Dr. Grew signs it. Or not."

"Fuck me," Summer tweeted to herself.

"Padre Balsio who said he was defrocked but still a partial celibatarian said Thomas must be dead."

"What? Balsio? Look, he's got no connection with the spiritual world, kid. He's defrocked. And he's defrocked because he was running a grift on the diocese and they caught him balls out. Believe me, he did enough money laundering for the gangsters in his time. He was laundering through the Vatican. Maybe the Pope knew. Maybe he didn't. So, don't talk to the guy. He's poison. He'll draw you into a laundering operation like milk draws pussy and pussy draws men."

"I really didn't notice," Alice mumbled, quickly taking out her phone.

"Defrocked: ejected priest. Grift: a strategy to get a hand in your pants pocket; Laundering: funneling illegal money through legal businesses to avoid taxes. Grifter: a person like Padre Balls who engages in a grift. Formerly, worked for the Pope; known to be a partial celibatarian."

"Put that thing away!" Summer ordered, reaching out for Alice's phone, which Alice quickly shoved back into her bag.

"Look, you're just going to have to stall them. Get back in there and play the Alice. You don't know what the fuck they're talking about. That's if they talk about the money Paul owed them."

"The gangsters?"

"The lenders. Let's hope they stay at that level. And, do me a favor? Try to talk to that thing on the down low. It will freak these guys out. And believe me, you don't want that. All magic is the evil eye to them. Malocchio."

Alice went back to the bar where Padre Balsio was stirring his drink. She was repeating the name Mal Occhio to herself. She wondered if he was in the Parlor.

Balsio laughed when he saw her.

"You know, I was thinking. Paul insisted on confessing to me even though I was no longer a priest."

"Confession: bad things done told gratis to a priest or at an exorbitant hourly rate to an analyst in confidence. See also: St. Augustine."

"He tells you what he thinks are the bad things?" Alice asked, "My mother and father were very divided over what was bad. She thought he was very bad. He said he never did a bad thing in his life. Why would anyone tell you their secrets?"

She didn't really think anyone would tell any secrets to Padre Balsio considering he had a laundering operation going with the Pope, no less.

She saw Summer heading toward them. She had to get away from Padre Balsio or be laundered. As Summer walked toward her, she saw her in a long fur coat, ready to be thrown overboard. Into Gray's Head Bay.

"Yeah, people tell you things in confession. But in words. Very carefully chosen words. They use words like a matador uses a cape on a bull."

Then he leaned close and whispered in her ear.

"They think Paul told me everything. Where the money is. He didn't.

When I asked him about ill-gotten gains weighing hard on his conscience, he said he didn't have any. Ill-gotten gains or conscience."

"He lied?"

She remembered Thomas telling her that the one thing God couldn't be was a person because people lied, and God couldn't lie. She always found it scary to think that God wasn't a person, not like her or anyone on the planet. Some entity from beyond the galaxy.

"Now, I think they're gonna get it out of me even if it kills me."

He backed away from her. Grabbed the shot in front of him. His hand shook.

"Who would . . . " Alice started to say.

"I don't think Paul trusted me."

"Probably had his reasons," Summer said, coming up to them and placing herself between Alice and Balsio.

Balsio wasn't happy to see her.

"We're having a conversation here, Counselor," he told Summer. "Why don't you go negotiate a plea bargain or something?"

"Goodbye," Summer said, and turned to Alice.

She was aware that a lot of Alice was rubbing off on her, at least the "Hello" and the "Goodbye." The other stuff she'd like to get vaccinated against.

"Coming?"

Alice followed her.

"I can tell you a lot about Tommy," Balsio called out. "Trip."

"This is a circus, my dear," Summer said, in her ear, "but not everyone is an amusing clown."

"He said someone will try to kill him," Alice said, her voice, Summer noticed, at the same, undisturbed pitch as if she had said, "I think it will rain."

"Yeah, welcome to the club. Everyone in here is paranoid. And they all have guns. Padre Balls is super paranoid. He was told something or maybe he wasn't told something, kind of like the spot you're in. I'm just talking shit. I don't know. I do know if Paul had told him where his money was hid, Balls would be somewhere spending it."

"Who's he?" Alice asked Summer as the two sat on the sideline, or what Summer referred to as the bleachers.

She pointed to a tall, wide shouldered man in a rumpled, baggy suit and a whole head of newly awakened hair. He didn't look at all like a gangster but then again, she wasn't sure what a gangster looked like.

"That's Angelo Bari. He and Tommy were good friends."

"He's the Prince of the Neighborhood?

"I did say that, didn't I? Yeah, he's a good guy."

"Not a gangster?"

"He and Picco run a grift now and then. Small time. They wind up going up their own asses, pardon the expression. They kind of get into a loop. End up where they started. Still, they don't give up. Like, maybe now. Don't say a friggin thing."

"What's going on, Ange?" Summer asked.

"I thought you were the one who knew what was going on around here, Counsellor."

"Hello."

"This is Trip's wife. Alice. Alice, this is Angelo."

"Hullo. Sorry for your loss."

"I didn't lose him. He left me."

"He means Paul. Not Trip. Thomas. Whatever."

"You knew Thomas. Trip well?"

"Me? Yeah, I grew up with the guy. I don't know what he became. And that's everything, ain't it?"

Angelo towered over them, wider than the two of them. He had come over to get a close-up of this woman with the pale face and mounds of hair swept every which way, including across her face. So, this was Alice. Trip's Alice. He had met her once. Years before. She was just a kid. Nineteen. Twenty. He didn't remember the eyes he was looking at now. She had less luminosity then was what he remembered. The eyes hadn't been on perpetual high beam.

"We all grew up with the guy," Summer said, sighing as if very bored. "Some of us didn't grow up. Like Little Johnny over there. Picco, picco. Some are dead."

"You can only hear from the live ones, right Summer?"

"Okay, Ange, just what are you hearing?"

"I'm actually the hear no evil, see no evil, do no evil monkey.'

"I'm sorry Thomas never spoke about you," Alice said, somewhat sadly. "Not ever having done any evil. He never spoke about any of his Brooklyn friends. I didn't even know he was really a man called Trip."

Ange gave Alice another once over. What he saw in her eyes, the first whatever color they were eyes he had ever encountered, was not the gaze of someone looking at herself in the mirror. She didn't look like the Selfie type. She looked kind of startled, like someone who had turned over a pillow and found a big surprise. Smart and nuts is the way he would put it. And she needed to work on her hair, which shimmered like a jar of bees' honey held to the light, but unruly like a haystack pitched every which way. The eyes, a dark grey encircled by turquoise, or vice versa, were kind of fascinating. They kept changing. Yeah, he could see Trip scooping her up like treasure from a sunken ship. The wackiness seemed to him right off like a splash of cream on an Irish whiskey.

Summer leaned over and whispered in his ear.

"She's on the spectral, or spectrometer or something like that."

"I'm here because Mr. Limone left me some money," Alice told Angelo.

"Yeah, he knows that, honey. Everyone here does. But you don't have that money and right now no one knows where this money is, if there is any money."

"Thanks for spelling that out, Summer," Angelo said, smiling. "I'm really not interested in the money. But I know Paul left some debts."

He looked around.

"Some guys are here hoping to be paid off. It could get out of hand. Trip and I were ... "

"Partners in juvenile delinquency," Summer interrupted. "And that does not give you any cred here fifty years later."

"It's the IRS money that they don't know about," Alice told him. "I don't know about it either. But the people who lent money to Mr. Limone think I am going to get it. But I don't want to get it."

He wondered whether she always spoke so publicly, loud like either she was trying to reach other people far away or wasn't even aware of them. But he was enjoying it.

Every time Alice opened her mouth and bugled, Summer winced in pain.

"I'd say Paul owed a lot of people a lot of money," Angelo said in a very low voice, almost a whisper, "And those people would go to a lot of trouble to get what they were owed. That's what I would say. So, I don't know what Summer told you, but you're in a lot of danger. You shouldn't be here."

"Thank you. We've heard it. Do this lady a favor and tell those people that Paul had nothing to leave anybody. And if he did, Alice refuses it."

"If Mr. Limone left any money to me, I would not accept it."

Alice made this an even louder, bold pronouncement that this time made heads turn toward her.

Angelo nodded. Maybe she was loud because she was half in the bag. Or maybe it was because she had lost her social filter sometime in the past. Usually with the quiet, shrinking Alice types getting them to say anything was like pulling teeth but this Alice was blabbing with a bull horn. Was she tipsy, clever, or just nuts?

"Let's get a drink," Angelo said.

He wanted to hear her talk more. It was the kind of voice that didn't register anything, as if she hadn't heard or what she heard meant nothing to her. She seemed to be responding in some other dimensions.

"She doesn't drink," Summer told him. She started to say any more but Aunt Rita, wearing something like a gypsy dancer's outfit, rushed up to her.

"They got your old man out back," she told Summer, breathlessly.

"What the frig?" Summer said, jumping up. "Where the hell is his nurse?"

"You mean the Home Care Professional? He ran. They say you're your father embezzled the money Paul owed them. "

"I'll be right back," Summer said to Alice. She gave Angelo a look.

"I'm out of this one," Angelo said and she cursed under her breath.

"Just keep an eye on her. She's . . . Just keep an eye on her."

Grabbing Aunt Rita by the arm, Summer said "Where?"

"I told you not to trust those HCP people. All they do is watch the soaps. I ..."

"Shut up, Aunt Rita and take me to them."

"The bar?" Angelo said, holding out a hand that Alice took.

Angelo drank two quick shots and Alice sipped her first one. They were silent for long minutes although all around them it seemed as if pandemonium was breaking out in ever new levels.

"Hello."

"Okay," he replied, sensing he was flushing. "Hullo."

"Are they killing an old man out back?"

"What? No. Just the usual mistaken identity at a Wake."

"Are these people a danger to me? And my daughter?"

"Yeah, I would say they are. But you and your daughter have nothing to worry about. Your backs are protected. Picco and me go way back with your husband."

Alice somehow felt relieved listening to those words, even

though she didn't believe that she and her daughter would ever be safe again. She had a feeling they couldn't go far enough away to be safe. She and Thomas had gone far away but they really had gone no place. They had gone to Iceland. Then he had gone some place and she had a difficult time thinking about where she went. She feared she might be on a journey even though the word frightened her.

"Whatsa matter?"

"Padre Balsio would pull me into a laundering operation he has with the Pope."

"Yeah, maybe decades ago but the only thing he can do now is pull up the pants he's laundered. There's a new Pope anyway."

"Summer said that you and Little Johnny were gangsters and would find some way to swindle me. That's if I talked to you."

"She said that?"

"She also said you were the prince of the neighborhood."

"There's some bullshit for you on both accounts. Tell me, what's your daughter's name?"

"She names herself according to many different moods and circumstances."

"So, what do they call her at school?"

"I think they've been calling her Alice this year."

"Another Alice?"

"No. My name is Cecily. But Dr. Grew sees no signs of Cecily in me. Alice is true to who I really am. Tell me, why did Thomas. I mean Trip leave me?"

"Hard for me to say. Like Summer said, Trip and me were street punks together. He went off to college. I stayed in the streets. I seen Trip a few times only since he left Brooklyn."

"He left me also."

"Let's just say Trip had a kind of wanderlust. Hence the name."

"Dr. Grew says Thomas disappeared into what darkness from the past he carried with him, inside him. But I think he wasn't a prince inside. He wanted to put his hand in rich men's pockets."

"It ain't there. It's invested. You gotta angle to get at it. Used to be you could get a gun and rob a bank. But with all these electronics and plastic money there ain't nobody smart enough to do that and get away with it. You need to angle, angle real smart. Just the right bait. Everything's gotta be perfect. You can't crash in with a gun. You gotta get the mark to want to give you the money."

"You think of doing something like that?"

"Me? Wrong location. You know when they say location,

location, location. My location sucks. Place, people, opportunity. The only thing I'm connected to is a barstool. And Picco. That guy."

"I think Dr. Grew would love to meet you."

"Yeah, who knows? Maybe he wouldn't want to meet me. You know there was a thing Trip and I could always do."

"What?"

"Spot a con and the guys working it. Summer told me something about this doctor of yours."

Alice wondered what a "con" referred to but refrained from taking out her phone to ask because Summer had told her to not do that. It disconcerted people. Then she remembered the Iceland cruise so many years before and how Thomas had explained to her about a con.

"I wonder what's happened to Summer."

Angelo shrugged.

"Probably picked her old man off the pavement. She's been doing that her whole life. Keeping the old fool from going down the drain hole. Wasted effort."

CHAPTER FOUR

EULOGIES

The third and last night of the waking at Torricelli Funeral Parlor was a whole new life experience for Alice.

Padre Balsio led them in the rosary, then Dino Kim, the young half Korean, half Sicilian funeral director, told them how honored he was to be hosting the death services of such a notable man.

What he got in return was a lot of abuse, mostly racial, from the mourners who seemed to have come into the place inebriated. They were on the last day of a three-day drunk.

Alice sat there in the first row of seats, dressed in a Bergdorf basic black, and wondered if she would now get a picture of the world Thomas had come from, the world he had left behind.

She wondered if this whole world had somehow been genetically transmitted to her daughter. Not telling Biel, which was her daughter's chosen *nom de jour*, would be like not telling a black child about slavery or a Native American about the Trail of Tears or a Jew about the Holocaust. You really, really didn't want to tell them. But choice, that overrated illusion. It wasn't here to have.

She found herself not paying attention to what Padre Balsio was now eulogizing because an image of the Padre at the Laundromat talking to the Pope kept intruding. But then after he ended and sat down, snippets of what he had said paraded through her mind.

The world was divided in many ways, Padre Balsio had said, but in one place, there were those who were always ready to seize the day and whatever property they could leave with by nighttime. There were also the salubrious and the confined nerve ends. The screwed up and the grifters. The one Prince and everyone else. These, Padre Balsio said, were just a few of the basic rifts among those still living. The dead had their own problems and rifts.

Alice wasn't quite sure if she had made some of this up, so familiar did some of it sound. She might have mingled some Oyster Bay grandmother, some of her father and grandfather. And some Commander something or other. For sure. Padre Balsio, the defrocked priest, the man who laundered money and not clothes, had failed to mention those who went and those who stayed behind.

The vodka was working on her. She had a memory of once being an alcoholic but Dr. Grew had told her it was an implanted memory. She just liked a drink on social occasions he told her. She didn't recall any social occasions in her life but Dr. Grew said he would be happy to implant some. Alice wondered if it were possible for a hangover, the kind where you couldn't get your head off the pillow, to be implanted?

She saw Summer Arpeggio looking at her and it seemed as if she were signaling something.

Alice got it and nodded, and Summer nodded back.

Something of great significance might be revealed by the eulogizers so Alice should attend closely to each in turn. She found herself doing that by trying not to blink. Summer had also pointed to the drink in Alice's hand and shaken her head. Her mother, she remembered, often had a glass in one hand and a paint brush in the other. Her father had told Alice that her mother was painting "Alcohorals," pastorals with an alcoholic motif.

She didn't want to think about that. She had listened to Angelo Bari explain how the pieces were arranged on the board. This was the way Angelo expressed himself. The life before them was a like a board game without a bottom to Angelo Bari. She found that funny. On that board and in that game, Summer was trying to protect her father and not Alice, so Alice had to be wary of her. She put that piece alongside Little Johnny who was trying to get into her pants. She wondered if Little Johnny who was also Picco were as different from each other as Thomas and Trip might be.

The eulogizers she discovered split between the egoists, the fearful, who seemed frightened, perhaps because if a great man like Paul Limone could die, so could they. The egoists, on the other hand, saw only their own immortality on this occasion.

All the eulogies mixed with the alcohol and the Chorus surrounding her. That Chorus sang over the voices of the eulogizers. Totally disrespectful. A Greek tragedy without Sophocles.

She heard a few kudos to Paul and then from the same voice something of triumphs driving various women in and out of his bed and how a lot of things people gave Paul credit for were really done by the eulogizer and how Paul would have been alive today if he had listened to this voice.

"Shut up and drop dead!".

Another voice. Crying. Why is he crying she asked herself? Someone whispered in her ear that this guy was a guy who had sympathy for no one, including his mother, whom he had put in a home for paupers so he could get possession of her house, which he now lived in with a goomara. Alice recognized the word.

Another eulogizer said he owed everything to Paul, which quickly led into how Paul owed everything to him. Paul owed him for pointing out how some things may look good but would turn to shit.

"Go fuck a duck!"

She heard about the time some breakaway cargo broke this eulogizer's head and Paul had half of what was on that skid sent to his home regularly until the Feds showed up and confiscated it as stolen contraband and put him in Federal prison for twenty years and he just got out and would somebody run a benefit on his behalf?

Another speaker thanked Paul for paying for his father's funeral, even though he couldn't say in front of a defrocked priest like Padre Balls that his father was anything better than a rat bastard but seeing as how Padre Balls was no longer a priest he could say that his own father was a rat bastard who should have croaked twenty years ago and been chopped up in a chipper.

Then a croak of a voice said that it was good that Paul was lying in there with all his friends around instead of having been exterminated, which was the worst way to go, although extermination still went on all over. He had in fact exterminated the rats just below us in this funeral home.

She recognized Picco. He thanked Paul for supplying him with an expensive French hair oil that happened to slip off the skid as needed over the last twenty years and also for drawing his attention to that bitch of his ex-girlfriend's extra-curricular lifestyle as well as getting some of the loan sharks off his back when the vig was about to swallow him whole.

That brought a lot of laughter.

The testimonies became stranger and stranger Alice thought and after a while she became drowsy, most likely she thought from the powerful fragrance of the many flowered wreaths enclosing all the mourners in a womb of deep sedation mixed with Picco's expensive French hair oil. She also wondered why he was wearing a suit that looked several sizes too small for him, even though he was a small man. Perhaps it had been laundered by Padre Balsio and shrunk?

Nonsense filtered her perception so that if there was any kind of message in any of what she heard, she hadn't gotten a glimpse of it.

She only got a glimmer of a question: how did Thomas ever break free of this world? There was more than enough mania here to swallow Jesus, Muhammad and the Buddha.

When a large man in a very shiny grey suit and a silver pompadour crowning a long, horse like face took the microphone from Padre Balls, the mourners suddenly dropped into a pit of silence.

"That's Gorgeous George," Angelo whispered to Alice. "Gigi is what we call him. Gee, for short. He owns the Pompey. Or, let's say the lenders do."

"I got advice, my friends. My enemies too Dead is dead. What you need to do is put your own money away and you go to lenders. Here's what it says. I'm reading here. Then you go to another lender to pay the vig on the first lender. You go to a lender who gives you some stock that you sell, then you take that money and buy the same stock when it goes down, you sell short, pay back the lender and pocket the difference. You go to a lender and put up collateral you bought with money from another lender so you can buy more collateral to go to another."

He paused and ran a hand through his thick steel grey hair.

"In closing. That's about it."

Alice heard someone yell "You know we love you Gigi." They were very strange, these mourners.

"That's Connolly."

"So, where the fuck is the Jamison, Paul? How could you have a Wake without Irish whiskey?"

He got booed, applauded, whistled at and escorted to the bar.

"It's true enough. A pint of plain is your main man. I quote my man Flann O'Brien."

Alice looked at the speaker at her elbow.

That was code certainly. A pint of plain?

"I'm sorry for your loss," she told the man, hoping to solicit more code.

"Not loss a'tall, darling. 'No man is taken till a black hole is hollowed in the world to the depth of his two oxters and he put into it to gaze from it with his lonely head and nothing to him but his shield and a stick of hazel.'"

That sent Alice into a tail spin.

"Is there a subtext to that?" she whispered. "A code?"

"*At Swim Two Birds*," he whispered back to her and walked away.

She was decoding "oxters" when Angelo got up and took the microphone, he was red faced and it looked to Alice like he had been crying, although she knew he hadn't been, at least not while she was awake. She thought he looked very messy for a prince, at least the ones she had imagined.

"Connolly. Go fuck yourself. I'm passing that on from Paul. It's bigger than Irish whiskey. Paul wasn't all about money. Paul's gone but we're here and we're like an amazing fucking whale got himself beached in Coney Island."

He had the entire place rattling in angry protest. It had come on sudden like a burst volcano.

"I sound old and over the hill more than Gee and I'm on the right side of 40. But I feel it.," he said in almost a whisper. "And there ain't nothing natural about it."

"Fuck it!" someone yelled.

That brought so many shouts, and then gunshots. Alice knew they were gunshots because she saw the guns in the hands of those all around her. She expected the police to raid the Wake, probably, she conjectured, not the first police raid of a Wake in Brooklyn history. She saw Dino Kim rushing through the mourners, begging those with guns being fired into the ceiling to put their guns away. And then he disappeared from view as if he had dropped through a hole in the floor. And the shooting and shouting went on.

And so, the testimonies ended, and they all went back to Parlor B, the bar room, leaving Paul, the Kingfish, in the casket surrounded by tons of flowers, wreaking to the high heavens the aroma of decay.

Before they left Paul, Padre Balsio managed to bring it all down several notches by taking the microphone and beginning to recite what Padre Balls called The Rosary. Few heard but he kept on and soon all were responsive as he called to them: "Hail Mary."

Then he was asking forgiveness, although it seemed to Alice that they weren't asking forgiveness from anyone. It seemed to her they wanted to throw punches, keep firing their guns, and break some heads. They were fired up.

Thomas had had that fire and now she saw where it came from. Dr. Grew had told her that Thomas had failed to subdue his anger, it had gone inward, and set off a raging fire against which reason, logic and common sense could not prevail. She wondered about that now because Angelo's quiet anger and his confusion had seemed to her so very grand.

Angelo had come to stand in front of her as soon as a shot was fired, and she felt safe despite the chaos all around her.

As this last evening wore on and the mourners went half or all in the bag, Alice did follow a trail of wonder as to how she and Thomas, like two alien planets, had ever understood each other. They hadn't, she decided. She had no religion you could surround in brick and mortar, but she knew the words "When I was a child I thought and reasoned as a child." She didn't know how she had reasoned then or who she thought Thomas was. He was so clearly some of this all around her now.

The laughter was louder and longer, tearful testimonies were going on throughout Parlor B and angry shouting sparked like bolts of lightning, flashing and then gone. A very small woman at the bar. A Little Person? Was screaming at a very large man in a rumpled business suit. What was going on?

Alice decided to stay and drink rather than leave. She felt that Thomas would walk through that door. This was his home and she had finally found it, though it was only this parlor of riot and not a home.

She found herself sandwiched between Angelo and Picco at the bar, her self-appointed protectors. They had eclipsed Summer.

It seemed to Alice that these two were saying a lot of strange things.

"Sometimes it's better to think somebody's alive than be thinking they're dead."

Angelo shook his head.

"Sometimes Johnny don't know what he's saying," he told Alice, who was glancing at her phone looking for the texts she was sure to be getting from Biel.

She hadn't told Biel about the Wake. Biel thought she was at a publisher's party.

"Boring. Be home soon."

Biel didn't know her father. Why should she know she had a grandfather who had just died? Why should Biel know any of these people existed? This was a dying place, soon to be an extinct place. Summer had told her that. Ashes in dust. Dust to ashes.

She had been noticing a steady stream of men and women going through a door marked Parlor C and she asked about it.

"Lady Aquamarine is in there reading the future," Angelo told her.

"She makes some good money at these Wakes," Picco said. "Everybody is thinking when and if they're gonna be next. They gotta know when their ticket gets punched."

Alice suddenly had to know the future.

They queued up and when it was Alice's turn to sit before this large, black, turbaned woman, she asked her if she knew where Thomas was in the future. Or not.

"If I don't know him, I can't find him," Lady A told Alice in an Island accent, though Alice couldn't target the island.

"You know him, Tanya," Picco told her. "Trip Limone. You went with him for a while back then, didn't you?"

"That prick?" Lady A responded, all Brooklyn accents. "I hope he's dead and buried."

"I married him."

"Damn, girl," Lady A said, giving Alice a "Are you for real?" look.

"Do her favor, will you, Tanya?" Angelo asked.

"It must be wonderful to see the future. I wish I could do that. I think it's better than the past."

"Yeah, that ain't gonna happen, white girl. The future is black. I'm black. We're like one. We're joined. And it ain't nothing wonderful. It's like a movie theatre. You go in and you blind. I go in and I see everything right away."

"Do you see Trip?"

Tanya gave Ange a look and he did a "no" flutter.

"Naw, he ain't there."

"Maybe he's at another movie theatre?"

"It ain't like that. The future is just one place. And he ain't there."

"Does that mean he's dead?"

"You go into a movie theatre, girl, and your mother ain't there.

That mean she dead?"

"She is dead. She didn't go to the movies. She said she preferred pictures that stood still and you could look at for a long time.

"Thanks, Tanya," Angelo said, putting some tens down at her table.

"Nawa," Tanya replied, a word Alice didn't know.

Alice decided to let that word go. Dr. Grew had told her that certain words needed to be pursued, some words need to be repeated, and other words needed to be let go, at once as if they were hot coals dropped into her mind.

"I think everybody here is wonderful," Alice heard herself saying.

"Thing is, everybody here," Picco told her, "shouldn't be associating with everybody here."

Alice started to say something, but she seemed to be slurring her words. Too many drinks. Too many different kinds of drinks. She should have left a long time ago. She shouldn't even have been there. She shouldn't hang around with these types of guys. Dese types. Even if one was a prince. And he was protecting her.

Why was she there? Here.

Ange took it upon himself to clear the place out and Picco went to bring the car around.

Alice found a comfortable chair near a lamp and sat down.

Everything in front of her seemed to be off kilter, dancing. Maybe they were. Dancing. Some still at the bar. She had to admit, in her own mind, everything seemed to be dancing free of any moorings, her memories, dreams and reflections like wave tossed boats on an open sea.

She began to recite her calming mantra:

'Twas brillig, and the slithy toves/ Did gyre and gimble in the wabe'

Wabe? What was that? She pulled out her phone and she touched Dr. Grew's App. She needed to hear his voice.

"Why am I painting more than writing?" she asked, afraid to ask, "Why am I here?"

"Your children's world is vanishing, becoming perhaps too dark to survive. You paint now in the very room your mother had set her own easel. She looked to the paint for explanation. The movement of paint, slow but especially fast when she wished it, gave her an escape route from her fallen, imperfect world. Painting for you gives you greater access to much that a single, linear sentence could no longer reach. The paint is a bigger door, a camino of recuperation your mother had found and now you have found for yourself."

Thomas had told her that they would one day escape from a world imperfect in ways they would not tolerate. Maybe he was talking about The Wake.

But she thought then and still thought that subtracting the intolerable, extracting and excluding it would suit her better than escape. She had asked Dr. Grew who to exclude from a perfect world and how to do it.

She used the Dr. Grew's Voice App and listened:

Maybe the solipsists should go, just for irony's sake.

And what about the narcissists who didn't seem to do any damage but the way to see them was like dark holes of society, pits of selfishness that swallowed the paltry few gestures of altruisms.

And what of those whose money wielded the power of monarchs? The ones who could adjust the world to their capriciousness, their obscene self-love, those who wanted to eat the whole world. The thieves of the human heart and soul.

She shut Dr. Grew up. The drink was talking. She didn't recall Dr. Grew saying any of that.

CHAPTER FIVE

PARABLES

She was laughing at herself when she realized someone was standing over her.

She looked up and saw a big, square shouldered man in an ill-fitting suit, tent size, standing there. At first, she thought it was Prince Angelo. No, different face. This one was big like Moose Monjoy in that old film noir *Mother, My Sweet*. All those old black and white films that Thomas had loved, and she would watch with him into the wee hours. He could be any of those guys, he told her.

"Hello."

Then she shut her eyes and opened them again.

"Don't tell me," she said, covering her mouth as if she was chewing something but actually, because she was giggling. "They call you Moose. Hello, Moose."

"I am full of regrets about Paul," the big guy said in a very tiny voice, holding his hand out.

"Thank you very much, Moose," Alice said, reaching up and shaking a hand that could probably stretch across a canvas, and wondering what kind of regrets Moose had and anxious to hear them.

Was this, finally, a message? Would she hear a parable? No, this was a Lender. Were all Lenders gangsters? Watch out for the con, the attempt to win over her confidence in order to swindle, you, Alice, she warned herself. It's coming.

As she looked up at that giant with a face as round and as blank as the moon, snowman black coals were his eyes, she could set him far back at the vanishing point and paint boats and water all around him. She saw that. He was a friendly giant.

She tried not to giggle.

"I'm sorry to hear about your regrets. Have you had them long? I mean have you been here long? At ... at the ... the service? The Wake services. For ... for Paul?"

And then she was laughing, holding a hand over her mouth.

She felt a sudden wave of nausea but when she saw the stupefied look he was giving her, she felt so sorry for him. He was a sad giant. Such a tiny voice.

"I don't get noticed sometimes.'

A wave of laughter, hard to suppress, covered another wave of nausea.

"I'm sorry," she told him, waving one hand in front of her as if warding off her laughter and feeling very sad for him at the same time.

"I just wonder why. You're not noticed. Sometimes. You can fill a doorway and you have a very, very ambitious, rowdy pompadour of hair shading the tiniest eyes I've ever seen. But they're profound eyes. I think they are wonderful. Eyes."

Profound eyes? She didn't know what she was saying. And then she realized, she hadn't spoken what she had been thinking.

"I'm sorry you're so sad. About not being noticed."

"Yes, but this is not the occasion."

"Maybe you were standing by a doorway. What? What did you say?"

"This is not the occasion."

"The occasion? You mean the service? The Wake? For Paul?"

"Not for nothing, Paul owed me some money."

She patted a chair next to her and looked around. A quiet pandemonium but nobody seemed to be paying any attention to her. Maybe Moose was right. He didn't get noticed. Where was the Prince?

Moose sat down.

"Tell me," she said, suddenly realizing that if she drank more, things would go better. "Do you want a drink?"

"I'm in AA."

"That's fine. You know, Moose ... "

"No, I don't know him."

"You don't? What does 'not for nothing' mean? That you're not a fan of nothing? Or not and nothing mean more than nothing? Sooooo, for something?"

"I need someone to give me the money, the stash, Paul owed me."

"I see," Alice said, trying not to slur her words and searching for the right words at the same time. "You need to talk to a whole bunch of people about that. Lots of people. Lots. But not me. You could speak to Thomas. Wait. He's probably dead. Or should be. Tanya couldn't find him in the future. Maybe he's just in the present?"

She caught herself.

"No, not him. Paul's lawyer. She's not to be trusted. Summer Arpeggio. It sounds like a villa in Tuscany. Or a concerto. Or a pigment. You could paint with."

She paused.

"Someone told you to talk to me?" she whispered, leaning into a shoulder that looked like a wonderfully comfortable bolster. "Listen. It's true that Paul left me a … stash. But I … no one knows where it is. If I had it, I would give it to you. I don't.

Moose cleared his throat. He seemed to be looking up at the ceiling. Alice looked up there and saw nothing. She saw that she had drooled a bit on his shoulder and fanned the spot rapidly.

"I'll have to hurt somebody if I don't get my money."

"You will have to hurt somebody?" she repeated, looking into a glass of whiskey that was suddenly in her hand. "That … that, Moose, is a very sad intention to have."

Suddenly. A very direct parable. Message.

"Did you come here to threaten me?"

Anger rose, instantaneously, as if, he had just threatened her. Had he, really?

This was the giant who was casting a shadow on Biel's life. This was the villain she had been waiting for all night. Biel? What strange names her daughter thought to call herself.

"Do you know that that there's not enough room in my world for people who want to hurt other people?"

She stood up when she declared this, her eyes closed.

"I wouldn't hurt you. But you need to tell Arpeggio. No more games."

"I need to … What? I need to stop drinking. I need to … to get my coat."

She looked around, and then fell back into her chair. Wasn't somebody going for a car?

She stared at Moose's blank canvas of a face.

"Moose, why me? I don't know why the stash was left to me."

"You're Alice, aren't you? They told me Alice got the stash."

"She did?" Alice asked, amazed that someone fictitious could have gotten all the money. "She got the stash?"

Alice realized she was sitting there with a mouth open, stunned. She finished her drink. Or somebody's drink. It was the last thing she needed then but it seemed to fit the need.

Did that make sense?

The wisest course someone in her head told her was just to look for her coat, before other enigmatic, threatening giants showed up. She also recalled the advice her daughter had given her: "Don't Panic!"

The problem was, she wasn't sure she could make a dignified effort to get her coat. She hoped Paul, wherever he was, appreciated her getting soused at his service. Dr. Grew had once told her that for her, alcohol was a short cut to sanity, one that like a hangover, didn't last long.

She suddenly saw Thomas at the bar with a drink in his hand standing next to the Little Person and the poor man she seemed to be still abusing.

"Aperitivo?" he called to her.

She blinked hard and when she opened her eyes, only someone who looked like him was there. Nevertheless, she wasn't at all surprised he had disappeared. It's what he did. Of course, she now knew that it hadn't been Thomas who had left her but Trip. That's what Trip did. Hence the name. Thomas would take her to places without alcohol.

She thought of Trip, a total stranger, who was probably sleeping like a baby somewhere right then, a giant's shoulder on which to lay his head, mindless of having left her amid whatever it was she was amid. Of which she was in the midst. Within which.

But he wasn't. What was she thinking? Thomas. Trip. They were both no more. Neither had a future. Nobody she had ever met before had been called Trip. Anyway, he wasn't. Sleeping way down below. Dark, deep, dank. The forever sleep. The sleep that had no end. You could hail Mary all you wanted but she couldn't wake him.

Why were little silk pillows put under the heads of the dead as they lay in their coffins? Was that part of the service, like Belgian chocolate left on the pillow? Or an origami towel folded into a giraffe left on a bed?

Before she could make up her mind to get up and walk straight, someone was speaking to her. She opened her eyes and realized she must have blacked out.

"Paul would have liked that everybody is enjoying themselves."

The voice sounded like it was Stephen Hawking's and he was under the lamp table by her chair. Not a baby tiny voice like Moose's but a mechanical, robotic one. Why would a famous physicist be here at the service? The physics behind death. Death had to have a physics.

Where had Moose gone? Oh, yes. People didn't see him sometimes.

She looked under the table.

"But it don't look like sadness to me. If this is mourning, show me what happy is."

Alice felt spooked and jumped up out of her chair and sure enough there was someone standing on the other side of the table, someone about three feet high and not a child.

The face looking at her was drawn, wrinkled and mottled, and he had a long, yellowed in the tooth smile.

She instantly thought that here was another gangster. Con man. Laundry man. Lender. She prepared herself to hear a parable.

"Mal Occhia," the little man said, sticking out a hand that was outsized compared to the rest of him. He was wearing an expensive looking dark suit and a big cravat pushed his outsized head to an upward tilt

"People say the name fits. Mal."

Alice took his hand and fell back into her chair.

Unbelievably, she remembered the name. Mal Occhia.

Mal ambled around the table and then hoisted himself onto a chair.

"Maybe you thought what I thought?" he asked her.

"What?" she said, trying not to laugh because she knew what he didn't know. If she said his name. Rumple Stell Skin. He would disappear.

Drunk, nauseated, confused, sad, tired, frightened, and ridiculous. She thought she had run the list in her own mind but Mal told her she had just summarized the human condition.

"You know, my dear, I thought that if there was any way for Thomas to get here, he would be here."

She didn't respond.

"I knew his father pretty well."

"I don't feel like talking, Mr. Mal. I don't feel like talking about feathers. Fathers. I drank too much."

"Never knew mine," Mal told her. "And my genetics have

prompted me not to be one."

"Do you have a message for me, Mr. Mal?"

"Call me Mal, sweetheart. Fairly well, let's say I knew Paul fairly well, but I knew his lawyer better. Mr. Arpeggio who is over extended now both regarding workload and regarding mental capacities. In short, something needs to be done."

Something needed to be done. She had to do something. No, this was the threat she felt coming. Or maybe it was the parable.

"I don't have it. I want to pre … pre something I want to turn it down. I mean I don't know where it is."

'Preemptively," Mal said, nodding.

Mal looked at her closely. He had very, very large eyes of a very strange color and in their blue, blue seas, she could see many tiny, tiny boats. Malocchia eyes. The evil eye. She felt him push her back onto her seat.

"Mr. Arpeggio is over-extended."

"What do you mean over-extended?" Alice asked, feeling another wave of nausea resulting from leaning so far forward and then being thrust backward.

Over-extended: to borrow more than you should; Also, to stretch forward and need assistance in regrouping.

"That's a sweet device," Mal said to her. "It has some wit, which the present circumstances lack."

Amazing, she said, perhaps audibly. She still had a glass of something. It was full. In her hand. Who had put it there?

"He went to lenders, established leverage, goes to other lenders, establishes greater leverage and lets it all ride on a housing development in Queens because he thinks Queens is going to be the next Brooklyn. Stupid. But stupid is what Mr. Arpeggio has become."

Alice wanted to say 'repeat that' but she really didn't want to hear it again. She thought of Trip. Trip? … peacefully sleeping. Like the dead. With his little pillow. Below decks.

Why wasn't he here listening to this?

Why was she here?

Mal had not stopped talking.

"We Brooklynites know that Queens can't happen because Brooklyn is a warm, suddenly exposed belly the rich want to lie on and Queens is an outpost for the banished potato. But real estate wise, lawyer Arpeggio, brains almost gone, thought it would happen. Brains say … " and here the little man tapped his forehead, "that if it does happen, it will happen after we are all dead. Not just

Paul. That's what a Mensa person figures out."

There was the threat and possible parable again. It seemed that the problem with parables was that you didn't know when they were happening, or they only happened when you were somewhat inebriated and then everything was of course a deep parable to be interpreted. These Brooklynite parables at the service? Not transparent at all, although she seldom found any words transparent, for which she was not to blame herself. Words were secret doors that often went no place. Dr. Grew's words.

Alice felt sure that she didn't know what Mr. Mal was talking about but it was most certainly a parable. A real estate parable. She did know that if she heard any more of that wired, grating computer voice, she would do what Moose would do: hurt somebody. She could put a thousand Mr. Mals on canvas but only one Moose.

She scanned the room for help. Picco, Prince Angelo, Fussy Mussy, Padre Balls, Gigi, Tanya, Summer, or any of them. They were alike anyway. All forged from the same piece of extinction, like the missing link. One was a Prince. But where was he?

What she saw was the Little Person who had taken off her bra and was now standing on the bar waving it. She was making a fuss. Alice shook her head in strong disapproval.

"Not any kin of mine," Mal told her, looking at the fuss. "Evangeline Solly. Nasty. Drunk or sober. Imbeciles stay up at 3AM to listen to her radio talk show. She trades insults with her co-host, Bratter. That's him standing next to her."

His face wrinkled into great displeasure.

"If Paul walked in on this, he'd walk out," Mal told her. "So, we sum up. As our brains are working. It was Paul's money that the lawyer Arpeggio used to launch his over-extensions. Now his brain is over-extended. Money gone. Mind gone."

At this point Mal put both hands together -- Money and Mind -- and clapped loudly.

She jumped.

"Mind gone?" she said, repeated.

She had heard of guiding your own dreams and she wondered if she could guide her inebriation to sobriety? Lucid inebriation. A clear mind and many drinks. Personally, she felt that in between rare occasions of both, she got tossed around a lot.

Who had told her that? Probably her father. Jonathan Darden. He was probably peacefully asleep also. He was probably in a Parlor A somewhere at that very moment. No little pillow for him.

No service at all. Pile of wood, torch it and float him out to sea.

"You might be asking yourself what all this has to do with you. Several million reasons," Mal said, smiling. "We sum up once again. Arpeggio's collapsed brain encouraged him to use Paul's money to get the first round of lenders to lend. That was his step up. Embezzler and swindler, in short."

"But not a grifter?" Alice asked, somehow drawn to that odd word.

"Many unsalutary words will pop up if it all begins to unravel," Mal told her in what he probably thought was a whisper but what sounded like a loud death rattle to Alice.

"And it will unravel unless one of the lenders is paid now with interest."

She realized her eyes were closed and that she might be sleeping. All along, she had been the one peacefully asleep on the service pillow hearing the word "unsalutary" repeatedly, though she had not found it to be a word at all. The secret door that went no place.

"All of this you must convey to the daughter who now controls the father. The finger she points at you."

And here Mal pointed a very long finger at Alice who realized that her eyes were open, and she was awake. The evil eye was still on her.

"Points back to her."

Alice studied the little man. She wondered how old he was. She had read that Tom Thumb sized people didn't live very long. Mal might have been immortal. More certainly, if she was asleep, he was a nightmare.

"I know who you are. You're a grifter."

He put on something like a smile but was, in her viewing, more like a grimace.

"I'm really that one lender who wants to be paid now with interest. That's the way to think about me. It's the smart way. The dumb way has a bad end. Non-compliant people wind up in dumpsters."

Still smiling, Mal took a snuff box out of his breast pocket, opened it and offered it to Alice who looked at it and shook her head and at the same time reached into the tiny box with two fingers and grabbed what she could. She watched Mal stuff his up his nose.

"Why don't you talk to Summer Arpeggio then?" she said, stuffing the stuff up both nostrils, hoping it would sober her up.

Mal went for his handkerchief.

"The will redirected our attention. Everything left to you. And now you are here. A person of interest as the Feds say. You can't be ruled out."

"I can't be ruled out?" Alice repeated, happily. This was the best news she had heard at The Service. There was life after this.

Mal was wiping his bald pate and looking over at the burlesque at the bar.

Several other women had gone topless and their admirers were wildly applauding them.

"Sometimes a great deal of sadness produces its opposite. People make jokes and laugh. Then sometimes it is what it is. Degeneracy. That's what it is in this case. But time is shy. You touch it and it will run out on you. The poet says there is fear to be seen in a handful of dust but it has the opposite effect here as we can see."

He worked himself off the chair.

"Everything will work itself out," he told her. "The true will find their peace and the false will be discovered. Sometimes, sadly, in a dumpster, the affordable funeral parlor. I wonder who is paying for this orgy?

He waddled toward the men's room.

Alice had to slap herself to see if she was awake. She probably wasn't because if your eyes were closed the Mal Occhia couldn't see you. Mal only appeared when you were asleep.

That's what Little Johnny. No, he didn't like to be called that. Angelo called him Picco. If you had your eyes closed, the mal wouldn't work. She felt sure that if she were sober, her Alice would easily resist and probably subdue the mal in the malocchia. She was also sure that if she could uncode why time was shy, she'd get the message.

Summer Arpeggio found Alice lost in the coat room trying to find her coat.

"Your father is an embezzler," Alice said when she saw Summer. "And a swindler. Both."

"You know you're drunk, don't you?" Summer said, noting at once that a drunken Alice was no longer spaced out. The alcohol was probably trumping the meds she was on. The stupefying meds her Dr. Grew probably had given her.

"Your father robbed money from Paul and now a giant and a dwarf ... I mean, Little Person, told me I can't be ruled out. Does this look like my coat?"

"My father's in the hospital. They did everything but eat him in that alley. How the fuck would I know if that's your coat?"

"Your father was eaten?" Alice asked, eyes popping and rocking back on her feet so that Summer had to grab hold of her.

"You're blitzed. Who have you been talking to?"

"People with parables, not transparent," Alice said, putting on what looked like it might be her coat though hers had been a fur coat from Bergdorf and this one was cloth.

"I think it's Aunt Rita's," Summer said. "It has her gun club pin on the collar."

Alice ignored the ID and kept the coat on.

"Wasn't Angelo watching you?" Summer said, anxiously, scanning for Angelo.

"A man who looks like four big men packaged in one suit told me he'd have to hurt someone if someone didn't give him the stash he says Paul owed him. He repeated the word stash several times. It made me sick. He's very large but he says people can't see him. And then a Little Person. Mal Occhia. Do you know that being little doesn't stop you from growing old? Well, he told me I couldn't give anyone any money because your father had already stolen it. Grifted it."

She leaned toward Summer as she said these two words.

"There's no sense in continuing this now," Summer told her, curtly and pushing her straight. "I'll call you tomorrow. And don't worry about Mal Occhia or The Lutheran. They're intimidating to an outsider but they're really just paper bags."

"Paper…paper bags?"

"I'll call you tomorrow. And that's not your coat."

"I shall be …. occupied," Alice declared emphatically, as she tried to button the coat and realized it wasn't her coat, but wrong coats were the last thing she'd trouble herself about. Be occupied with. With which. The last thing. Coats were not wrong in any important way. There were far more important matters to be wrong about. Of which. With which. To be wrong.

She had to get home. Biel would be wondering what happened to her. And after that, she'd be wondering what happened to her. Herself.

Outside, the cold air hit her hard, like a cold, cold hand slapping her brain to sobriety. She took a deep breath and welcomed it.

Little chance of getting a cab in that neighborhood. Trip's old neighborhood. He would probably know where she was.

She had her phone out and was saying "Uber" when Picco came out the door and, coming over to her, took her arm and told her he'd drive her home.

He had the kind of vintage flashy car that she thought fit his clothing style. Naples yellow with Egyptian hubcaps, he told her.

As Picco drove, she told him about the giant and the little old person.

"The big guy was The Lutheran," he informed her.

"Dr. Grew says sometimes everything is easier in life if you have a religion," Alice told him.

"The Lutheran ain't a Lutheran," Picco told her, turning and smiling at her.

"The Lutheran ain't a Lutheran?" she repeated, suddenly more fatigued than nauseated or angry. Focus remained a problem. "I mean, isn't."

"The big guy you were talking to. Don't pay any attention to him. Paul owed him squat. He's in a bad way since Sonny Woe and Ronny Pains let him go."

"From what was he let go? Of," Alice asked, knowing she should not have asked but intent on proving to all that she was sober.

At the same moment, she felt that the more questions she asked the more she felt like puking.

"He lacked the finesse needed for a top ranked lobbyist firm like Woe and Pains run."

Something flew across her mind, but she quickly let it go.

"Naw, I'm just kidding. Those guys ain't top ranked anything. They're morons. Lobbying is a grift, sweetheart. One too far a reach for them. They're in the bargain basement of the Grift Hotel."

She didn't understand that, but it was her own fault. Once again, despite her better judgment, she realized she was asking questions. The more questions she asked and the more answers she got the more she knew that getting her confused was the real Kingfish here. It seemed like a return to something, but she didn't have any better hold on it than the first time. She felt she was tackling her drunken mind with a mind lost in a rabbit hole. She wondered about the usefulness of that fight.

"Woe and Pains back in the day conned tourists into buying swag wristwatches and phony theatre tickets on Broadway. They'd give their left ball to lobby for Walmartz or anything to do with cement, like Famazon and Starfucks. Organizations like that."

Despite the sober counsel she was giving herself, Alice pulled out her Smartphone:

"Lobbyist: A person who attempts to influence powerful people to make decisions that profit other powerful people the lobbyist represents: See also, The Blackmail Grift" and Old-time extortion."

"They call it lobbying but it's just old-time extortion. The Lutheran enforced when promises weren't kept. It's like now they call torture `extensive interviewing' or something like that. We call extortion and bribery lobbying now. But in the hands of a genius, like Ange, it's a small, dirty part of a beautiful grift."

"Who calls what what? Who's Ange?"

"Do you know what I call embezzling?" Picco said, grin still holding fast on his face. He was amused.

"Embezzling?"

"I call it swindling. Don't think I'm not on top of things."

"I don't," she said, having no idea where he was on top of, unless he was on top of her head, pushing her into a migraine.

"Good," he said, reaching out and giving her leg an easy pat. "You ain't no easy boozie. I kind of like you better this way. You know, less zombie and more pluck. Maybe me and you could team up on a couple three things."

One hand was inching up her skirt and he was leaning toward her.

There was something she had to say. She remembered.

'I didn't think you needed women to force you to come around if you were a sharp guy. Which you are. So, there's no force. Involved."

He laughed.

"I am popular. But I think Ange told you to say something like that, right?"

"Who's Ange?"

Alice pulled the hem of her skirt down.

"No worries about funeral costs," he told her after a while.

She had her eyes closed. Now she opened them.

"I don't think I was. Why should I worry about funeral costs?"

"You inherited the money and the debts. Payment due."

"Wait, you mean I'm supposed to pay for this ... what do you call it? The Wake. I think I left without paying. For what?"

"The service."

"The service. Yes. Body in a parlor thing. Hail Mary. Wait. Pull over. I'm going to be sick."

Picco made a sharp turn to the curve and had barely come to a stop when Alice had the door open and her head out.

Picco grabbed her coat and held her as she vomited into the street. When she was finished, he pulled her back into the car, gave her a silk, monogrammed handkerchief the size of a shirt and continued driving. She noticed she had puked some on the coat. Somebody's coat.

"Feel better? You always feel better after you get it all up. It's one of those bad but it's good experiences in life, like taking a ... like relieving yourself."

She thought she did feel better. This voice was very soothing.

"Angelo got Sally Franklin to cover the funeral expenses."

"Sally Franklin?" Alice mumbled, feeling so much better but not yet able to stop digging the hole she was digging. "Why did she cover whatever."

"He makes Hamiltons in his basement. He's a real artist. Of course, his name ain't really Franklin. Or Sally. I think it's Sid."

"Hamiltons? You mean like ten-dollar bills? He counterfeits money?" Alice repeated, amazed and then amazed that she was amazed. She somehow clearly saw the face of Alexander Hamilton although she had never met the man.

Talking to Picco was worse than talking to Mal Occhia.

It was all one big nightmare. What she was going to do was take Biel out of school and both would go off to her favorite remote hamlet in Braga, Portugal and just stay there. Where the dwarves and the giants couldn't find them. Better yet, they could both sail away on any of the beautiful schooners she painted. The thought made her happy and she smiled.

She felt something hard pressing on her hip. She pulled a small, black gun out of the coat pocket. She opened the window and threw it out.

"That he does," Picco was saying.

"He paid for the service in counterfeit money?"

"It's his gift to Paul. This funeral is not cheap, my dear Alice. Open bar. Actually, the way it works out it's a grift gift."

"A grift gift?"

"Thus far. If Dino takes the Hamiltons. You know funny money is in the toolbox of a good grift. Dino will know they're queer, but he knows how to unload them so he's not out anything."

"Grifters have toolboxes? Like carpenters and gardeners and green grocers?"

She was stunned, before it was the alcohol, now it was the alcohol plus thoughts. She sat there thinking that she was now being dragged into a crime. She was surprised that she didn't feel any different.

"Tell me," she said, turning to look at Picco's profile. "This is my last question. If I ask another one, kill me."

She panicked.

"Wait. Don't do that. But … Okay, is there anyone you know who is not a criminal, gangster, grifter, anyone with a toolbox? Isn't there any Sweet Baby somethings or Good Neighbor somebody? Saint Judases or something?"

Picco showed all signs of thinking deeply about that. He finally said:

"Sure."

And then; "Okay. Nobody. Sweet Baby is a hooker and Good Sammy just says "good" a lot. He choked his brother with a wire hanger."

"Oh, my God!" Alice exclaimed, sinking as low as she could get in her seat. She was beginning to sober up and freeze up at the same time.

"Look, you're not asking the right question. Bad people become criminals. Good people become criminals. When you get caught, you're bad. If you don't, you're good. You should be asking me, "Picco, who can I trust?""

She took a deep breath. She smelled bad. Her breath and the coat had its own cheap perfume deal going on. And his French hair oil.

"Okay. Who should I trust?"

Picco glanced over at her, taking his eyes off the road for too long in her estimation.

"Depends. The better question is whom or who shouldn't you trust when it comes to the way Mr. Lucky … that's Paul. They called him that cause he looked like Cary Grant in that movie. When he was young. Trip. . ."

"I trusted Thomas."

"See? That was a mistake. Look, Angelo wouldn't want me to tell you. Get you in deeper than you have to be."

"Please stop the car and let me out."

"Okay. Look. Summer Arpeggio for one. Don't trust her. I already told you that. If anyone knows where the money is stashed her old man knows. Off shore account or something like that. But he got himself demented and I don't think she's gotten the info out of him. Yet."

"They ate him Summer said."

"Eat or get eaten they say around here, just kidding. They roughed the old guy up a bit. Fats Bracciole took a bite out of him.

Just to make him remember. Summer now. Well, hey, she's still around. She'd be sailing off into the blue if she had the dough."

Alice's head was pounding, her mouth felt and tasted like a warmed-over gym towel was wadded inside it, but she couldn't stop dealing with what Picco was telling her. She wasn't letting go of the words she should be letting go. They were taking her nowhere.

"Goodbye."

"Yeah, goodbye but wait until I stop the car. We ain't there yet."

"Now, you take Summer. She just wants to throw everybody off her case. We know she's got it. Or close to getting it."

Alice didn't respond.

"It. Whatever Paul left you. The interested parties ... ."

"The Lenders?"

"You know you work a grift right the lenders think they borrowed money from you. That's when it's sweet. Look, Ange and me just don't want anything to happen to Trip's special lady. And her daughter."

"Summer said Trip was a prick."

Picco laughed at that.

"That's because he dumped her in the 8th grade. She never forgot. Summer's a Tartar when it comes to revenge. She's always packing."

"To go where?"

When he pulled up in front of her Airbnb, she told him that she wasn't a special lady, just a forgotten one. She had been figuring that out in her silence.

"I've spent the last ten years down a rabbit hole."

"Hey, now you're out. You're in Brooklyn."

"I'm trying to be. Do you think I'm crazy?"

"I couldn't tell, being half crazy myself. That's what Ange tells me. It's a crazy world. Half the population is trying to get at what the other half has. That's what Gee says. He says it's more like 60% totally fucked over, 20% working a grift, and 20% kissing the asses of the 1%, who are inventing the robots and jacking the organs they need to live forever."

"A hundred and one percent?"

"Exactly. So, lighten up. You're among the redistributors now."

"What?"

"Redistributors redistribute. Like me and Ange."

"The numerical value of redistribution in Chaldean Numerology is: **2**;

see also, envy economics and the redistribution of time in pre-modern societies."

"That from your phone?"

"You know, it doesn't help."

"You know what would do you a world of good? Going out with me on down to Mill Basin. Island Channel, like that. Gravesend Bay. I got a long keel, masthead sloop. I call it *Baby Cheeks*. Get the wind in your hair. You'll feel like a million bucks. You know what a sea breeze in your face is like? It's ..."

"Goodbye."

CHAPTER SIX

SAILOR

Alice and Prima, her daughter's *nom de jour*, were deep into their plans to take an extended trip to Malta, which they had picked out of a hat filled with destinations, when the doorman buzzed. Someone malodorous and very odd looking saying he was Thomas's cousin wanted to come up. Should the doorman tell him to move on?

Alice looked at Prima, who was on her phone telling yet another of her friends that she and her mother were off to Europe and of course they should come and visit them in Paris.

Fully expecting not a cousin but a gangster or a lender or a grifter but still curious, she said:

"Let him up."

She thought of warning Prima but she didn't know what to warn her of. She could text her:

"Prima, you are about to meet a grifter. Your father's cousin."

No, that wasn't right. She wasn't sure what a grifter looked like, so it seemed proper identification was not possible. This one was malodorous and oddly dressed. Was the doorman supposed to provide that kind of description, or any description at all?

The idea that Thomas had a cousin was fascinating.

She wondered if he was Cousin whatever the way Aunt Rita was an aunt, of no one really. She thought about working up to reality by connecting the cousin to the Pearl stories. This cousin, whom she was about to meet, was Donny Ray Pickles in the *Pearl in the Foxler Holl'er* stories. Dr. Grew had told her that it was a gifted way of

71

seeing the world and the people in it, and most especially those who weren't in it, never were and never would be. The imagination, he told her, was fulfilling in this way, especially for his patients.

She opened the door on a man, not at all shaped like a pickle but more like a pear, red faced, straggly dirty brown hair hanging to his shoulders, wearing a Metallica tee.

Her imagination failed her, and she stood there, staring at him, open mouthed.

"Tim Kerplowski. They call me Sailor, but I wasn't on any boat. But I got … thing is I got a boat I live on. I was in The Sands. Iraq. Thing is. That was back then. In the Sands. I got a boat now."

"Goodbye," she said, closing the door.

He put a hand out to stop the action.

"I'm Thomas's cousin. It's a long story but that's who I am. Cousin Tim but they call me Sailor."

Alice continued to close the door on him.

He looked very much like a type of person Dr. Grew had described: The Sloven Irrational often referred to by politicians as "The People" and the police as "The Perpetrator." He was an Everyday American in Leap Year. "What it is is that," Sailor started, wedging a torn track shoe of enormous size against the door. "Okay, I'm Paul Limone's sister's son. I'm Pollock Kerplowski's son."

She repeated her goodbye.

"I'm what's left of the family after you leave out all the dead ones. And I got a right to be here representing on account of I'm entitled and you ain't."

Sailor peered into the apartment.

"Can I come in?"

He didn't wait for her response but pushed passed her.

She was glad to see Prima had gone to her room.

"I thought I heard you talking to somebody," Sailor said, dropping down on the sofa.

"That was my daughter, Prima. She's gone to bed."

"Ah, the kid in your Foxler Holl'er stories. I like to read those kinds of stories. When I'm on my boat. It's like not the Internet of Things but just things."

He stared at her, a faraway look in his eyes.

"Children like to tell themselves stories," Alice told him, "of things that are not visible. I'm an adult but I still do."

"I go on boats to stay as far away from The Sands as I can."

"Boats," she repeated. "Do you know this one:

Should you ever put to sea
In Equatorial clime
You may chance to witness
The Crossing of the Line,
On the Indian, Atlantic
And Pacific Ocean too,
When e're you cross the Equator
While on the ocean blue."

Sailor looked at Alice as she recited this, beady, woodchuck eyes blinking, uncomprehending and said nothing.

"Crossing the Line by Neil McLeod," Alice told him.

"I'm here to claim whatever … wait … you know Thomas and me were tight, right? First cousins and all."

"Not Trip?" she said, startled.

This man … this cousin who was …

"Tight: Not loose; also, bonded like first cousins since the first grade."

"Satellite talk," Sailor told her, shaking his head like a hand rattle.

"I don't like that. You telling them where I am. I don't want you to do that.

She wondered who "them" might be but she didn't ask. What Cousin Tim might tell her could be disturbing.

"The thing is I'm alive. I ain't dead. I've been in the VA hospital but I'm alive. This is what it is. You got what I'm supposed to get. That's what it is. The thing is," Sailor went on. "No, wait. Here's what it is. I don't get enough money from the VA to live on."

He looked, sounded and smelled mad, bad and dangerous to know Alice recited from memory. But this Sailor from The Stands didn't seem at all bad or dangerous to her. Just smelly. And befuddled.

He seemed to understand the look she gave him.

"I fit only one description in the DSM," he told her. That thought angered him. "I fought in a war," he told her bitterly. "One I didn't start. The thing of that is I didn't come out ready to start a business. Or invest wisely. I told them to stop so many times that's what they called me Stop."

He was standing now, and she asked him to sit down. She thought about offering him something but then again he didn't look like he was a member of the AA, like Moose. The Lutheran.

"Water?"

Alice wrinkled her nose when she walked by him. He did indeed smell worse than he looked but really, she thought now, it wasn't a bad smell. He smelled of the ocean. Of salt water and seaweed. She decided she liked it.

"The thing is," Sailor told her, taking a deep breath. "Okay, here's what it is. It's like this."

Alice waited, long ago having decided that "the thing" was everyone's sad attempt to talk about the world, which they could not hold clearly in their imaginations. She never painted that sort of nebulous, amorphous thing nor did it appear in her stories.

She watched Sailor pull a wrinkled pack of cigarettes out of his pocket and light up.

"*No fumar*," she told him.

"Exactly. Any chance for a coffee?" Sailor asked her, blowing smoke upward. "Black."

His beady eyes were hidden behind puffy lids and his lips were swollen as if bee stung.

He took another puff and immediately began to cough, soon a paroxysm of coughing and choking. His face went purple.

"Are you alright, Mr. Sailor?" Alice asked him, thinking she would ask Dr. Grew to give this man some money. Dr. Grew had told her that money was the best defense.

"I have PTSD from the Gulf War. And the 16-inch guns fired my ear drums to ash."

Alice saw that he wore an NA pin.

"Oh," was all Alice managed to say. *"Beware of strangers who knock at your door."* Summer's text. *"Don't listen to whatever they say. It's code."*

That made her want to listen. To the code. This was a cousin of Thomas's who had been tight with him since the first grade.

"The thing is everybody thought I was dead, but I wasn't. Just missing. Okay. Here's what it is. I'm alive. They had me in a facility out on Long Island. Otherwise I would have been at the Wake."

"You missed the service?"

"The way it is," Sailor said. "Is that I'm the son of Paul Limone's sister and she's dead and everyone else in the family is dead. But I'm alive. I'm Paul's nephew. You're not. You're nothing. But I'm entitled. That's the point. I'm the first cousin. The nephew. By blood. Excuse the expression."

He seemed very nervous now.

"I mean nothing personal," he told her in a less aggressive voice.

"I should tell you, Sailor, before you go any further that I wasn't given any money. And if I had, I would give it to you. As the first cousin. But I think that Mr. Limone's lawyer embezzled all his money. There was none to pass on to anyone."

At that, Sailor jumped up, held both large reddened beefy hands to the sides of his head and screamed:

"Oh, fuck me!"

He began to jog back and forth in front of Alice.

"Okay, here's the way it is.," Sailor said, stopping inches from her face. "I don't have access or agency. I've got negligible capacity."

Alice gave him a bewildered look.

"Access or agency," she said into her phone. *"Agency is the capacity of an actor to act in a given environment. The traumatized who show up at your door seldom possess it."*

"Satellite talk!" he screamed yet again.

Alice cowered in a corner of the sofa. She threw the phone on the coffee table.

"Look, here's what it is. You see what I'm saying? It is what it is. An agent does something for a principal. But not for himself. Okay, for himself. The thing is look out for yourself and let the other guy do the same."

Alice began to shake, a sudden trembling in all her limbs.

This was not a Lender or a Gangster or a Grifter. This was a lunatic.

"He was an embezzler and a swindler," Alice told him, her voice quaking.

Sailor started to cough again and fell back on the sofa. Alice reached over and took the cigarette from his fingers. She looked up at Prima who had crept out of her room, unseen by Sailor, and had just taken a photo of Sailor with her ubiquitous I-phone companion.

"Could you not do that and go make us some coffee?"

Prima made a face and then disappeared.

"Okay," Sailor said, wheezing, barely able to speak. "Where's the kitchen?"

"Never mind that."

"The coffee? Black."

"There is none. Of any color."

"Okay."

They sat and looked at each other for long moments. Sailor's anger had settled now into a pathetic confusion. He sat there with both ham fists resting on his thighs. He began a mumbled disjointed account of some of his experiences in The Stands or The Sands and the ease at which people were reported missing and accepted as missing by those who should have known better.

It didn't make any sense to Alice, but she found herself making consoling sounds at what she saw as the right moments to do so. She retained this feeling that she always missed the right moments while other people seized them. They seized the moment and she didn't. She found it as impossible to seize the moment as to seize the breeze or the age of two when you're four.

This Cousin was very frightening. She opened her eyes and saw Prima, once again, standing behind their cousin.

Alice tried to avoid paying any attention to the wide-eyed curiosity expressed in Prima's eyes as she peered at both of them. Alice waved to her to go to her room before Sailor saw her and launched him once again into his interminable self-identification and perhaps, almost as bad, screaming outrage if he saw Prima's I-phone.

"The thing is," Sailor continued, tapping his knee, "It's like the stockade. Court ordered. What it is with the ins and outs of that, I don't know. But I'm not screwy is what it is. The long of the short is that my life has had its ups and down, ins and outs and what have yous. And whatever. Like everyone in the whole country. To some people around here I'm like North Korea or some country hiding its nuclear bomb production, if you listen to them. But money helps. That's why I need to get my hands on …. Okay. I'm the entitled here. I've got a few problems but I'm entitled."

"No money was given to me. None. But if you need money, I can help. I have a considerable amount of my own money. I'm in the top .01%."

"Okay," Sailor said, nodding his head several times. "But here's the thing of what it is. There was a ship come in."

He paused, leaned forward and stared at her unblinking. He was ripe. She wondered why he was whispering?

"A ship?"

"A ship with a cargo. Long time ago. They're still looking for it. But the thing is. Here's what it is. He took the cargo and sunk the ship out on Gravesend Bay. Or maybe further out in blue water."

"I know where that is," Alice said, remembering that Picco's boat *The Baby Chicken* was docked there.

"Money was made," Sailor told them. "A lot of money. Here's what I'm saying, the cargo was boxes of gold dust. Where's that? is what I'm saying."

"I don't have it."

"Sure. You don't have it. And I don't think anybody else has it. You know what I think?"

She wanted to say goodbye, but she said she didn't know.

"It's missing!" he screamed, jumping off the sofa once again.

"It's fucking missing!"

Prima, once again behind Sailor's back and taking photos, mouthed the word "Really?"

He dropped back on the sofa that shook with the assault.

He had his head down now and was sobbing.

"You should know, Mister Sailor, that my husband left me. He was a grifter and he went on a trip. Hence the name. Trip. I've had sanity empowerment care for the last eleven and a half years. I too lacked capacity. Some lenders who are also gangsters think I know where to find money that Mr. Paul Limone left me. I don't. Know. Are you giving me a coded message?"

"I ain't stupid," he told her, looking up. "You want to cut me out of this thing. Here's what it is. I'm in the package. Where there's me, there's me. The gold ain't missing. I ain't missing. I'm here to find it."

"It's not here though."

"No, it ain't," he said, looking around. Alice was glad Prima had gone back to her room. How really to explain any of this to her?

"But we need money to find money," Sailor told her. "I can rely on you for that?"

"It will have to go by Dr. Grew," she told him, nervously.

"Fuck Dr. Grew!" he screamed. "It's me. It's you. Is what it is. You know when they say it is what it is. Well, it ain't. It is what somebody who sends you there and then forgets about you says it is. I ain't missing."

"Okay, so, where are you? I mean where can I reach you? I'll come to you. You can take us to the gold dust."

"Us?"

"Me."

Sailor chuckled.

"I got a boat. It's where I live. On my boat. It's an 18' Parker. It's comfortable when there's chop but then, you know, it's steady when I'm just drifting and casting. For fish. Eat'em. Sell'em. Dead Horse Bay. Island Channel. I got my docking spots. I haven't lived on land for a long time. I ain't never going back to The Sands. I wasn't living on land when I saw what was owed me. I was on the water. I don't even go to Coney Island. The sand."

"I see."

"That's why they call me Sailor."

After he left, Alice just stood by the door. She could sense that a flood of thoughts was cascading through her daughter's mind at that moment. She knew everything she was thinking. She felt Callie's hand on her shoulder. Or was she still Prima? She forgot. Callie handed her a tissue. It was life's greatest gift to her to have brought this daughter to her to soothe and calm her at these moments of despair. The daughter is like an avenging, fiery force within her but that could not be wiped out. It too had its purpose. But now the consoling daughter made up for whatever else she was created to be.

She looked up at Callie and for a moment, she saw Thomas looking back at her. She heard his voice, quoting, always quoting people whose names she couldn't remember.

"The only people for me are the mad ones, the ones who are mad to live, mad to talk, mad to be saved, desirous of everything at the same time, the ones who never yawn or say a commonplace thing, but burn, burn, burn like fabulous yellow roman candles exploding like spiders across the stars."

CHAPTER SEVEN

SOMETIMES IT'S THE ALZHEIMER TALKING, AND SOMETIMES IT'S NOT

Sailor Kerplowski promised to take Alice to the spot where boxes of gold dust lay in a sunken ship at the bottom, a ship that Paul Limone had sunk.

Alice listened to him, wondering how he had gotten her number. She could tell Callie that Sailor had called. Callie was looking for him, intent on finding him, the gateway to her father.

"It's at the bottom. I can show you where. Alls we need is a salvage operation. It's up near Ten Mile River. We can get there on the Harlem Railroad line. I lost my car. What it is I never had a car. You got a car?"

Alice said goodbye and hung up.

She thought about conferring with Dr. Grew. He had been calling. He wanted her to be on her own, but he didn't want her to get mixed up with lenders, gangster, grifters and troubled people. He didn't like the sound of "The Sands." He told her sand symbolizes instability. She had made a mistake texting him that night about the service. She had told him about Mal Occhia and The Lutheran and, oh yes, meeting a prince, but not a real one but one who they said was like a prince. He told her meeting a prince was also a sign of instability.

Instead of going to see Dr. Grew, Alice decided to confront Summer Arpeggio with the charge that her father was an embezzler.

"Embezzler: one trusted with funds who runs off with them: See also, a

type of insect."

Alice told Summer immediately upon seeing her that everyone she had met at the Wake thought Arpeggio had stolen Paul's money.

"Why don't you sit down before you start throwing unfounded accusations all over the place?"

Alice sat down.

"Drink?" Summer said, pouring two and giving one to Alice.

She had seen that her client here was much more fluid in every way with a couple of drinks. She had also witnessed the results of too many drinks. She needed to strike a balance in her approach to this client between whatever meds Alice was on, the crazy that seeped out anyway, the whiskey that seemed to juice her to a conversational normalcy, and too much fantasizing.

"Unlike everyone else, I don't think my father embezzled anything from Thomas's father," Summer told her calmly. "I might have gotten my law degree a little late to step in and prevent my father from screwing up but that's another story. I did law school on one of those matchbook level promos. Anywho, my father screwed up because he's got Al Heimers Or dementia. Or both. Or maybe he's just old. He's an old man, Alice. It hasn't been easy witnessing his mind going further away from me each and every day."

She had tears in her eyes.

"I'm sorry," Alice said, a tear coming to her own eyes. "And he really wasn't eaten?"

"No, dear, he was just bitten. Regardless of what you've heard about this section of Brooklyn, we don't eat people. We prefer to drink. Salud!"

"Skol!" Alice said, hoisting her drink and then drinking.

"Don't get me wrong. My father made mistakes. But he didn't run away with Paul's money. Whatever Paul had, is still out there."

She saw in Alice's eyes that she was someplace else, those big umber brown eyes that didn't seem to blink but didn't seem to be looking at anything in the room. Was that the same color eyes she had previously?

"You got to be careful listening to those guys," she told Alice. "I told you before they're not particularly politically correct."

"Buried under volcanic ash," Alice said, nodding.

Alice then told her about Sailor's visit and what he said about the sunken boat and the gold being at the bottom.

"We're going out there to take a look."

Summer gave her a pitying look.

"You are really something, Alice. Don't you know a scam when you see one?"

"A scam?"

"Scam: You know it as a grift."

"You mean a grift?"

"Yes. He's running the old cash-for-gold on you. Did he mention salvage costs?"

"He said salvage would be required. And a car."

"Have another drink," Summer said, downing her own.

"First off, anybody starts talking about the bottom, getting to the bottom of it, the bottom line, it's at the bottom, sweet bottom. All like that. There ain't no bottom is the truth of it. So run."

"The world is a chess board without a bottom."

"Yeah, that too."

Summer could see that Alice wasn't fully absorbing what was going on. She wondered not for the first-time what kind of meds Dr …. what was his name? Doctor Groan? Grope? Grain? He had her on some powerful stuff whatever it was. She reminded herself to run this by Sal at the *Pompey*. Sal knew meds better than he did whiskey.

"You haven't given him any money, have you? Or a car?"

"No. I'd have to see Dr. Grew about that."

"Dr. Grew," Summer repeated, sending herself a memo to check that son of a bitch out. He had obviously found a passage to a mind in which Summer herself was rattling around.

"Okay, look, here's what I think you need to do. First, forget about embezzling stuff. You should face the fact that if my father did embezzle money, it was money the IRS knew nothing about. There are no books to audit. And if you made criminal charges, they would fly all over Brooklyn. You and your daughter would be front page."

That thought visibly frightened Alice.

"I won't make any criminal charges."

"Now, I know that prick Picco …

"He's a prick too?"

"Piccolino. He probably told you that I had Paul's stash. Well, I don't. Everybody knows I don't have it. If they thought I did, I wouldn't be here now talking to you. I'd be either in Parlor A or on the run."

Alice felt a shiver going through her.

"But let me tell you, if I had my hands on any money, I'd be gone. Really gone. The Brooklyn I grew up with got covered with volcanic ash. The Brooklyn jumping out at us now is, in short, an Indiana invasion. Twits. A fucking millennial safe space. For twits. We been invaded. They go around looking for Pokamen like the streets ain't real. I hate it. Freemiums. What the hell is that?. I hate it."

Alice was sitting there agape. It was clear that Summer's words were violating her safe space. Her words were a micro-aggression.

"Okay. Another drink."

After her third, the kind of fluidity Summer was looking for began to run through Alice's mind and body. No longer sitting there agape.

"Okay. My offer still stands. We can get these gangsters off your back by honoring legitimate loans made to Paul. Or, you can slip out of Brooklyn as fast as you can. It won't be safe. You pay up or you run. There's no in between."

That thought turned Alice's eyeball backlights on. Summer had to admit the kid had a fascinating look to her. Those eyeballs reflected light like collapsing suns and rising moons. Summer snapped herself out of that drift. Space-Ex Muck could send her to Mars, and she'd fit in.

"You're thinking. Why not run? True, going after you for these guys would be like the Brooklyn cops going after somebody in Cyprus with a bench warrant on them. Too costly. Too much trouble. I'm sure you could go to some geography these guys never heard of."

"My daughter and I were going to Manarola."

Summer suddenly looked very worried.

"Oh, yeah. Your daughter. That's what I'm saying. Running is not an option. You run, you'd be risking her life. It would be better just to let me pay these guys off."

"A Mister Mal Occhia and The Lutheran approached me at the. service. The Wake. They said they needed to be paid."

"Good. I'll talk to them. I'll see what it takes to get them out of the game. Then I'll let you know."

"Thank you. I'm sure Dr. Grew will honor whatever your services cost."

"Oh, I wouldn't worry about that. I just take my usual percentage. Which is 50%. Salud!"

"Where you going now?" she asked as she escorted Alice to the door.

"I'm meeting Angelo and Picco at a … "

She checked her phone.

"The New Pompey."

"The New Pompey: an old Brooklyn bar frequented by loan sharks, known gamblers, sap artists, social workers, bass players, drifters, grifters, shipping clerks, embezzlers, translators, house painters, parolees, hookers, enforcers, the precariat, fourth story men, drug brokers, poets, and an occasional Prince. See also, Sal, rated the best bartender in Brooklyn. Frequent hangout of the attorney, Summer Arpeggio."

"I wouldn't go there, if I were you," Summer said. "The place is crawling with guys working every con from short to long. A lot of low lives frequent the place. They died a long time ago, but nobody told them. Type of place. They haven't even kept up on what war we're in.

Alice was about to ask Summer why she frequented the bar, but she didn't get the chance.

"Remember what you found out about Pompey."

"It's covered in ash."

"Right."

"And I've got to tell you that Picco and Angelo may be working a long con on you. I don't know anything for sure, but I have my suspicions. So, reveal almost nothing to them. Besides, they wouldn't have anything good to say about Trip. When Trip left, he left them right in the middle of a long con that would have put enough money in Picco and Ange's pocket to sail out of here. Touching them is like touching the tar baby, sweets. Just some counsel I hope you'll take."

Alice gave her a puzzled look. Summer addressed the jury once again.

"See, some stuff people tell you is real. Some fake. Most is in between. A lot of it is alternatives to facts that idiots make up. The alternative to facts and evidence is bullshit. Not saying, you can't go a long way on bullshit. Anywho, it's a mixed bag. Know what I mean?"

"I find so much so different in Brooklyn."

"Same as life anywhere, honey, maybe here it's more like a slice of bread toasted on one side. The burnt side."

Alice remembered those words about toast, real stuff, fake stuff, alternative stuff. It all went into a mixed bag.

CHAPTER EIGHT

TOO COOL FOR THE ROOM

It was the first time Alice was in *The New Pompey*. She had had no trouble getting there although she didn't know the address, but the cab driver knew it well.

"Back in the day, this place spilled over with the hottest ladies, the fattest marks and the sharpest grifters," the cabbie told her without being questioned. "No matter how many got themselves fleeced, new fools just keep showing up. Never killed nobody so the cops never had reason to shut it down. You know, the cops liked the place too. No bodies dropped and the bartender pours doubles."

He pulled up in front of the bar. He turned to look at Alice.

"They work a salting con in there," he told her. "Sprinkle some gold dust on a pile of rocks and sell it as a gold mine."

"Can you do that with a sunken ship? It's at the bottom."

"Wha?"

"Goodbye," Alice said, handing the driver some bills.

"This is a big tip, lady."

"You don't think I'm one of the fools who show up here?" Alice asked him, hand on the door handle.

"Naw. No way. You ain't got the look. You got more of the look of somebody what's got her head screwed on right. Just go in there telling yourself you're too hip for the house. Too cool for the room. Too tight for fright. Too bold to be old. Young and hung. Tits out, mouth in a pout. Works every time. Got it?"

Inside, Alice found a great darkness to her right and then to her left a blue glow shimmering off bottles whose own glass was reflected in the mirror that ran the whole length of a long bar. She saw colorful lights from a jukebox and a cigarette machine straight ahead. She saw a small sign by the door that read "Maximum occupancy - Infinite. No jerks allowed." There was too much smoke and it was all too dark to see if the maximum occupancy law had been violated. Obviously, the cigarette machine worked. Judging by the noise, all of Brooklyn could have been in there. Like angels on the head of a pin, she thought. There was a voice above it all coming out of the jukebox. She didn't recognize it. It was a nice voice but sad.

She told herself she was too old for the tomb, too tight for fright. Too hip to dip. It didn't help.

Everyone seated at the bar had their backs to her. There was a funny looking young man with sandy tousled hair in an open collared white shirt behind the bar. He seemed surprised to see her.

"What can I get you, Miss Lovely?" he said to her. "First time in, the sin is in the bin."

"I'm looking for Mr. Bari," she told him, confused. She didn't want to drink anymore.

"Why?" Sal said, leaning across the bar. "When I'm here? The best-looking mixologist on Utrecht Ave."

"Goodbye," Alice said and turned to leave.

"Hold on. The goodbye hullo girl. I heard about you. I get the clue when I won't do. He's over there."

He made a motion to someone seated, called out "Ange!" and then Angelo turned around and saw her.

He came over to her, pulling on his pants and shirt.

"Hello."

"Hey. Alice. Right?"

He led her to a booth across from the bar. She could see now that although it was only late afternoon, the place was indeed crowded, an infinite number of people in booths, at small tables, and seated all along the length of the bar on high bar stools.

"So, what's going on?"

He could tell by her eyes that she had had a few.

"I went to see Summer. Before that ... "

She was interrupted by the bartender who came over with a tray holding two drinks.

"Rye okay?" Angelo asked her.

"Okay."

"No intro, Ange?"

"This is Sal, don't have anything to do with him. Goodbye, Sal."

"Don't listen to him. I just appreciate beauty. I'm built that way."

"I'd appreciate the drinks, Sal."

"Of course. From now on she's special in here."

Alice watched as he walked back to the bar, stopping to kibitz here and there.

"He's the best bartender in Brooklyn," Alice told Angelo.

"Yeah, for sure. How do you know that?"

"I'm not sure. Some things you know but not how you know. The unknown knowns."

"Okay. So, what were you telling me about Summer? You went there?"

"She says her father didn't embezzle Paul's money."

"Some people think he did. They put him in the hospital."

"Someone bit him to eat him," Alice said, looking at the shot of rye Sal laid in front of her.

Angelo picked up his.

"Salud."

She did the same.

"What else did she say?"

"She said that if she had the money she would be gone. Because Brooklyn is Indiana now and only the living dead live there. That's a contradiction, isn't it? Or a miracle. She also said if I wanted to get out from under, I should be gone also. Because I have my own money to go wherever I want."

"Yeah, well, she's hanging around because she knows wherever she goes people who want to find her can find her."

Alice found herself listening to the song:

She gets too hungry for dinner at eight. I am starving. She loves the theater but she never comes late. I never bother with people that I hate. That's why this chick is a tramp. She doesn't like crap games with barons and earls. Won't go ...

"She say anything about me and Picco?" "She said that you and Picco may be working a long con on me. She didn't know anything for sure, but she had her suspicions. So, I am to reveal almost nothing to you. Besides, you and Picco wouldn't have anything good to say about Trip. When Trip left, he left both of you right in the middle of a long con that would have put enough money in your pockets to sail out of here. Touching you and Picco is like touching the tar baby. It was just some counsel she'd hope I'd take. I don't understand some of what she says. I haven't been in Brooklyn long enough. I didn't know I was under something and had to get out."

"You're not. Under. But you didn't take her counsel. Obviously. You're here. I think that was smart but why?"

"I've never wanted to be smart. My father was smart and my mother said it ruined him when he was very young. And then after too, when it was too late for him to wise up. Wise up. Wise down. Funny."

"Okay. Well, you give me the chance to defend myself. In fact, me and Picco were talking about this the other night. It looks to us like Summer has pulled you in to take the heat off her. Got the lenders on you. Not her."

"You think I should go? Be gone, like she says. I could go to the provinces."

"Where? Listen, never make a desperate move if you can help it. I thought you wanted to find out what you could about Trip. You knew the Thomas in him. But not the Trip. Trip was the guy who left you. Don't you want to be able to tell your daughter something real, like who her old man really was?"

Sal came over with another two drinks on a tray and two water chasers. There was also a cup of dry nuts.

"Benny Tonto says the Sailor has been over to see the lady here."

"Thanks, Sal."

"What did Kerplowski have to say?"

"He said he was Trip's first cousin and that he was entitled to whatever money his uncle had left because he was the only living blood relative. He said he and Trip were like brothers. He also spent a great deal of time in The Sands. He also has PTSD because they wouldn't stop when he told them too. He smells of the seashore and wears an NA pin "

"Coney Island. Look. Trip thought he was too unstable, too reckless. Never hung around with him. Sailor's homeless. He lives on a skiff, under a tarpaulin."

"*Skiff: a shallow, flat-bottomed open boat with sharp bow and square stern. See also; the homeless who are not boatless.*

"That thing tell me who's winning in the fifth at the Big A?" Angelo asked, pointing to the phone Alice had in her hand.

"Sailor calls it satellite talk with them. I think them means extra-celestials."

"Okay, listen. Sailor made a pitch. You told him there was no money. You weren't given any money. But you felt sorry for him and you said you'd give him some money. Right?"

"For the salvage operation."

"What salvage operation?"

"Paul Limone sunk a freighter he had loaded with boxes filled with gold dust. It's at the bottom. Sailor knows where it is. All he needs is money for the salvage operation. He's going to take me there "

"What? Look at the water? It's a scam. There's no boxes of gold dust in a sunken freighter out in the Sound or wherever. It's the oldest scam in the book."

"That's what Summer said. She called it a cash for gold scheme."

"That it is, and Sailor is too stupid to pull it off. Did Summer put the bite on you?"

He saw that question immediately made Alice jump.

"I mean did she ask you for money?"

"Only to pay back the lenders the money Paul owed them. This way I can get out from under. Am I under?"

"No. Go on."

"I can get out from under either by being gone from here or by paying off the lenders."

"How to get out from under she said into her phone:

"*To get out from under: to extricate oneself from troubles, esp. financial troubles. See also, an enticement or lure that ropes in naïve marks seeking to escape the bonds of their messed-up lives.*

"You have any intention of handing that kind of money over to Summer? You know, to pay back Paul's so-called lenders, which I expect will multiply like fish in the Bible."

"I will talk to Dr. Grew."

"Yeah, run it by him. Sooner the better."

He picked up his drink.

"So, you tell me all this to hear what I have to say. Smart. Even though you don't want to be smart, you are. You know that if you tell me nothing, you can't know what I think."

"I'm also attracted to you," Alice said, putting her empty shot glass down and running a finger over her lower lip. "Not so much on the outside but more on the inside."

"Damn. What can I say? Right back at you. The outside for sure is attracting me. And the inside? That's more fascinating than anything ever walked into this bar."

"I'm not too far for the bar?"

"You know, this makes it a whole lot easier trying to, you know, help you out the way Trip would want me to. I mean the two of us getting along and all. I mean not that he'd want me to take his place."

"People say you are an unmade bed of a man, which is a line from a movie Summer saw."

Angelo ran a hand through a mass of hair he always hoped to send a brush or a comb through one of these mornings. He had been contemplating parting it on the left side but Picco said that style went out after the Civil War. He had been thinking of using some Picco's French hair oil.

"Okay, let's get off me and back to you. I think you should get this Dr. Grew off your back. That's first thing. Forget about Summer getting the lenders off your back. She just wants to take your money and run. I mean I don't know this guy Grew but it sounds like he has too much to say about what you can do and cannot do in your own life. He's not leaving you to be free to choose, if you know what I mean."

Alice stayed silent, probably, he thought, because he didn't know what he meant. It was a stupid slogan he had picked up.

"Don't you want to find some way of taking your own life back?"

"Thomas tried but then he went away."

As Angelo considered that comment, Picco came into the bar, saw them and came over.

"Sit down, Picco. I'm just about to go over for Alice here the kind of web being weaved around her."

"Fuck yeah," Picco said, squeezing in alongside Angelo. "Webs are being spun right now and we don't even know it. The president is caught in a dark web that The Deep State ... "

"Just listen up, Picco."

Sal came over with a drink.

"It's a web of grifters," Angelo said. "First off, Paul Limone. He drew Alice in with this bogus inheritance. Why? What he's doing bringing you to Brooklyn, to all this?"

He made a sweeping gesture with one hand.

Alice followed the hand.

"You texted me to come here."

"I bet you never gave Paul any respect when he was alive," Picco told her.

"Maybe I did. But I never met him when he was alive. I met him for the first time at The Wake. He was laid out, Mr. Kim told me."

"See? He's dead but now he's got you into his world, to which you basically said, 'Fuck off.' To him and everything that meant anything to him. Including his son. Am I right here?"

Alice looked dazed. Angelo made a gesture for Picco to back off.

"Paul was a fucker when it came to revenge," Picco told her, stirring the tall mixed drink Sal had put in front of him without a request. "He was like a gypsy when it came to that and the moon didn't have to be full. It could be half or even quarter. You know what I mean?"

Alice stood up.

"Goodbye."

"Sit down. Please. Picco, shut up. Forget about Paul. Summer. She sets you up as a target for the lenders. And, once she finds out you're loaded, she comes up with a con to get a paycheck out of you."

"Are there not true lenders? Are they all gangsters?"

"Tell her, Picco."

"Mal Occhia and The Lutheran bought up all the paper on Paul. They're the only lenders. They found Mal in a dumpster this morning so now it's The Lutheran holding all the paper."

"Mal Ochhia is in a dumpster?" Alice exclaimed, visualizing instantly the tiny man with the wrinkled face in a dumpster, which she was not very familiar with but pictured as a vehicle used by gangsters.

"You need another drink," Angelo said, calling Sal over.

"And I wouldn't worry about The Lutheran. Ange and me got him tied into a long grift which leads to him being happy to pay us instead of anybody paying him."

"It's a Ponzi," Picco whispered to Alice. "But our own version. We borrow from Peter to pay Paul and then from Paul to pay Peter. You extend that to couple of hundred guys and then the clock strikes Bingo! And you take off. It's show time."

"Stifle that crap, Picco. Truth is, that's a scheme we never got off the ground."

"Yeah, but we do got a margin call out. The Lutheran will be forced to liquidate his position or front more capital to keep his investment. But there's no stock and the money will come to us."

"Someone killed Mr. Occhia?" Alice said, as they watched her digest what Picco had said.

"Mal looked in the mirror and put the evil eye on himself," Picco told her, smiling. "Mal was a prick anyway. He would have fit in a garbage pail where he belonged."

"Let's get back to the web around you," Angelo said. "Summer and Sailor. I told you what they're up to, right?"

Alice nodded.

"They're bad eggs," Picco said. "They'd slip their mother a mickey for a buck and leave their kids in the wind if they had to scram. Me and Ange. We're the good ones. We stay cool. We stay on the spot. Right here. We don't move. We hold it down. We're here for you. We make the stand."

"Would you shut the fuck up, Picco?"

"Goodbye."

"Okay, wait," Angelo called out. "I know this is what any good con artist wants to convince you. He's the good guy. You know why you can trust us? We haven't put the bite on you for any funding, have we?"

She shivered.

"I mean have we asked you for money?"

Alice shook her head.

"Okay," Angelo said as Picco waved to Sal and pointed to Alice.

"I think Alice is at the perfect mellow point, Picco. Too early in the day to get sloshed."

"Sloshed: I drank a lot of wine and got sloshed."

"It's a lot quicker with straight rye shots," Angelo told her. "Okay, now we got the good Dr. Grew."

"He's a grifter?"

Both Angelo and Picco laughed.

"Lady, he's got all your money in his hands. So, I'd say he's running a good one on you."

"Yeah, how the fuck did he work that one?" Picco asked, shaking his head, and still smiling.

Alice seemed puzzled by that and went to her phone:

"How did I wind up with Dr. Grew?

"After Thomas left you, you crashed. Total dive to a black hole. Your father confined you to a rest home, aka a mental asylum. He died and his estate, or, the money he stole from your mother, was left to you. Dr. Grew, a staff member at Ravine Farm Rest Home, became your personal analyst. Consider that both Grew and the rest home are bogus. They did so based on a generous gift made to the administrative judge. The man calling himself Dr. Grew petitioned the court to appoint him the conservator, guardian and protector of your money. You escaped his control when you received a letter from Summer Arpeggio inviting you to Brooklyn to receive an inheritance. You have not been in communication with Dr. Grew since you told him about The Sands. You can assume that he is looking for you.

"Holy fuck!" is all that Picco said, after listening to Alice's phone.

"What else does that phone say about Dr. Grew?" Angelo asked.

Alice asked that question.

"Dr. Grew may be a legitimate guardian seeking only the best for Alice.

See also, Dr. Grew may be running a very sweet grift on Alice; See also, Dr. Grew may himself be a part of a long con being run by someone unknown; See also, The Commander; See also, Dr. Grift may not exist outside Alice's own mind."

"That's not a fucking phone," Picco shouted so loud that people nearby turned to look at him. "That's a fucking witch. Who gave that to you?"

"I think I bought it online. On eBay. However, Dr. Grew may have given it to me. Or if not him, one of my friends at Ravine Farm Sanitarium. Actually, I think it suddenly appeared."

"That phone is worth a cool billion," Picco said, pointing to Alice's side pack to which she had once again returned the phone.

"Forget about that phone, Johnny," Angelo snapped. "You know what's new that I'm seeing here? I'm seeing the fingerprints of our friend, Trip."

"Trip? How's that?" Picco said, shaking his head. "I mean he's dead, right?"

"That was never confirmed was it, Alice?"

"He was there and then he was gone."

"Like he was alive one day and dropped dead the next? Or like now you see Ange here and then you don't because he left the room?"

"The living drop in and the dead drop dead. One morning I woke up and he was gone."

"That's Trip alright," Picco said, lighting up a cigarette.

"The thing is why did he leave then?" Angelo said. "What happened just then?"

"Just then? That's like when, isn't it?"

"Maybe it was a money issue?"

"My mother died, and my father got all the money."

"So, the Manhattan Princess was a broke ass Princess," Angelo mumbled.

Picco's eyes lit up.

"Then the father dies and she's a flush Princess again."

"And Trip hears about it."

"Dead people don't hear anything. But I think they listen anyway."

Picco gave Ange a look. Ange told him to shut up.

"Okay, think it through. What's he do if he's not dead? He starts a grift to get Alice's money back in her possession and to get Alice back in his."

"Yeah, but what's the grift?"

Angelo slammed the table.

"We stick close to Alice and we find out."

"It could be disappointing, but I'd like that."

Picco saw his buddy blush. Angelo wasn't the one who ever got it on with the ladies. He didn't primp to pimp; he had no game at all with the ladies; he rarely shaved or got a haircut. Even the French hair oil didn't put him over the line with the ladies. He was a big mess. But clearly, the young lady here was attracted. The dead don't hear but they listen kind of lady. The goodbye and then hello kind of lady.

CHAPTER NINE

MINDFULNESS

One of the stories Angelo and Picco told Alice was about how they, Trip, and all their buddies had spent summers on the Coney Island beach. And though Trip got seasick when they took a boat of Paul's out of sight of land, they lived more on the water, hugging the shore line, than on the land.

Mal de mer. She remembered.

That story somehow captured Kitty's --- her daughter's *nom de jour* -- imagination and so Alice arranged for a small apartment in Coney Island for her and Kitty for the summer. Just to be close to Trip's friends.

In the day time, Alice found herself on the boardwalk or under it or close to the shore sketching each day different segments of sky, ocean, sandy beach, boats on the horizon. She was responding to a kind of urge to paint the sea, the shore, the great expanse of faceless ocean, and the tides that were like the earth's own meditative exercises.

But most especially the boats, to her they were transformed human bodies, silently embraced by the waves, lulled into a forgetfulness of what their lives had been like on shore. Thomas had told her they were star stuff, but she felt now that the waters had been for a very long time their home. And somehow too the way out.

It was pleasant to have the ocean nearby and recall what Ange told her about him, Trip, and Picco going up on the boardwalk and finding a place that served them beer although they were under age.

Almost all that Ange and Picco remembered of the boardwalk and its honky-tonk joints had been torn down, nothing in their place but a clean, sterile emptiness. It was an early gentrification they despised but to Alice it was still a step closer to Thomas's world. Trip's world, however transformed. What she had were the shards of what had been his world and she found herself, as with a painting, projecting a rich life into it, exploring both on the canvas of her own mind and the canvas on her easel the hidden layers of a life.

At around nine every night she went to *The New Pompey* where she always found Angelo and Picco. They called the place The Clubhouse.

"Hey, why don't you take the lady somewhere sometime?" Sal said to Angelo that night as Alice and Ange sat at the bar.

She knew she was drinking too much but Angelo told her drinking wasn't her problem. Her pills were. So, she stopped taking them.

"Dr. Grew said they take the edge off. Nothing more."

"Without a doubt. Take everybody's edge off and then herd'em wherever you want. Thing is, Allie, when you can't trust a goddamn thing around you, you better keep your edge. You wanna stay 100% alert. Comprendo?"

"They call it mindfulness now," Sal told them. "Reduces stress, which occurs when your mind is not as full as it should be. Truth is, I don't know what the Saviour they're talking about. I say, what if your mind, like most of the minds come in here, are full of merde?"

Alice responded by looking around her. The usual suspects, which was what Picco called them, were at the bar. They were all partners in crime, the crime never specified.

She loved the names. She remembered all of them as if they were characters in her stories. Her imagination was aided by the nicknames they all had. She had sketched some of the faces.

"They've all kept their edge," Angelo told her. "Couple three drinks just whet it, like a knife. You gotta stay sharp. Are you staying sharp?"

He had put a hand on her shoulder and was looking straight into her eyes. Behind him, she could see Sal wiping a glass and smiling. She remembered Sal telling her that ... how had he put it? -- Angelo had a thing for her. She thought that the thing he had for her had most likely been encouraged by her confession that she was attracted to him. That had been over a month before, so his emotions had taken their time. Maybe his mind was too full to give her a space?

Still, she wasn't surprised when Ange finally showed up at the Coney Island apartment late one night.

"Come by to see if you want to go sailing with Picco and me."

When Alice ushered him into their small living room, she saw that her daughter, Camille, who had been on the sofa looking at her lap top was now gone. That pleased her. She wanted Ange to herself. Camille --- where did she get her names? -- made it difficult. Somehow, she had been seeing less and less of her daughter. She seemed to have found her own friends.

"Okay," she told Ange as they both sat down on that same sofa. "Is there a special reason?"

"You don't need a reason to get on the water for a day of sailing. It's a getaway most people don't think of when they think of Brooklyn. But this is a peninsula. They talk about the Great Lakes. Well, we got the Great Atlantic Ocean all around us, feeding the rivers, the channels, the Sound."

"Real places aren't on any map."

"Okay, I'll remember that."

"I didn't say it. I read it. Sometimes I fear the ocean. Sometimes I don't."

"Not any of my fears. My fears are all about being stuck in one place, like a fly on the wall. The couch and grouch life. I wasn't made for it. I'm seeing the dark at the end of the tunnel and what I want to do is get to the light. You gotta keep moving to get there."

"But they didn't call you Trip."

"No, they didn't. I never went anywhere. Look. Brooklyn is on the map. Brooklyn is sticking three quarters of its ass out into the Atlantic. Mostly spent our summers on Coney Island, Far Rockaway, and Jones Beach. Johnny's family comes from Broad Channel. You walk through their house, out the back door and there's the channel leading to the ocean. There's no fear there."

"That's a wonderful world. Truly. A true place. Aren't they rare?"

"I don't know. Is it set? The sail?"

She nodded, smiling.

"Six AM launch. Picco will pick you up around half five."

"You can borrow my wind breaker," Camille said, coming out of her room as soon as Angelo had left. "You'll need it."

She had been listening.

"This is a Bermuda rigged cutter. Small single-masted boat, fore-and-aft trigged with a triangular mainsail and two foresails. It's an old one. Heavy sail cloth and no winches so me and Picco have our workout but when sails are full in a good wind, there's nothing like it."

Now, Angelo took her below and gave her a tour of the interior.

"Oh, what a small world it is!" she exclaimed.

"Yeah, great design. It was the old man's. Paul. He thought of everything. He could plan. See, the galley is aft in order to take advantage of this large hatch overhead for standing room. The settee and forward double berth extend around the mast, and the table here is right aft of the mast. Comfortable seating. Try it."

"This cabin is extended right to the deck edge. The seating area here is over eight feet wide."

They could hear Picco making noise on the deck.

"Time to launch. Come on up."

It was a beautiful day and for the first time in a long while, Alice felt she didn't have a problem in the world. As the cutter's sails went up and they sailed straight into Jamaica Bay, everything in the past that had troubled her seemed to blow away with the same breezes that filled the sails.

They lowered sails and dropped anchor about noon in the Great South Bay. Picco went below to make lunch. He seemed to Alice to be an entirely different Picco now, as if the sun, the wind, the water and the sails had made him silent, reverent, a man too awed to puff and display his own vanity. There was clearly a bond of work between Ange and Picco that went beyond the need for words.

"I'm jumping in for swim before lunch," Ange told her, taking off his shirt and before she could respond, he had dived in.

She watched as his head rose for a breath on the swell of a wave and then disappeared in the crest. She watched him until it seemed to her that he had gone far enough from the boat. He had disappeared. She called out to Picco, who came up from below in a rush.

"He's gone!"

"Naw. Paul had us swimming from bay to bay in Coney Island when we were kids. Don't worry.

Ange only looks like a couch potato.

"I've never seen one."

"Lunch'll be ready by the time he's back."

When Ange reached the boat, Alice held out a hand.

"Thanks, but I'll pull you in," he said, lunging up and grabbing the bulwarks. The whole boat seemed to tilt, and Alice almost fell overboard but Angelo grabbed her.

After lunch, Picco excused himself and went below for what he called a "snooze."

"You know, Trip's father gave this boat, the *Mrs. L* to him. Johnny and me was the crew. When Trip left, he gifted it to me and Johnny. Johnny renamed it *Sweet Cheeks* which I went along with. Shouldn't have but I give in to Johnny. I'm thinking this boat should be yours. It's part of your inheritance."

"Are the lenders after it?"

"Going after something isn't getting it, Alice."

She could see clearly that he had a thing for her. And he wasn't a lender here for her money. But she didn't think he always told the truth.

"Sal has a boat. He wanted to take me sailing."

"Yeah, but you came with me."

There was an awkward pause.

They could hear Johnny snoring.

"He gets a workout out here. We both do. Beats sitting on a bar stool."

"Why do you it? I mean, sit on a bar stool?"

"The Club House? I don't know. I guess it's kind of a departure point for Picco and me. Has been for a long time. Thing is we don't depart. Launch. Thing is, I don't know what the hell I'm talking about."

"I like the sun on the water," she said, tearfully.

"What's going on?" he said, putting both arms around her.

"Dr. Grew wants me to come back for a respite. He thinks I'm refractive."

"What the fuck does that mean?"

"Weeks. Maybe months. I … I don't want to go."

"Hey, this guy can't own you."

"The court … I'm legally incompetent because of my … They say I don't know what's real."

"Fuck the court. It's your life. You need it back. You're real.

Very real. Nobody seen anybody like you don't make you unreal."

She put a hand up in front of his face.

"You frighten me when you get angry. Don't be angry."

They remained silent for a long time. And then she opened her eyes,

"Was Thomas's father a gangster?"

"He taught the three of us – Johnny, Trip and me -how to what he called fathom minds. Know how people thought and then use it to game them. It was hard. What people said got in the way. But then we got good at it. Actually, Paul said Johnny hadn't the head for it and Trip couldn't put his own self out of the way and do the fathoming of other minds. That's how Johnny and me got into the grift game. Trouble was we didn't have money minds to get into and work our game. It's all broke minds we're living with. We've been small time so far."

"And Thomas. I mean Trip never got into this game?

"Trip came out of college with one thing in mind, grab the gold ring like we always tried to do on the carousel in Coney Island. Grab and run."

"And he found me? I was the gold ring?"

Angelo shook his head.

"I don't think he knew what he had. In you."

"I was his Manhattan Princess."

"Well, he didn't learn any of that from Paul. Trip didn't think much of his father."

"Maybe it's not best to see too much of your father if he hurts your mother. Your father, was he something to you?"

"Didn't Balsio tell you? I'm the orphan of the neighborhood. Went from one foster home to another."

Picco came up from below, yawning.

"Jeez, I really conked out. Sorry."

"Why don't you jump in, Picco? Wake you up."

"Yeah, I think I will."

Picco pulled off his sweatshirt, kicked off his sneakers, ran to the stern, jumped on the bulwark with one foot, and then dove into the water.

"Wow!"

"He doesn't look it now but Picco was our all-round athlete in the neighborhood. You're looking at me like what happened? The ladies. The ladies broke Picco's training, let's see, when he was, about 16." "The Ladies?"

She was thinking of the Sirens and a man struggling to get back home. Trip. Jessica, her Classics professor, had talked about the Sirens in class.

"Funny thing. Picco and me come out here on the water and nothing else matters. It's always like we're just starting out on this long voyage. But it all ends when we get back on land. Know what I mean?"

They looked out to where Picco was on his back, floating.

"Anyway, me and Picco. We try to hold the edge. What else can we do? I got the one mind I can't fathom. Now, with you. It's two."

CHAPTER TEN

RAVINE FARM SANITARIUM

Ravine Farm Sanitarium was a large, institutional looking building, built circa 1960s, without anything around it of a farm nature.

"Jesus, look at this place," Picco said driving through open gates and then down a long drive.

"These places don't file shit with the Feds," Summer said, seated in the passenger seat, Angelo lounged in the back seat of Picco's Roadrunner. "They've got a front like they're some kind of soul saving tax write off."

"It could be a Hairy Krista recruitment center," Picco said.

"I don't hear any finger bells," Summer said, as Picco pulled into a parking spot marked "Reserved. Doctor Grew."

"Mount up," she said, getting out of the car.

They had brought her in to the con because what they needed to pull it off was exactly what Lawyer Summer could provide. And she wanted to get this doctor's hands off Alice's money as much as Angelo and Picco did.

"I got all we need to persuade," she said, a briefcase in hand. She had a severe business suit on. Angelo and Picco were wearing black suits they had used on a few scams before. They called them their FBI suits.

They walked passed a "No Hunting" sign which caused them to stop, a genuine WTF moment. When they looked to the right, passed a field all November brown, they saw two figures on a hill. Both were carrying what looked like rifles.

It was a faux FBI credential that Angelo flashed at the reception desk.

"Dr. Grew," he told the young receptionist.

"Do you have an appointment with Director Grew?"

"The FBI doesn't advertise it's coming," Angelo told her, stone faced.

"You know, sweet cheeks, if the FBI needed to make an appointment, Dillinger would still be on the loose."

Summer looked at Picco and sighed.

"Look, Miss, just point us to his office before you become an accessory."

"It's on the top floor. The fourth."

"What's with the hunters?" Picco asked. "Deer?"

"Two of the Stakeholders wandered off."

"Stakeholders?"

"Residents."

The Director had a secretary, but Angelo flashed his FBI badge and they were in the office before she could respond.

An old man was behind a huge desk. He didn't look up.

"Bonny told me you were in the building," he said, scribbling away."I'm Dr. Grew."

Summer and Angelo sat down in the two chairs in front of his desk. Picco sat down on a sofa under shelves of books.

"I need to take a close look at your credentials," Grew said, looking up. "We must fix our attention almost fiercely on the facts actually before us,"

"Chesterton."

He had a mass of white hair that billowed like a halo, a pinkish face and tiny hands. But what immediately caught the attention were one bright blue eye and one dark brown one.

There was some background music, sea shanties? There were seascapes on the walls.

"You like to sail?" Picco asked, studying a painting of a yacht.

"My wife calls me a doctor on land and a commodore at sea."

He stood up from his desk and began to recite:

"'To sail into an unknown spring, or receive one's baptism on storm's promontory, where the solitary albatross heels over in the gale, and at last come to land. To know the earth under one's foot and go, in wild delight, ways where there is water.' Malcolm Lowry."

"Okay by me," Picco said, giving Angelo a "WTF?" look.

"Down to business. Here they are," Summer said, taking some sheets of paper out of her briefcase and laying them on Grew's desk.

He picked them up and gave them a cursory read.

"And what is this supposed to be?"

"Those? Those are charges that will be brought against you for mishandling the financial affairs of the well-known children's author, Cecily Darden. Aka Alice. The Alice you told her went down the rabbit hole."

"Ah, those stories are superb, aren't they? Far from the sea yet somehow the stillness of those mountains evoking the expanse of sea and sky. Both draw us in a way that promises a revelation of the deepest mysteries. All else dwindles to an insignificance before the vast empty blankness of life as the Sun has allowed it."

"Whatever. I'm Ms. Darden's attorney. And I'm prepared to sue your ass into a vast empty blankness for gambling with her money and causing her monumental mental anguish."

"Monumental?" Grew repeated. "Is that a legal term? Like, suing my ass?"

Angelo leaned forward, his whole body challenging the strength of the chair.

"You've not been acting in her best interests, Doc. We're going to take that legal guardianship away from you."

"Yeah, and we've got everything we need to do that," Picco called out, cheerfully.

"So, you gentlemen are the crew attached to this piracy?"

"Us?" Angelo said. "Naw, we're the guys who know you've been losing truckloads playing poker. At the track too. You've got the kind of gambling addiction that requires therapy, Doc."

Summer took a rubber band wrapped bundle out of her briefcase and tossed it on Grew's desk.

"Photocopies of checks from the Darden trust you wrote to pay off your gambling debts."

He fingered through the pile.

"Withdrawals. 7% of the trust fund yearly. That's legal. What I do with my money is not illegal."

"Maybe not," Summer told him, "but we're going to impeach you anyway. We're prepared to make a case in Federal Court. And what you need to know is that I've got Cecily Darden ready to testify as to what kind of voodoo you've been subjecting her to."

"This place will close down," Angelo told him.

"You won't be draining anymore of your Stakeholders' bank accounts,"

Picco said, getting up and standing in front of Grew's desk.

"And most likely you'll go to jail," Summer said. "We're going to bust your game wide open, Doctor."

Grew began to hum something.

"It's a long road in the courts to any of that. We must all set ourselves for a long voyage. I have the resources, including proper lawyers."

He smiled at Summer who shook her head and looked at Angelo and then Picco.

"What is it about me that don't come over as Harvard law?"

"The Brooklyn inflections?"

"But that's not going to stop you from preventing him from dipping into all those resources with his patients' names on them."

"I've already taken steps to block the good Doc's access to any of those funds."

"She's not Harvard, Doc," Picco said, "but she's sharp."

Grew sat back, sighed deeply and studied the three of them.

He began to sing in a low voice:

"I've sailed the seas until I'm broke; I drink and swear and gamble and smoke; But I can't swim a bloody stroke, Says Barnacle Bill the Sailor."

Summer gave Angelo a WTF. look. Angelo wasn't amused.

"We've got you, Doc. You've played your last game with Alice's mind."

"Alice? Yes," Grew said, his eyes lighting up.

"If I had a world of my own, everything would be nonsense. Nothing would be what it is, because everything would be what it isn't. And contrary wise, what is, it wouldn't be. And what it wouldn't be, it would. You see?"

"So, you're more the patient than the doctor, right?" Picco, said after another WTF pause.

"She's adopted the Alice self for her own protection."

"Bullshit!" Angelo shot back. "You've got her on all kinds of drugs that fuck with her mind so you can tell her any shit you want to."

"Attend, please," Dr. Grew said, standing up. "After a long, costly court case, you can take the guardianship away, but Alice remains Alice. She lacks capacity to make decisions that will not harm her. Someone else will be assigned as legal protector."

"That's not going to happen," Angelo said, angrily.

"I see. She's got you, I suppose. And you think you've got her, but you don't really know who she is, do you?"

"She gets away from you and the meds you've been feeding her, and we'll find out."

"You'll have her. Alice. And her daughter. What is her name? So very many names. Have you met her?"

Angelo hesitated, and then shook his head.

"We're getting away from the brief here," Summer said. "You've fucked up the daughter's life. Young girl. Fucked up the mother's life and that fucked up her daughter's life. Poor kid is so fucked up she doesn't get out of the house."

"She can't even decide what her name is," Picco added.

"Now that's fucked up," Summer said, nodding.

"I'm thinking that everything being fucked up is your courtroom style?"

"Fuck you!" Summer shot back.

"Well, on that indictment, which is, fucking up the daughter's life, I win. She has no daughter."

"Whatya mean?"

"The daughter may be a reflection of some ideal somewhere but she's not in this world. Alice made her up. She dreamed her up. Sometimes I think Alice believes she's her daughter's dream. The whole Taoist butterfly thing. Whatever. The fact is that Alice needed someone to express thoughts she herself couldn't express. The daughter is a kind of prosecutor from her own mind. A convenient, though non-existent, interlocutor. None of you have seen her, have you?"

"Whatya you mean she made her up?" Picco repeated.

"She's always talking about her," Angelo said.

"Well, our Alice was a one-woman crew and she was in wobbly seas. She watched her father drive her own mother into insanity. She married a man who thought she had money and then found out she didn't and so went out to milk a cow and never came back. She needed another crewmate. It's always easier on a long voyage, which is what life can be, to have someone in the foc'sle you can talk to. An imaginary friend. Or daughter. Even a Prince. What's more chimerical than a Prince?"

Grew gave them time to digest this.

"Which means of course that she's seeing and talking to a daughter that was never born. Never existed. Which means she won't be allowed to testify against me."

Angelo leaned forward, nervously rubbing both hands together.

"Just what is wrong with her, Doc?"

"I've told you. Childhood traumatized topped with a lover leaving her. She was very attached to her mother who was apparently torn about in sadistic ways bit by bit by her father. Alice is a witness forever in her mind to all that. Probably a lost pregnancy in there also. At the crisis moment. Her mind toppled. Fractured into small islands of awareness, forgetting, dreaming, and hallucinating. Back and forth, like a seesaw."

"What's with that phone she's got?" Picco asked. "The one that works like a genius out of a lamp. We call it the Alice App."

"The Alice App? Let me see. I recall that I implanted a chip with an algorithm of my own design that fuses Google search with a privacy violating invasion of her own mind's fears, suspicions, and expectations. That's her inner voice you hear representing that fusion. Some fact mingled with unreliable social media, private screwball and some mystery of an extra-planetary nature, genuinely off the algorithm."

"What the fuck!" Picco exclaimed. "Where'd you implant all that?"

"In her frontal lobe."

"And why the fuck did you do that, Doc?" Angelo said angrily. "Turn her into a freak? You're no shrink. No shrink would call their patient a screwball."

"I was joking. I didn't even know she had a phone. I was just feeding your friend's fantasy. On occasion, it's best to do that. But I do employ unorthodox methods. It's not my aim to turn her into a freak. I intended the device to be a stabilizer. A kind of defragging of her own aberrant neural networks so that she could experience some control of the world around her."

Angelo tried to make sense of those words. Finally, he said to Grew:

"Just joking? We didn't come here to amuse you, Doc. You get out of her life."

"Or you'll take me to court?" Grew said, amused.

"Or I'll break your fucking head."

The two stared at each other.

Summer was the first to interrupt that contest.

"You know what? You've been her legal and psychiatric guardian for a long time and she's still fucked up. Because you need to keep her that way so you can soak the trust fund in perpetuity."

"In perpetuity? Now that's an improvement in your courtroom delivery."

"You're a total fucking fraud," Summer told him angrily.

"I'm an explorer, Ms. Arpeggio. I am the psychiatric equivalent of an astrophysicist who has been to outer space.

I am the Elon Musk of psychotherapy. I find psychotic aberrations in humans to be an unexplored frontier, as much a marketing frontier as space exploration is. To me the askew mind is like a vast ocean and I am a Captain James Cook exploring every Cape Horn and Gulf of Guinea of the human mind."

Grew had begun to hum again, watching them, and it seemed to Angelo that he was in the place they should have been in and they were in the place he should have been in. In short, he was in command and they were cutting bait.

"But she does have money," Angelo finally said. "I mean she's a marketing frontier?"

"Yes. She inherited her father's estate after the gentleman passed on."

"I couldn't get access to the size of the trust," Summer said, "but we've followed your spending trail and it's over a quarter of a million."

"There's about thirty million in a well-managed stock portfolio producing a two digit return plus a settlement or slush fund of about ten million."

"Trip walked away from a sweet inheritance," Picco said, whistling, and Angelo turned and gave him a look.

"Why open the books to us?" Angelo said, turning to Grew.

The way everything was now going made him increasingly nervous. It didn't seem as if they were in charge any longer. They were getting fathomed and fucked.

"I want to give the three of you an appreciation for the goose who lays the eggs."

Summer was the first to catch on.

"We don't go to court with any of this and we get some of those eggs?"

"*Full leisurely we glide,*" Grew quoted, "*For both our oars, with little skill.*"

Picco expressed another WTF look.

"I believe the trust can put another attorney and her crew on retainer," Grew said, "for say 2% of the total worth per annum?"

"One quarter of a million each if split three ways," Grew told them.

Grew waited.

"Clearly good news, judging by the looks on your faces. You came in here seeking what? Maybe ten thousand?"

"We came in here looking to get Alice shuck of you," Angelo told him. "And put your ass in jail."

"Don't get annoyed at me for pushing your Hurrah moment forward. You had your eye on the money and not putting me in jail."

"So why fork over?" Picco asked, genuinely curious.

"Because like the sharp attorney here says, there's a case to be made and it's not in my interest that it be made. And now it's not in your interest that it be made."

"We're going to think about this," Angelo said, smelling rats all over the place but unable to see them. They should have brought the old exterminator, Mr. Mensch with them.

"What? We're waiting?"

"Shut up, Picco," Angelo said. "You'll be hearing from us."

"Certainly, Captain. As soon as you all get together on a name, you'll get your first check. How about monthly retainer remittances?"

Grew came around from his desk, hand held out.

Angelo looked at it, sneered and walked out of the office. Picco followed him out. Summer gathered up her papers and shoved them in her briefcase.

"At least you should be very happy, Ms. Arpeggio. You won your case. And you're going to be rich. You can sign on to a new voyage. And new crewmates."

Summer felt at that moment like she was tied up and knotted in several different places. And this weird guy had done the knotting.

"You better figure that Angelo Bari is not happy. Money aside. That guy will find a way to pay you back for fucking with Alice's head."

"I'm passing the difficulties that Alice's head presents to Mr. Bari. And I wish him luck."

"Fuck you. I'll text you deposit details."

"I'm sure you will."

When she left, he was humming his Barnacle Bill song.

"That was very sweet," Picco said as the three were back in the car. "What did Glue say to you when we left?"

"I asked him to board my old man as part of the package."

"Whatya he say to that?"

"He said the world is everything that is the case is what he said."

"What the fuck does that mean?"

"I don't know and I don't care. I'm sending Aunt Rita over to him with my father end of the week. Let him know he wants our silence this is part of the package."

No one said anything for another few miles.

"I'll have to arrange for that monthly to be sent to an off-shore account," Summer said. "My father had one in Cyprus."

"Is that where Paul's money went?"

"Fuck you, Piccolino."

They drove in silence for about four lights.

"What's bothering you, Ange?" Picco finally said.

"I don't know. I can't put my finger on it. But something's not right."

"You mean besides he's got staff out hunting for escaped patients?"

"Stakeholder, Picco. Stakeholders."

"I don't think it's safe to send your old man there. He'd escape and they'd shoot him."

"Aunt Rita will be with him. She's got gun club trophies. Hey, Ange, you think maybe there's more than the 40 million? That's what's worrying you?

"It's not that. It was like he was ready for us. That we walked into it."

"Like a grift and we were the marks?"

'Yeah. That's the feeling I got. He knew everything about us. He didn't bat an eye what we had on him."

"Come to think of it, when I left, he called me Miss Arpeggio."

"He did?"

"Your face gets around."

"My fist will go into your face, Picco."

"Hey, Ange, look at this way. We got Alice free of that guy and we cut ourselves a steady flow of cash. We're earning, brother. What's to cry about?"

"I'm not crying, Picco. I'm reviewing how the whole thing went down."

"And so?"

"And I don't like it is what. There's going to be a next play here."

"What the fuck does that mean?"

"It means we may be way over our heads. This is not the short con you're used to playing, Picco. I think we're right in the middle of a very long con. And I can't see what our parts are."

Summer who had been quietly driving and saying nothing was now nodding her head.

"I'm with Ange on this. We're in the middle of something here. We're not on the inside. So, what I'm asking is who brought us to this guy? Dr. Grew or whoever he is."

It didn't take Ange long to say,

"Alice."

Picco shook his head.

"That poor kid is the roper? No way. I think what you need to do is figure out what you're going to do with a steady … let's see, a quarter of a million in twelve monthly payments."

"Almost 20K a month," Summer told him.

Picco clapped his hands.

"Baby, I'm going to run out the thread in my spool like nobody's ever seen before."

"You'll be spending forty thousand a month on a thirty thousand income. And when guys like The Lutheran come after you, you'll come running back to the neighborhood for protection."

"We'll see," Picco snapped back. "I heard they put Mal's murder on The Lutheran. So, it's death row for that big jerk. "

When they pulled up in front of *The New Pompey*, Angelo cautioned both to stay mum on everything.

"You go out and buy a yacht in a year or so, Picco, and the IRS will be all over you. That's if we ever see a dime out of this deal."

"You think he'll renege?" Summer asked.

"Fact is, I can't see through this. If I'm right and we are at stage one of a long grift, the final chapter is not going to be us going anywhere with anybody's money. Whoever is running this is using us, not making us rich."

Nothing felt right.

"Grew agreed to giving us a lot of money. Too easily. And I can't see why he did it in the first place. Not that amount. Not any of it."

"You know what I think?" Picco asked. "I think you're paranoiac. And even more than that. I think you're seeing people and problems that just ain't there."

"What are you going to do about that daughter thing?" Summer said.

"Ask to see her," Picco said. "When she don't show up, tell Alice it's because she ain't there. Maybe that will clear her head because I got to tell you, if that kid ain't there, this Alice is scaring the hell out of me."

"Strong women always scare you, Piccolino."

"No way. It's the crazy ones."

"You say crazy again, Picco and I'll shut you up.

"Maybe it's like Dr. Grew says. She needs an invisible daughter to talk to. But now she's got you."

"Yeah, she's got you, Ange. That's a good thing."

"Yeah, she's got me," Angelo replied, getting out of the car, and wondering if she had all of them.

CHAPTER ELEVEN

J.J. PICCOLINO

If Angelo had any suspicion of Alice, it was immediately vacated when he saw the tears of joy that came to her eyes when he told her that she was free of Dr. Grew.

"From now on, you do what you want with your money. You throw those pills he gave you away. You forget about ever being under Grew's control again."

"Hello," she said in almost a whisper.

"Okay. You'll be okay."

Yeah, she was really Alice. Not so much in a rabbit hole but still Alice. And that was okay with him. It was Alice he wanted.

"I'm ready."

"Oh, yeah? For what?"

"For you. To be with you."

They were in her Coney Island apartment. She started to take off her blouse. He wondered where the daughter was. But not for long.

"Summer says she sent Grew the Cyprus transfer info," Picco whispered to him at *The New Pompey*. "So she sent him Aunt Rita with her old man. Wonder how that will work out?"

Angelo looked at him and shook his head. Picco worried him. He was wearing a new leather jacket. It looked like the Zegna jacket Picco had shown him on his phone, more than once over the past couple of years. He was still the Picco he ran these streets with, the guy who wasn't big but had big plans to do big things and go to big places and spend big and just do everything big. There was no way that guy, grown up but still inside the same guy yearning to be big, was ever going to handle a flow of some 20K a month without stepping into the spotlight. You know, where the cops can get a good look. Those thoughts darkened Angelo's mood considerably.

"J.J. Piccolino looks like he won big last night," Sal said, putting cups of coffee in front of Angelo and Picco. "In every way."

"Let's get a table and talk," Angelo said and Picco followed him over to a table.

"What's up?"

"You make any plans to get out of Brooklyn?"

"No. Did you?"

That annoyed Angelo.

"I'm not you. I can keep my mouth shut and my money out of everybody's face. You can't. I'm also not leaving Alice. I've been thinking of marrying her."

Picco seemed surprised. And amused.

"Really? You sure about that? What did she say?"

"I haven't asked her yet."

Picco stared into his coffee. It was already cold. He saw a marriage leaving him out in the cold. In and now out. He felt queasy all of a sudden.

"You'd cut that freak Dr. Grew right out of the game. I mean, you'd be her husband. Take over handling her stockpile."

"I'm not doing it for that. And if I did, you and Summer wouldn't be cut out of the deal."

"We wouldn't? Why's that? We got leverage on Grew. Summer and me, we got no leverage on you. You don't have to give us a dime."

"Can it, Picco. I'm not marrying her to cut you and Summer out. Friendship doesn't compute with you? It does with me. It's Grew I'm after."

"We could cut him out without you having to run the store."

Angelo shook his head.

"I ran that by Grew. It wouldn't work."

"You ran that by Grew? When?"

"I called him. I told him Alice didn't need him. She'd be running her own affairs. He said maybe after a long court deal, we could get him detached from her, but the court has her down as mentally incompetent or what they call legally incapacitated. Some other shrink would be appointed guardian. Not me. I'm not a shrink. And he made it clear that the court would in no way recognize me, given my rap sheet, as a proper guardian."

"And marrying her would be something that could happen? I mean Grew wouldn't get in the way of that?"

"Yeah, he would for sure. I didn't bring it up. But he'd go to the mat on that. He's still got his beak in now."

"And so do we. That's the sweetness of our arrangement. Why fuck with that? I want the monthly. I don't want to grow old waiting for the courts to put that whacko in jail."

"Yeah, okay," Ange said, upset at himself for running his mouth without studying the moves that had to be made.

"Yeah, Ange, I know you. It bothers you that we had to leave Grew in place so we could dip into that special lady's honey pot. Makes us no better than him. I get that. But we unhooked her from that freak's chain, didn't we? That's something."

"Yeah, okay. Let's drop it. But that changes nothing with what you've gotta do. You've gotta get out of Brooklyn. Right away. Look at you, you're already sporting a what? Four, five-thousand-dollar jacket? And we haven't seen any money from Grew yet. Who did you tap for the money?"

"I went to Gigi."

"So goddamn stupid, Johnny. What did you do for collateral? You tell Gigi about our deal with Grew?"

"I'm not stupid, Ange."

"You didn't mention the deal with Grew ..."

"Okay. I told him Alice was loaded and you two moved in together."

Ange clenched one fist and then suddenly the rage drained out of him, like air out of a balloon.

Ange hunched over the table, staring at both his hands.

"You're tying yourself down to somebody ... Look, you see Gee as a good guy. I do too. He's been like a father to me. But he's a dangerous guy. Especially now that everything he has is costing him a lot more to keep. The developers want him gone. Believe me, Gee is like a bear cornered in his cave. "

"Look, Ange. You don't know where she is. You're crazy about her. Sure. You remember Gloria Brown?"

"You went out with her in the 8th grade?"

"No, listen. She was married to that cop she was crazy about. He tried to arrest her. They had an argument over, I don't know, coffee wasn't hot enough. The cat was on the mat. Whatever. He handcuffs her and runs her in on some bogus charge. She loved him. He was nuts. Love and crazy. It's a bad mix."

"Look, Picco. What are you gonna do when you can't even pay the vig? I say that because I don't think we're gonna see a dime out of Grew. We're being played. Right in the middle of something we can't see. I told you that. But you jump in like we're winners already. Somebody is making chumps of us. And you're helping them by acting stupid."

"Okay, Ange. You know what? It's my life. I go stupid and you go crazy."

Angelo jumped up suddenly and banged the table.

"I'm gonna get Alice free of whatever this is she's in and I'm in. I got no patience for you anymore, Johnny."

"Yeah, why do you need friends now? I could just drop dead, disappear. Be in a hole in the ground."

"You're putting yourself there. Not me."

"Yeah, well, I'll pay Gigi back as soon as that Grew money ... "

"You're not listening. No money. Gee will be pushing through that door once you don't come up with his money."

"I'll disappear."

"With you gone, he'll have to come to me. He'll have to walk through me to get to her. You know why? Because you used Alice and me as collateral."

He pressed one finger hard into Picco's chest.

"Capisce? None of this shit would have been on my plate if you had checked your fucking greed like I told you."

Picco watched him walk away.

"Have you seen the daughter yet?" he shouted but Ange didn't turn around.

Picco took the shot glass in front of him with a shaky hand and then knocked the drink back. He would go but he didn't know where. He would vanish but he didn't know how. Angelo hadn't told him.

Someone was screaming at the bar. Or maybe they were laughing.

CHAPTER TWELVE

THIS PLACE IS FRAGILE

That evening Alice told Angelo that her former theatre professor was performing in a new show she had seen announced in the papers. Could they go? She had been a favorite student of his, a colleague of Thomas's.

It was a "why not?" deal for Angelo so Alice bought two tickets and she and Angelo made their way to the Medicine Show Theatre on W. 52nd and 11th. He didn't like going into the City. The City, as if Brooklyn was the boonies. Now it was …what did Sal call it? Brooklyn was the new Paris. A new curated Brooklyn and Manhattan was eclipsed.

Alice's former theatre prof, Warwick Marune, had half dozen lines as a drunken malcontent, making swashbuckler moves with his arms and flashing smiles at the audience in an inane manner. This would be dramatic Angelo thought if only because the guy was about Angelo's height and thin as a broom stick.

When the curtain opened and Alice looked up from the program in her hand, just having read the words: *"Setting: The Lodge, a boarding house for the Nutserati, the last radicals on the planet"* her whole body tensed and she felt chilled, iced as if a current of electricity had passed through her body. She didn't want to go down this road of hurting memories, but this play was going to take her there.

She remembered what Dr. Grew had told her about a past she couldn't go back to without pain and a future that was no more than a wall built against the past but doomed to repeat it. What then was the present? she had asked him. Something that never happens while it's present. She had told that to Angelo. It had been pillow talk and he had said that time only ran out when you watched it. Otherwise, it didn't exist. Like now, with her, it didn't exist for him. She thought that a lovely thing for him to say. The words of a Prince.

"The Lodge was where Thomas and his friends lived. I did too," she whispered nervously to Angelo who said, "Okay."

He pictured elite, highbrow lunatics in a big, log cabin, the kind on the syrup bottle.

After the performance, Alice struggled with the idea of taking Angelo back stage to meet Warwick. Oil and water kind of thing but she thought it might be good to talk to Warwick because "The time has come to talk of many things," she recited to herself, not knowing why.

They found Warwick leaning against a prop, cigarette hanging out of his mouth, his long body arched over two women still in costume. Theatrical maids.

Alice didn't remember anyone having a maid at The Lodge. Warwick was out of costume and in his street clothes. He looked gaunt as if he had missed quite a few meals, but taller for that leanness, a pencil mustache precisely shaved, his clothes rumpled, his shoes, scuffed, worn leather. He looked sixty but was pretending to be much younger and the pretense shown through conspicuously in the way all artifice did in the presence of the harsh light of reality. Alice's painter eye had taught her that. You try to paint the past the way Disney or Rockwell would, and it went nightmarish. She saw that in her mother's paintings.

He didn't recognize Alice at first and then a light of recognition.

"Come, we shall have some fun now!" he shouted.

"Exactly so!" Alice shouted back.

When she broke free of his embrace, she introduced him to Angelo.

"Angelo? I hope not any kin to Shakespeare's Angelo who makes fornication punishable by death."

"I'm not that guy."

Alice told Warwick that she now had her own child, not a child really, all of seventeen years old. Sandra.

"Thomas's daughter! My God!"

He reached down and wrapped his arms around Alice once again.

"I share a dressing room," Warwick told her, apologetically, releasing Alice.

"How is Thomas? I haven't heard anything in eons."

Angelo was just about to say he was dead when Alice said, "We don't know. I was hoping you knew where he was."

He didn't and he wished he did, and he was about to go for a bite to eat and would they join him?

Once out on the street, Warwick told them that in his opinion, the country was becoming too uncivil for actors. The everydayness of the young was so strange to him. Theatrical philanthropy was at an hysterical low point. And other comments that made no sense to Angelo. The guy was wired like he was on something but not drugs.

"I've got plans," the actor told them. "Jessica … "

He paused and opened the door to what he called "his steak house." The smell of pan grizzled fat rushed to greet them. Angelo looked around and saw diners who looked like they lived under a bridge.

"High Line Public Park residents," Warwick told him proudly. "Some mole people too. A masterless assortment. Jessica does not approve of the impoverished."

"Jessica still with you?" Alice asked, realizing that she had not thought of her friend in years. Everyone connected to Thomas had been expunged.

"I was about to adjust the sails of my life. But Jessica was impatient and abandoned ship. Nevertheless, we will sail passed all those nets of entrapment. She has sailed into a very promising port. She lives now with Senor Robert Bellator. Original family name something else. He made up that name for himself. Bags of inherited gold doubloons. A facsimile of a Las Vegas pleasure dome as a cozy home."

"I'm sorry to hear you and Jessica broke up," Alice said, sadly. "I always thought you two were soul mates."

"We are! We are! Monsieur Bellator is nothing more than a fleece in our lives."

"A fleece?" Angelo repeated.

"A fleece indeed, Angelo. In this case the fleece, Lord Bellator, is a Wall Street financier, a stock analyst, a banker of Croesus proportions, a man doing God's work alongside Goldman Stacks and the president's son-in-law, an advisor to the elite, a monarch with hundreds of quant minions who dive to the bottom for the Brooklyn of great worth. He uploads, downloads, unloads, loads, ejaculates. In short, a regurgitated man of the new financialized, giggy sharing Millennium. A mogul as approachable as that salt shaker. An unstable paranoiac and a scion of ancestry that course in his blood like tape worms through intestines. In short, a low, godless figure divided from Art and Nature."

Angelo was running the circuitry of connections here in his mind and seeing that they all led to a dark muddle, a muddle he wasn't rushing to make sense of. His focus stayed on the word "fleece."

"So, Waswick, this senor monarch Mexican guy, the fleece, is your ex-wife Jessica's new husband and you don't like him?"

"Call me Warwick offstage. Purely a business relationship. And he is not Hispanic. He is what obscene wealth makes of our human clay. A twist of gnarl, a rock of root."

Angelo looked around the steak house and noticed a bouncer like guy eying them.

"Jessica should have re-married me. I am, as far as immortality goes, a hot prospect. Money in hand is nothing compared to being married to raw talent whose potential is staring you in the face."

"She should have held on to you until you panned out, right?" Angelo told him, smile on his face. "When you hit retirement age in a few years."

"Time is a staged event, Angelo. I choose to play the part of a young man on the dawn of great things. And in what stream are you panning for gold, my youngish sir?"

"I try to make a few bucks here and there. Off the cusp. These days I'm mostly trying to keep people from making money off me."

"A proper mission. Be no one's pawn or play the fool for those no better than yourself."

"Angelo sails a good deal. He's on the water every chance he gets. Brooklyn is surrounded by water. It's a peninsula."

"Ah, Brooklyn! A true place yet shown on every map."

He forked a bit of steak he had ordered and plunged it into his mouth.

"The Nutserati? Remember them? I'm an exception. Among those already exceptional."

And then he laughed so heartily that the diners around them stared at him.

"I was very young," Alice mused, sadly.

"My dear," the actor her, *"Bliss was it in that dawn to be alive but to be young was very heaven!* We all lived as one in The Lodge, the hearth of all our rebel ways. *Build thee more stately mansions, O my soul, As the swift seasons roll!"*

"You were with us in "The Uprising" of course?" he suddenly and very seriously asked Alice.

"They wanted to upend the world," Alice explained to Angelo.

"And I went down a rabbit hole after Thomas left me. Like Alice. I think it's where the world and I were upended. Or maybe it was just me and the world is stable and makes sense."

"Some of it is a ball of confusion," Angelo told her. Uplifting comment he thought and told himself to shut up.

"My dear, you were always Alice. You saw the white rabbit looking at his watch before you ever met Thomas."

Alice gave Angelo a frightened look.

"Yes, I guess so."

"That was Thomas's fiction, to upend the world," Warwick went on. "I never thought he was serious about it. A bit of a poseur was our Thomas."

"He wanted to be an actor. I guess he was because he played the part of Thomas. He was really Trip, you know."

"He was really a trip, you say? Ah! so much has changed Cecily. Brooklyn is a peninsula. Thomas is now a trip. You are now Alice. So wonderful. Do you remember when you thought people were bombs? Baghdad was being bombed nightly. You became so confused. You thought you were one yourself. Thus, you magnanimously wouldn't go near people. Ah, so long ago."

He saw Angelo giving him an open mouthed WTF look.

"May I roll out our cast of characters and their battles with "The Resident Constabulary"?

"Go ahead," Ange told him. "Knock yourself out."

"I was for swashbuckling drama," the actor told them, swiping a last potato bit around his dish. "Acting in each classical form: Oedipus Wreck, Beowulf's mother, Don Corleone, Sancho Vino, a tall Lautrec, and Alexander Burr, fatally wounded. Jessica was Greek tragedy and advanced feminist vitriol. Tee was classics, aperitivi and Dada; Cutter, Reign of Terror, Communard and Guillotine. He called himself Reynard. A cruel fox. He put his wife, Joan's head on the block every day. A destined divorce. Jean-Louis, faux languages and Cannabis sativa distribution."

"And Thomas?"

"A seafarer and wanderer in every sense of the word."

He cleared his throat and then proclaimed:

Lest man know not
That he on dry land loveliest liveth,
List how I, care-wretched, on ice-cold sea,
Weathered the winter, wretched outcast
Deprived of my kinsmen.

"That sounds like Trip," Angelo said.

"Trip? Yes, our lives. A mere trip in the rolling emptiness of eternity."

"Trip was Thomas's childhood name. He was always leaving. On a trip."

"And so you said, my dear. I thought it was the meds speaking. My apologies. I am so thrilled that you no longer identify with a bomb. You have matured into a flower. I must tell you, Angelo, that when Thomas quoted poetry in the class room, he drew every lovely into his sphere of influence. Like a sun to its planets. To turn into a dark star hence."

"He drew me. I wasn't much older than Sandra, my daughter, is now."

"Sandra? Did you know that it's a feminine form of Alexander? Defender of men. Is that what she's like?"

What she's like is invisible Angelo said, but to himself.

"She likes to change her name. Yesterday she was Kitty."

"From *Gunsmoke*, I guess," Angelo said, and they both gave him a questioning look.

"How marvelous! A star is born. All parts await her. All names are hers!"

"She doesn't get out much," Angelo said. "I've never seen her."

"She's a very private, shy person," Alice said, in almost a whisper. "Withdrawn."

"Like Emily Dickinson. How marvelous. Throwing her sonnets out the window."

"Maybe not her," Alice said, timidly. "She's more taken with her phone."

Angelo could see that for the first time, the wind had gone out of the actor's sails. He glanced at Angelo who shrugged his shoulders.

Alice stood up.

"Goodbye."

"Goodbye, my dear?"

Angelo told him that they had to go. He was parked in a tow away zone, though he wasn't parked anywhere, not owning a car.

"You do? Wait, I seldom have a chance to talk to a man who sails in blue water."

"Mostly along the coast. Though blue water sailing is what we do in good weather. I don't sail much now. I lost my first mate."

"I have always desired a schooner two masted sailboat, in which the aft-most mast or the mainmast will be taller than the foremast. You understand the importance of height, being a man of considerable proportions yourself."

"I don't say I understand it."

"My dream boat will be gaff cutter rigged, with a topsail set on the mainmast. I personally believe that of all the different types of sailboats, a schooner under full sail is one of the most beautiful sights afloat. You can sail anywhere, at any time. And off you go, into the wind."

He stood up this time to recite:

"'To sail into an unknown spring, or receive one's baptism on storm's promontory, where the solitary albatross heels over in the gale, and at last come to land. To know the earth under one's foot and go, in wild delight, ways where there is water.' It's a quote from Malcolm Lowry. I'm going to stencil it in the salon. A glorious salon."

"We gotta go."

"I will be in charge of steering. Sextant and celestial navigation."

"Wonderful," Alice told him. "What a wonderful voyage."

"Good luck in getting the funding," Angelo told him, beginning to get a whiff of grift going on here he couldn't figure. Was he hitting Alice up for the funds? Or, just maybe, the guy was a hot air balloon, flying too high to play the part of his own wounded life.

"I can see you and Jessica with the wind in your faces," Alice exclaimed, clapping her hands.

"Jessica followed the money right up the arse of the Golden Fleece," Warwick cried out, waving one arm as if it held a sword.

He was still standing, a towering presence in that small restaurant.

A waiter came over to him and mumbled something into his ear.

The actor stepped back and exploded.

"We want the finest wines available to humanity, we want them here and we want them now!" he shouted. "I quote Withnail."

"You better pay up and get out, with or without," the waiter told him. "Twenty-five. And no more screaming. The customers are fragile."

"Fragile?" Warwick repeated as if the word had some magical power. "What is this dump? The glass menagerie?"

Angelo reached out and pulled at him and he sat back down.

That didn't stop the waiter who grabbed Warwick's shoulder. Angelo smacked his hand away.

"Don't jam him," Angelo said, looking up at the waiter.

The tone had a chilling quality that drew the actor's gaze up from the wallet he was rifling through and on to Angelo's face, which showed no emotion.

"Cash is safest in this emporium. But I seem to be a trifle low."

"I got it," Angelo said, handing the waiter cash.

"This humble, indigent artist thanks you. You have the heroic manner of my hero, Errol Flynn."

"He's called the prince of the neighborhood," Alice said proudly.

"What money has your ex-wife ... Jessica? ... been following?" Angelo asked as Warwick sat down.

"She follows the man who follows the money," Warwick replied, winking.

"And you follow them both."

"And on to a marvelous voyage!"

"To us a bon voyage," he said, raising the glass and knocking it back with one swallow. *`I must go down to the seas again, to the vagrant gypsy life. To the gull's way and the whale's way where the wind's like a whetted knife; And all I ask is a merry yarn from a laughing fellow-rover. And quiet sleep and a sweet dream when the long trick's over.'*"

"You mean you want us to go with you?" Alice cried out.

"Of course. You think it's by accident that we have met? Everything, my dear, happens for a reason."

"Except all the shit you don't see coming and don't know why it's coming."

"Wise and heroic, my dear Angelo, if not truly Shakespearean."

He was beaming at Angelo as if he had finally found a friend.

"I don't think I can go," Alice said, drawing back from the enthusiasm she had expressed two seconds before. "I have been there. Goodbye."

"Take it easy, Alice. It's all imaginary with your friend here."

"It is?" Warwick asked Angelo, his bonhomie shot through. He immediately snapped out of it.

"Of course, it is. If we couldn't imagine, where would we be?"

"Back in the real world," Angelo mumbled.

"Pardon, monsieur?"

"So, this monarch guy has no problems with you hanging around his wife?"

Warwick studied Angelo's face as he considered that.

"I am most certain that once he sees Jessica and myself together on the bow with the wind in our faces, he will realize that our immortal love transcends his aged lust."

"You think so?"

"Why not?"

"Not for me to figure out, pal. I got my own chart to read."

"I have faith in the underlying magical order of all things," Warwick told him, laying a hand on top of Alice's "And there,

Jessica and I are forever united. It cannot be other than that, sir."

"Any chance," Angelo said slowly, "Jessica might see you aren't playing with a full deck?"

"`He is the half part of a blessed man, Left to be finished by such as she; And she a fair divided excellence, Whose fullness of perfection lies in him.' King John. I also bring to your attention, my dear Angelo, that all geniuses must be slightly out of their minds otherwise they'd be completely within the minds of ungenius."

"If that's what you think."

"And what is it that you think?"

"I think crazy plus swindle doesn't put you close to anything but jail time."

He leaned across the table.

"In short … "

He paused.

"In short," Warwick repeated, smiling. "I sense the drama."

"In short, I think there's a good chance this mogul guy can figure out you and Jessica are working a grift on him."

"It's hard to say what moguls are thinking. That's their gift."

"They think about money. How to get it, how to hold on to it, and how to spot people who are trying to take it from them. They can see your hand trying to get into their pocket is what they can see."

"I like this man. He's flourish and daring. A true hero in our time. A true prince, as you say, my dear."

"You've got the market on that, don't you? All flourish?"

"Here's what I say. Why do algorithm and finance billionaires buy newspapers and cattle ranches and rocket ships and Indian tribes and baseball teams and Little People and cotton fields and the Buddy Holly archive and the Magna Charta and dinosaur bones and the livers and kidneys of people sleeping under a bridge?"

"Thomas's first cousin sleeps in a skiff."

"We don't know why," Angelo said, "and we don't care."

"Because what they do tells the whole world to fuck off!" Warwick screamed.

There was loud growling coming from the invisible, fragile regulars at the far end of the bar. And in the dark interior of the restaurant drums could be heard.

"We better tone it down. Those gentlemen think somebody hired us to get the authorities here so the bartender, who owns the place, will lose his lease. It's something that's happening all over these rent control neighborhoods. I impress you, no doubt. I came upon a whole dramatic plot with just several visitations to this historic establishment."

"Goodbye," Alice said, for the third time, not moving.

"You must come to Senor Bellator's, his digs near the Delaware Water Gap."

"Why?" Angelo asked but Alice said she would love to go.

Alice gave Warwick a long, tight hug.

"Crew members. Sailors one and all" was what Angelo heard as they left the restaurant.

Angelo wondered whether he had just signed on to something, and then, looking at Alice, he realized he already had.

CHAPTER THIRTEEN

JESSICA MARUNE

"There's a call for you Ange," Sal said that night as Angelo sat at the bar. "Jessica Marune. Who's that?"

"Give me the phone. You don't have to know everything, Sal."

"Hey, believe me, half the stuff I hear, I don't wanna hear. What I know is based on not hearing anybody."

"This is Angelo," he said when he was snuggled in the now totally unused phone booth that went along with all the other extinct artifacts in the bar.

"Jessica Marune. Would it be alright if I came by to talk to you? I need to clear up some matters Warwick may have confused. You're at *The New Pompey* on New Utrecht?"

"That's where I'm at."

She told him she'd be over in twenty minutes. He went back to the bar.

"Where's Johnny Picco been, Ange? Funny seeing you without your shadow."

"He's gonna be on the road for a while "

Sal whistled.

"Flying solo in the big, wide world? Bout time. Dije hear about Aunt Rita? Had a shootout with some private cops over at some private rest home. Summer's old man got shot in the foot. You hear anything about that?"

"No."

"Summer got her out on bail. Seen her?"

"No. And I don't want to. Either one."

"Private cops. Now they got private firemen. Private soldiers. Private prisoners. Who gets shot in a rest home?"

"Shut up, Sal and listen. A woman is going to come into this bar pretty soon. I want her tailed when she leaves here. Can you see to that, Sal?"

Jessica Marune showed up a little later but by the looks she instantly got from those at the bar, she was worth waiting for. She was a tall brunette, looked early 30's Ange figured but probably older. She dressed and walked with the kind of style that disdained the place and enjoyed it at the same time. Nose in the air and a smile on her face.

She walked right up to Angelo just as Sal was set to spark.

"Mr. Bari? Jessica Marune. May we sit in one of those booths?"

"Sure."

"I seem to be getting a lot of attention," she said, smiling and turning to look at the men at the bar who were looking at her.

"Place is full of pigs," Ange told her, shrugging. "They've all been #Metooed. Like the President."

As soon as they were seated, Sal came over to them.

"I'm Sal. Short for every woman's salvation. I have the pleasure of serving you."

"Hullo, Sal. I love the look of this place. It's vintage wrapped but actually real."

Sal looked around.

"Yeah, it's real now but it used to be a movie set. Black and white. Brooklyn noirs. Never no plastic is our motto. What can I get you?"

"Whatever Mr. Bari is drinking."

"Well, Mr. Bari here drinks straight Jim Beam Rye and sometimes he drink's Zubrowka out of the freezer and sometimes he drinks…"

"Give us some Jamison and quit the gab."

"I have the feeling I can smoke in here," she said, taking a pack of cigarettes out.

"You'd be the only one not smoking. We don't get cigarette patrolled."

"Fascinating," she said, as he lit her cigarette and she blew smoke upward. "I hate these gentrified snob bars. The fop curators and connoisseurs of everything. They've taken the dirt out of sin. The burnt off the toast."

She paused and he lit her cigarette.

"The sin out of sinning," she told him. "Did you know you can't curate sin?"

"I don't know. I don't sin. Nobody in here does. What do you want with me?"

She studied him to see if he was burnt, like the toast.

"I go by first impressions. Malcolm Gladwell says they count awfully. They're important. I think you'll do."

"For what? Loading trucks?"

"From what Wally tells me you've kind of caught on to what we're up to."

"Who's Wally?"

"Warwick. Mr. Bellator nicknamed him Wally because he said it suited him. Warwick doesn't like it."

"So, you use it anyway. Look, spell it out, so I can know what you think I know, and I can know it too."

Sal came back with their drinks.

"Cin-cin," she said, hoisting her glass and knocking back the drink.

"Salud."

"I've rushed here to talk to you because Wally invited you to Mr. Bellator's, though he says he didn't. He's a liar. You should know that. He thinks he lies for dramatic effect, like Oscar Wilde, but he lies with evil intent. Thank God he hasn't discovered Twitter. He'd be giving your president competition. Anyway, you need to know certain things before you meet Robert Bellator."

"Like what? I know he's mogul."

"He's our mark."

Angelo admired her coolness.

"You're the inside on this or is it Wally? I don't get the feeling he could manage a long con."

"Mr. Bellator keeps Wally around for his own amusement, being, as such with all moguls, in need of amusement. Anyway, I ask Robert to bear with Warwick. We are, after all, soul mates. Whatever. I was lying. Warwick isn't evil. He wouldn't know how to be. But he does lie for dramatic effect. Also, I'm not absolutely certain that I have a soul. I suspect no."

"Okay."

"I see I'm boring you. In short, our Warwick is all drama and very little reality. It's a terribly sick world. With all the wealth in the hands of people who roller coaster from depression to sadism. I can't convince Warwick of that. He's as much in wonderland as Cecily. Alice. So very fey.

"She's leaving it. Both worlds. Sick and wonderland."

"Yes, I see. And coming? Where? Here?"

"You got some sadism in you, lady. It's filling up the place."

"You mean why don't I free Warwick or tell Bellator to find his amusement elsewhere? I won't and I think you know why."

"You're the real sadist?"

"Guess again."

"It's part of your grift. Keeping your mark hooked."

"Precisely. Besides, Warwick hasn't always been a good boy. He's not good. He's not evil. But he's not good. Maybe Alice is. Maybe not. But he's weak. Punishment is not unmerited in this case. Crimes cannot go unpunished, Mr. Bari. Weakness is a sin in my world."

Angelo looked over at the bar where Sal was gesturing. Angelo shook his head. He needed to stay sober. This lady was not a novice at the game. He still didn't know what the grift was or where he fit in. Things were true and then they weren't. He was bad but then he was good and then he was bad again. Alice was good underneath or maybe bad underneath. What crimes was she talking about? What did a depressed sadist look like? This Jessica was a walking fucking mind torque and he was running out of patience. He figured what he was getting was a tiny look at something from the wrong direction.

"What are you bothering with me for?"

Her face, which was lovely but not an Alice face, most definitely not an Alice in wonderland, but a hardened face no amount of face product or lifts could conceal. No, she wasn't good. And she wasn't weak either. That's the only way he could describe it to himself. She lowered her voice and leaned forward.

"I've convinced Bellator that he's an heir to a Ponzi scheme fortune and that if he wants to clear himself, he'll have to launder millions. Our need is for a laundry man."

"I don't want to know more. Besides telling you I don't own a washing machine. I just want to know where Alice fits in here. That's my need."

"Don't worry. She's everything she seems to be. Let's just say she wandered in and led us to you."

Angelo thought about that, and then he shook his head.

"Naw, that don't sound right."

"Why not?"

"Because I'm thinking Dr. Grew is where you want me to lay Bellator's money. And he didn't just wander into the game. He had your whole scam down pat. Knew his lines. He was waiting for us."

"I'd say he's working his own short con," Jessica told him, putting out her cigarette.

"Nix to that," Angelo told her, trying to stay good humored even though the lady was trying to spin him. Probably she was too used to spinning guys like two tops. She was the kind of hustler he and Picco always needed to get into the big game. Now, here she was but she wasn't opening a door to let him in. It was more like he was a piece that could be played.

"He's set up to launder Bellator's money and you set him up. So, I ask again how did Alice get into this? And don't fucking waste my time. You're in my bar. I can throw your ass out of here. You can shake it on your way out."

"Okay, I'm trying to give you the short of the long. As a favor."

"I'm seeing a long grift in this, so long fits. Hit me. Or goodbye as Alice likes to say when things go sideways. I'm a two-bit hustler and you know that. My worth is in being with Alice. So, that's what I know."

"Bellator doesn't like the dirty spot his ancestors have put him in. He's obsessed with purifying himself. Filthy lucre. The Devil's excrement but he doesn't know how to live any life other than a mogul's. I tell him let's launder the money. Make it clean."

"I heard that. Alice?"

"She's got that wonderland allure. Innocence adrift. Personally, I don't see it. But Bellator will. I'm betting on that. She's the pure soul he wants in his life. She's better than cleaning the money. "

"He won't get the chance to be around her."

"You won't let anything happen to her and we'll get the money. You can take Alice wherever you want. Understand? Nod, if you understand and can accept that."

"Grew says she's loaded. There's a trust fund."

"Empty. We set up Grew to be the guardian of Alice and a trust he can pretend is loaded by throwing around some working capital. He left a trail of expenditures. Gambling debts and such.. You picked those up. Grew gets his thrills out of conniving. He has restless brain syndrome. He threw out a hook and you went for it."

Angelo nodded.

"And then the deal with us for millions that ain't there."

"Bellator will know about that. That deal makes Alice's trust millions really real, as the idiots say. He's got a penitent's hunger for absolution but he's also very fearful of being taken by people like his own ancestors. They're dead but they're also still in the world. He's got an eye out for a confidence game. We need to play very carefully. Alice is a so very real innocence, beyond being stunned and blind. It all makes her magnetic. It didn't take much to go through the legal hoops to get her out of the sanitarium and under Grew's care and so on. Dr. Grew is a true genius. He can make you whatever paper credential you need. We come up with some front money and he works wonders spreading it around the market. Makes two fish look like a million."

"Good for him. Picco and me ever got into a Big Store. As you can see, we can't even get ourselves out of this bar. Or this neighborhood."

"Well, you're in one now if you want it. A real Big Store."

He waved to Sal. He needed that drink now.

"What makes you think Bellator will trust me? Isn't that kind of a crap shoot? I show up and he says 'Here's ten million. Launder it for me and bring me back fresh, new greens.'"

"I can't know for sure if he'll trust you, but I know he won't go direct to Grew. As I say, you're the man now in Alice's life. You've already pulled the reins out of Grew's hands. Bellator will see that. Why deal with Grew now when you're the man?"

Ange puzzled over that, not as sure as Jessica seemed to be that he was an indispensable piece here. But he had to be otherwise this lady wouldn't be spilling it all out to him.

"You're the proper lure is what I suspect."

"And what's that?"

"An old school grifter who fell for a lady slightly off her rocker who fell for a masterless man she calls her prince. Bellator will see you as dirty. He'll do everything he can to save Alice from you."

"You're kidding me? Why the fuck would he hand money over to me if he thought that?"

"Beating you is beating those bad genes that have been passed on to him. Beating you is also winning Alice."

He knocked back very quickly the shot Sal put in front of him.

"Warwick and I are going to build you up to Bellator. Put one hundred per cent trust in you to deliver as promised. He knows he can't trust me. I tell him straight up I'm like his great grandfather. Every trick in the book to get what I want. If I tell him you're okay, he'll figure you'll scam him."

She laughed.

"It's a game we play. He fears his soul is dark, greedy, narcissist. He knows mine is. I'm Medea. I remind him that we humans put self interest first. He keeps me around to show himself he's better than that. It's so sad when wealth has such a diseased mind."

She gave him a wink, as if he were in on something he knew and she knew he wasn't in on. A kind of double mock wink he figured.

"I don't know that kind of twistedness. We don't get within ten feet of those guys, so I wouldn't know. But you? You get close?"

She stood up and held out her hand.

"It's taken me a long time but I'm a pillow away."

He stared up at her. He hadn't ever gotten this close to someone like her either.

"Been lovely chatting with you., Angelo. Warwick will be sending you a dinner invite to Bellator's. Connivers' Dinner. It's what he calls his roundup of fools and miscreants who have shady deals they think they can put over on him. Emissaries in a way from his own dead corrupt, conniving ancestors. In his own way, you know, he's as unglued as our dear Alice."

"I'll kill you if anything happens to her."

"You are a Prince, aren't you?"

CHAPTER FOURTEEN

DINNER WITH ROBERT BELLATOR

Alice's meeting with Jessica was strange in Angelo's view.

Angelo had driven to the Bellator compound, which was at the end of the Garden State Parkway where Bellator had his own ferry service, a thirty-foot ketch that took them across Delaware Bay to the compound close to Rehoboth Beach.

Alice stood in the bow of the boat, a scarf keeping the wind from blowing through her hair, sun glasses on and a small fur jacket that she held tightly to her body with both arms. Angelo towered beside her, the wind and sun smarting his eyes, but wondering if he had ever felt a more glorious day. A glorious November. He could feel her lean and press against his body as if he were for her a wall of safety. Her mainsail in the wind. Wobbly seas.

"You know I really don't remember you," Jessica said, greeting Alice. "I remember your name "Cecily." But that's not the same thing as remembering you. I mean it's just a word that stuck with me."

"It doesn't matter. I'm Alice now."

"You know I had so many students back then. But apparently only one Cecily."

Angelo stood there trying to imagine Jessica as a school teacher. He was still trying to figure out how big a part Alice had in the grift Jessica had told him of and at what point Bellator would become fascinated with her. Like he was.

"I of course remember my colleague Thomas Lemon. The wild

rover. You ran off with him, didn't you?"

"What's the deal here, Jessica?" Angelo asked, wondering why she was bringing this shit up.

"No deal, Mr. Bari. I was just saying I remembered Thomas. He was something of what some uncharitable people would call a prick."

"That was Trip," Alice corrected her. "That's what everyone says about him."

"And so true. I mean after running off with you to that awful place he called a refuge of the soul. Those were his words. He wrote to me. A bower of happiness. Blah blah. He was so full of himself. And lies. Wasn't he, Alice? Full of deceit and self-loving. You must have celebrated when he left you."

"I went into an asylum."

"Don't we all? Of course, I liked Thomas. Lost boy is what I called him."

"Lost to me."

Jessica, with half closed eyes, studied Alice.

"You know, my dear, I somehow get the feeling that if you found him, you'd shoot him. Did you know being shot in the head unexpectedly is one of the better ways to die?"

"Are we going to stand here talking all night?" Angelo snapped.

"You know now that I see that face in my mind's eye," Jessica went on, ignoring Angelo. "Thomas's, I mean. So very handsome in that Italianate way. But I don't blame you for wanting to shoot him. I'd do the same. We women need to stick together. He was a real shit for leaving you. That's what he did, didn't he?"

"I think you should change course right about now, "Angelo mumbled, angrily. "Otherwise, we're out of here."

Angelo reached out a hand to Alice, but she didn't move. No one seemed to be paying any attention to him. This thing, whatever it was, was going to play out and he couldn't stop it. He had no idea how any of the crap Jessica had told him would execute. He was a piece of standing wood. Dogs come, they piss on him.

"I feel for you," Jessica said to Alice. "I honestly do. When we get caught in a sick relationship like yours and Thomas', it's a kind of bondage."

"Bondage," Alice said into the phone that was suddenly in her hand. *"A relationship not freely chosen. Also, weird sexual play."*

Alice looked at Jessica who was staring at the phone.

"You must be talking about Trip. I didn't know that about him then. Angelo and Summer have been telling me about Trip."

"I'm so glad," Jessica said, reaching forward and kissing Alice on the cheek. "And you mustn't feel disappointed because I recall only your name and nothing at all about you. Warwick has a thorough memory of you. He says you were one of his finest acting students. He told me that you were the finest Ophelia he ever had in class."

"I don't remember playing that part," Alice said, the same anxious look she got on her face when she couldn't remember anything about who she had been.

"Of course not, dear. He didn't say you played the part. He said you were Ophelia. You know, it's funny he only had you in his acting class. I only mention it because in those days charges of moral turpitude hung over Warwick's head as if he were a Catholic priest visiting a flock of choir boys. Only they weren't boys but girls. Like you."

"What did you think?" Jessica asked Alice after they toured what Warwick called The Big House located at the center of The Compound, a 40,000 square foot chateau built in the Loire Valley 16th century style. "It's grand isn't it? 'Let no one untrained in geometry enter.'"

"I failed geometry or maybe I didn't take it. Either way, we're already in."

"Just words over the entry to Plato's Academy. I think he was teasing."

"You see Warwick has not changed," Jessica told Alice nodding to where the actor was standing and drinking with several other guests, some in formal dress, some not.

"I had to let him go. He still thinks in his usual delusional way that he and I will be together again. "

"He's delusional?"

"Well, my dear, he thinks he's a great actor and perhaps he is. But not on stage."

"We saw him," Ange said. "In a play."

"Oh, was there a stage? What do you think of this dream castle?"

"I'm too puzzled to think," Alice told her, sitting down next to her on a sofa, one of many in the exhibition hall sized room adorned and strewn with enough bibelots, museum pieces, ancient artifacts, *memento mori*, hides and heads, and Orientalia to bail half the country out of poverty if ever directed to that purpose.

"Nice paintings," Angelo said, looking around.

"They're Hitler's. He did them before. Robert says his ancestors sat for most of them."

Angelo started to say something and then didn't. He glanced at Alice. She was looking elsewhere. He was sorry he had come.

"He keeps it all pretty private, doesn't he, your friend Robert," Angelo said. "A hundred acres never seen by your everyday slob."

"Hundreds, Mr. Bari. Hundreds. This is the right place for the right people. Enormous wealth seeks out safe havens. For the wealth and for themselves. Consider it a rare opportunity to come inside Robert Bellator's haven."

"I do," Alice said. "I hope he'll like us."

"He'll make his entrance. Right now, he's in his monitoring room watching what a multitude of video cameras all over the compound are capturing."

"Can he hear us?"

"On and off as his interest piques and wanes. Say something spellbinding. He likes spellbinding."

Alice was looking everywhere now, wide eyed, looking for the cameras.

She spun around, looking up at the ceiling.

"Hello! Hello! I'm Alice!"

Jessica reached out and put two arms around Alice, as if to bring her to ground.

"Hello, Alice," she said to her, smiling. "Tell me some more about poor Thomas. That lost boy."

She led Alice to a sofa where they both sat down. Angelo remained standing.

Alice began to tell Jessica about the inheritance that had been taken from her but had been rescued by Angelo. She smiled shyly at Angelo.

Jessica snuffed her cigarette out and lit another. She lit it with a tiny gold lighter she took out of her pocket.

"Thomas never talked much about his family," she told Alice, "but we all figured…I mean everyone but you and Warwick…Something of a different wavelength I suppose. But it was as clear as good vodka that they were mobbed up, as they say. That's all gone now. I wouldn't worry."

"I'm not worried. I know that Angelo will keep the gangsters out of my life."

"So reassuring. Unless of course Mr. Bari himself is a gangster."

"I cannot think so," Alice said, looking at Angelo. "Goodbye."

"Don't leave. Think how disappointed Mr. Bellator will be, very disappointed if you and Angelo leave now. Besides, if you stay, I have so much to tell you both."

"Like what?" Angelo said, taking a drink off a passing tray. It looked bubbly. He put it back on the tray.

"Any chance I could get some rye neat? Start telling me."

"Well, there's an idiot who calls himself Mister Sailor who was at the last roundup of Bellator's Connivers' Dinner who was so much more a greedy pig than every other greedy pig present..."

"I know Sailor," Alice interrupted, somehow energized by that knowing. "Sailor Kerplowski. He's Thomas's first cousin. He's still alive and he claims whatever money his uncle left him. He's from The Sands."

"Naturally. But he thinks he's a sly one. He told Robert that with some funding he could lead us to boxes of gold dust lying at the ocean bottom. I hope the bags are tightly tied."

"He told me the same thing," Alice said, upset that Jessica was amused by Thomas's first cousin. "I think he's an honest man."

"I wouldn't think so," Jessica said, shaking her head. "Anyone who you expect to tell you where a treasure is buried -- sunk in this case -- has already dug it up and run off with it. I learned so much from the greatest thief of all, Autolycus, such a successful thief with the power of metamorphosing both what he stole and himself."

"Is he here?" Alice asked, looking around.

"Autolycus or Mr. Kerplowski? Neither, dear. Mr. Kerplowski came in an old rowboat with a put-put engine and left the same way. You must wait to get the latitude and longitude of the sunken treasure in the mail. So many cereal box tops, I suppose, or is that scam over?"

"I don't think Thomas's family were gangsters."

"How did the *pater familias* die?"

"I don't know. Ambiguously they said. I ... I went to the ... The Service. The Wake. I was supposed to be watching out for people who were interested in me. They tell parables, as in the Bible."

"Were there any? I imagine there were mobs and mobs of them."

"Parables? I don't think so. I drank too much but I remember there was a giant and a dwarf. Really. They both said Paul Limone owed them a lot of money and they expected me to pay them back. From the inheritance."

"You know what I think?" Jessica said, blowing smoke up at Angelo. "I think we're at least two drinks behind the rest of the world."

"That's what Thomas always said."

"Of course, I remember he liked it when I first said it and he said he'd borrow it. Taking things was a habit of that poor lost boy as I remember him."

One of the many servants announced dinner.

The dinner was served in elegant Downton Abbey style, as all the house staff were English and wore the livery of the bygone age of the Mother Country.

"He doesn't look like a mogul," Alice had whispered to Angelo when first seeing Robert Bellator. "Not a mound at all."

Angelo inspected the man seated at the head of the table, about two and a half yards away from where he and Alice were.

Bellator wasn't roundish but tall, thin, in his 40's with receding sand colored hair. He had on a loose cardigan sweater over a T-shirt.

Bellator stood up and welcomed them all to his semi-annual Conniver and Pitch Dinner.

Angelo heard what sounded like a muted Alice voice and out of the corner of his eyes, he saw Alice staring at the Smartphone in her lap:

"Conniver: one who conspires secretly, also a grifter who conceals what he's doing, which is most often to swindle a mogul by making use of shills, dupes and the off-key working-class types."

"The idea of a conniver's dinner started with my great grandfather, Wallace Tewks. He thought his own father was a conniving thief and so with a sense of reparation, Wallace being a very religious man, held a dinner once a year in which as many as could sit at this very table were invited to connive him out of his own inherited wealth. You see, he wanted to fling back to a contemporary surrogate of his own father what Wallace felt were ill-gotten gains. `Such are the ways of everyone who is greedy for unjust gain; it takes away the life of its possessors'* Proverbs."

Angelo could see that Alice's eyes were wide with attentiveness. The man's voice was gravelly, husky but nervously hesitant and not at all what Angelo had expected. He in fact sounded Bronx.

"The consequences of that first Connivers' Dinner was not as my great grandfather expected. He gave away a fortune to a man fascinated with steam engines and locomotives. As fate and irony and the strange twists of life would have it, that man returned what Wallace had given him one hundred-fold. It was a destiny that greatly unsettled Wallace. But he took the words in Ecclesiastes to heart: 'So there's no use arguing with God about your destiny.' And there you have it, my friends. The wealth rose and fell rose and fell from generation to generation but as at an early stage it was mostly in land, real estate, engines and oil, it was passed on to me in abundance. So much abundance I've never had the need to practice the law I studied. I've kept on with the Connivers' Dinner as a tradition. I am equally disposed to fulfilling Wallace's wish to give it all away as well as invest it with one of you and await a hundred-fold return. I thank you for being here."

"You seem so sad, dear." Jessica said to Alice after the dinner, as the three wandered from one spacious room to another.

"I'm not but it's so sad about Wallace. He wanted to amend an injury. And he couldn't."

"Not to be sad, my dear. Cheering wine, as the Greeks say. Thomas lit you up, didn't he? He did have the romantic soul of a poet, didn't he?"

"I thought you said he was a prick?" Angelo said.

"Words are just tools. You should know that. Thomas saw himself as a poet. He didn't see himself as a prick."

Tears came to Alice's eyes.

"Ease off her, Jessica," Warwick said, coming up to them.

"Calm down, Warwick. And try to be less pathetic. Why are you crying, Alice? Thomas or Wallace? Or is it Warwick here? Remember, great grandfather Wallace died a very rich man, whether he willed it or not. And he's long dead, Alice."

"You know, I just don't think Thomas went anyplace. I don't think he wanted to go anyplace. I know that but I don't know how I know that. But it's why I don't hate him. I ... I didn't expect him to flower. But I didn't expect him to leave."

"Perhaps he's vanished into a whole new paradigm, my dear. It's what they say we do nowadays."

Angelo had tuned out when during the dinner the connivers had each made their pitch. Too many stories heard would be like laying down hundreds of crumb trails and so make any one impossible to follow. He wasn't going to do that. He was having a hard-enough time trying to follow what Jesssica was up to and figure out what Bellator was all about. He didn't seem to be what Angelo had imagined. Besides, as he had scanned his fellow diners, he saw only what Sal called the worn shoes types. He couldn't say what that meant but he knew he was looking at it now. But he got a more than a whiff of grifter. It was in their words too.

Alice had suddenly stood up right after a conniver had made some pitch for an online family curating service or something like that.

"I'm Alice Limone. I write children stories about my daughter, called Pearl in the books. I use the name Cecily Darden. Which is my real name. I'm here because Warwick and Jessica invited me. And my friend, Angelo, who is a prince but not comfortable being here right now ..."

The table full of grifters eyed him. Competition.

"But he's here for me because that is what kind of person he is. Warwick and Jessica were instructors of mine in college. Jessica remembered my name but not me. I married a colleague of theirs. Thomas Limone. He left me and my daughter. Why I don't know. Angelo knew him years ago as Trip. He was called that because he would suddenly pick up and take a trip. He liked to leave. Places and people. So, that's why he left me I suppose. He thought the world would be a better place if some people put their hands in other people's pockets. I don't hate him for that or for being Trip. How could I, as I never knew him? As Trip. Thank you, Mr. Bellator, for inviting us to your magical castle."

She addressed this last to Bellator, whom she turned toward. He seemed from what Angelo could see very touched by what Alice had said. And in truth, he had to admit that her voice in that cavernous dining hall had an angelic sweetness to it that he could see had reached every conniver and pitchman in the room. Not much of a line to grab in what she had said but it had a true ring to it. In fact, Angelo thought she had hollowed out everyone else's words. They should hate her for that, but it looked like she had touched the hearts of all the worn-out shoes. And her presence, with swatches of yellow ochre hair moving in unseen breezes and emerald green eyes that seemed to look at each and everyone in the room at once, clearly magnetized Bellator's own gaze.

Just at the point where Angelo was ready to leave the circus behind, Bellator walked in to the museum-like room Alice had chosen as her favorite.

He went right up to Alice.

"Our dead forebears are like a plague in our lives, Alice," the enchanted Robert said. "They occupy us from the inside out. Taint our purest being. But your name tells me you are noble. **Old High German** *Adalhaid*, literally nobility, of noble kind."

"However," Jessica interrupted him, "Her real name is Cecily, a name based on the Latin 'coccus' meaning 'blind'. Which seems appropriate as Alice tells us she was blind to who her own husband really was."

"But we are all blind, are we not, Jessica? First, to what we are, and then, as a result, to what others are. We children are blind to what our ancestors have done to us."

"Angelo is an orphan," Alice announced.

"I thought so. Bari is a port city on the Adriatic Sea, and the capital of southern Italy's Puglia region. Its mazelike old town, Barivecchia, occupies a headland between two harbors. Surrounded by narrow streets, the 11th-century Basilica di San Nicola, a key pilgrimage site, holds some of St. Nicholas' remains. To the south, the Murat quarter has stately 19th-century architecture, a promenade and pedestrianized shopping areas."

"Robert doesn't travel to real places. He imagines them."

"I try not to indulge myself as if I were deserving of my wealth. But I do read a great deal."

"That's great," Angelo said, not knowing what to say besides he didn't travel at all and he read even less and had less wealth than that and he didn't know what imagination was.

"I don't know how much good it does anyone if a rich man such as myself traipses over the world. An idle rich man's idyll. Idyll."

"Sometimes I wish my mind could photograph my memories," Alice told them. "And sometimes I hope I won't."

"Memory, the warder of the brain," Warwick recited.

"By the looks of you, Angelo, I'd say you were Scandinavian or more likely Dutch. You have a Dutch doorway frame for a body, which leads me to that conclusion. But you weren't raised in Holland. Very definitely Brooklyn. Not a gentrified Brooklyn either, I am happy to note. New money is as bad as old money. Don't ask me why but there it is. But you may be a descendant of the Dutch who at one time owned Brooklyn. New Utrecht being an example."

"New Utrecht," Angelo repeated to himself. WTF? This guy had gotten into his life.

"Warwick tells me you're a man of your word. I never knew what that expression meant. Words are very unstable entities, not entities at all but counters. And like all counters, they can represent variously. My father taught me that coin had meaning. Not words."

Angelo looked at Jessica who just shrugged.

"I have purged that fatherly lesson."

He turned to Angelo who was taking advantage of the booze wagon.

"I take it you are more than Alice's lover? Also, her protector?"

"He is," Alice said.

"You know, Mr. Bari, women have fought hard and long to be released from the patriarchal protection of men. Take Jessica for example. She is, in many ways, my protector."

"She's always had me," Warwick told him.

"As a burden in my life, wouldn't you say?"

"I wouldn't say that was fair, Jessica," Robert told her. "He's devoted to you."

"Words, right, Robert?"

"We'll talk at length then at some time, Angelo. Jessica has mentioned a small project."

"I know him," Alice whispered to Angelo. "That's Captain Wolf."

Angelo looked at the burly man in a black suit standing by a doorway.

Warwick, who had heard, laughed.

"One of Bellator's Myrmidons. McCord."

Angelo saw one of the butlers winking at Alice.

"Ret," she said, eyes wide in amazement.

"I've decided to announce the winner of the last Conniver Dinner," Robert told them. "And that winner is Mr. Sailor Kerplowski."

The man Alice called Captain Wolf leaned over and whispered in Robert's ear.

"Where did he go?" Robert said loudly.

"He went off in his boat."

"I think we need to talk," Angelo said to Jessica, later when they were on their way out.

She gave him a headache. They all gave him a headache. Alice seemed a bit tipsy. He hadn't monitored her alcohol consumption, but he had learned from experience that the lady shifted oars when she had a few.

"Of course, let's talk. You know when I look into those dark, pupil-less eyes of Bellator's I recall the name. Diabolus. He was *Diabolus,* who flowed downward taking them all with him. He wears those shaded glasses because like the Mephistopheles of *Faust* he shunned the light. I taught Classics. Warwick probably told you that."

She also seemed half in the bag.

"You did. Good for you. That guy doesn't read for me like he was Metholees or anything out of any Devil's ass. What did you say before?

He's a sicko because he doesn't like having his own money? Kind of a dopey mope of a mogul. All clown to me."

"I warned you, Mr. Bari. Get ready. The curtain is going up."

143

He's a sicko because he doesn't like having his own money? Kind of a dopey mope of a mogul. All clown to me."

"I warned you, Mr. Bari. Get ready. The curtain is going up."

CHAPTER FIFTEEN

THE MERCHANT QUEEN

It was much later and already dark when Angelo was once again steps from getting Alice out of there when the man Alice said she knew appeared, menacing.

"Hullo, Wolf," Alice said to him.

"McCord. I don't know any Wolf. Mr. Bellator wants to see both of you."

"Tell him some other time," Angelo said, taking Alice's arm and moving toward the doors.

"Mr. Bellator's the captain of this ship," McCord told him, putting a hand on Angelo's chest "You need to obey orders."

"Never did. See no reason to start now."

Angelo was tightening a fist when Alice's hand went on his face.

"Don't worry. It's never real with Captain Wolf. Just a game."

"What kind of game is this we're playing here now, Captain?" Ret said, coming out of nowhere. He winked at Alice. "Whatever it is, let's see what it is."

"Hello, Ret."

Angelo looked at her. The game. And Alice knew these guys.

"Why don't you talk to Mr. Bellator, Alice?" Ret said. "Really an okay guy. He's just hard on himself."

"Let's talk to Robert, Angelo," she said, smiling.

Angelo unclenched his fist but held onto the feeling that hitting either one of these guys would ease a lot of the frustration he had been feeling for … how long? Since Jessica. But he was in it. The game.

There was a small glow in a fireplace the size of Stonehenge. McCord and Ret positioned themselves on opposite ends of the room. Angelo wondered if every room in the mansion had its own décor appropriate pair of body guards. And if they did, were they *faux* bodyguards like he thought these guys were? And how did Alice know them?

Jessica was walking back and forth in front of the fireplace. Robert was seated in a large leather chair under an old-style floor lamp. Old as in a previous century. Drink in hand. He nodded as Alice and Angelo entered and motioned to a couch. They went over and sat down.

"Are you serious? The man's PTSD from head to toe. And underneath that is an idiot."

"Why so harsh, Jessica? Sailor has enough troubles visited upon him."

"This sad, sad man claims he knows where there's millions in gold dust in boxes, an absurdity at the start, waiting to be brought up from the Sound. His first idea was to sell you the Brooklyn Bridge."

"He's asking for very little funding, Jessica. And he's fought for this country. Something I allowed my wealth to protect me from."

"Look, he's been in the sands so long his brains have turned to sand. And he thinks he can run a scam on you. He's so obvious I can't see how you don't see it. You'd be the bigger idiot to be taken in by this scam artist."

"My ancestors started their rise to the top one tenth of one percent with a scam. More than one. I recognize it. It's not here with Mr. Kerplowski."

"You are kidding yourself, Robert. You are doing penance for them by getting yourself taken for a ride by this man."

"Allow me a few words, my dear. To acquaint our guests with the back story."

Jessica plopped down angrily next to Angelo. He didn't know if her anger was an act or not. He didn't know if this Robert was an act or not. The whole scene … First rule of the grift, run when you can't see all the corners in the game. And he couldn't. He could barely see the board.

"Since Mr. Kerplowski was with us," Robert began in his gravelly voice, "I've had some research done. A man named Paul Limone, caught as I see it between gangsters and his own greed, had an arrangement with an Argentinean gold mine to ship gold into this country illegally. He could do that because he had both ILA and ship owner connections. He was also deeply indebted to mafioso type lenders who would seize the gold. Hence, the scheme to sink the ship and leave the gold for future rescue. On February 10th, 2003, a ship, *The Merchant Queen*, sunk off Montauk Point. Mr. Kerplowski was left a chart locating the wreck and with the help of GPS, he tells us he can put us right on top of the gold. All he needs is some financing, which I tell you I am prepared to provide.

Jessica shook her head.

"It's a cash for gold scam," she told him. "One of the oldest. And tell me why Limone didn't go after the ...."

She hesitated and looked at Alice.

"Thomas's father?" she asked.

Alice nodded.

"Trip's too."

"Perfect," Jessica said, leaving Angelo wondering whether Alice's family ties or her madness was perfect.

Jessica was off kilter for a second but only a second. She turned back to Robert.

"Okay, why didn't he go after the gold himself?"

"He died," Alice said. "I was at The Service. The Wake. His friends laughed and drank and cried. I think some were paid to cry. And prayed to the Virgin Mary. But he was dead throughout."

"It must have been very terrible for you, Alice."

"I got drunk and stole someone's coat."

"Those things happen my dear at sorrowful events. At my own father's funeral, I pissed my pants. Not from laughter but sheer biology. I was 9."

Alice seemed deeply moved by Robert's confession.

"No one was sorry, I think at the Service. Mr. Limone's friends spoke but I don't think they really liked him. I know Thomas didn't like him. Trip didn't like him either. I believe that was his first trip. Away from his father."

"You are aware aren't you Alice that Thomas and Trip are one in the same?"

"Lay off, Jessica," Angelo snapped.

"Yes, Jessica, your harshness is very unbecoming. In fact, I don't like it. You've upset Alice."

"Goodbye."

"Don't leave, my dear. Stay a bit longer. I promise you that all will be well."

"Yes, I believe very few things are really impossible."

Angelo was looking at Robert whose eyes went wide as Alice spoke, like the Spanish guy coming from behind a bush and finding the Pacific Ocean.

"I'd advise you, Alice, as your friend, to always keep your meds handy."

"She's not your friend, Alice. Let's bounce."

"Calm yourself, Mr. Bari. Jessica knows when she's crossed my line."

"It's best to stay calm," McCord warned.

Before Angelo could respond:

"Go for a walk, Captain McCord," Robert commanded in a loud voice.

McCord nodded and left the room.

"Are we done with the Kerplowski matter?" Jessica asked.

"He was Thomas's first cousin," Alice said, a kind of sad gladness in her voice. "I think they played in the sand together long ago."

"I sense that whatever doubt we may have had regarding Mr. Kerplowski's petition has been vacated by Alice's confirmation of his pedigree. He comes from The Sands. Not from miscreant genes."

"She's not drinking," Angelo said to Ret, who was about to refill Alice's glass. "Just me."

"Excellent, sir," Ret said, winking at him.

"Do you have a cash for gold scam to offer, Angelo"

"No," Angelo said emphatically. He didn't have any scam to offer for a variety of reasons. Number one being you don't lay out your game to a mark who wants to know what it is. He saw Jessica giving him the malocchia. Fuck her, he thought. He'd get Alice out of there. But where's the fuel for the getaway? He didn't have a dime and neither did she. The scam. He had to do the laundry it seemed.

"I got a simple laundry operation," he told Robert in a very disgusted voice. "Not big. Modest. Very modest. A few shirts at a time. But it's solid."

"Thank you, Angelo, but I don't need a laundry service. I have no illegal assets to hide."

"Okay, then. Thanks for the dinner and the talk."

"Can you do a load of whites of say between ten and fifty kilos a month?" Jessica asked him.

"No," Angelo replied and he saw Jessica cringe.

"Wait a moment," Robert said. "How do you feel about Angelo's laundering operation, Alice?"

She shook her head.

"I …I don't know anything about it. I didn't know he had that business. I haven't known him that long."

"Well, I don't know anything about it but I'm thinking we could learn. Angelo could teach us? Perhaps some honest money could come out of all this. What do you think, Angelo?"

"I think none of it is worth the trouble. To anybody."

"Big oaks rise from small acorns, Angelo. In the beginning there was nothing. And then there was everything."

He was looking at Alice when he said this and everything Jessica had said about this guy was ringing its bell for Angelo.

"Sometimes everything is really like multiplying zero here," he told Robert.

"He's too small time for this, Robert," Jessica said, giving Angelo a sneering look. "Everything about him."

"Go for a walk, Jessica. But first, I'd like you to apologize to Alice. You have been very rude to her."

"Alice, dear, I am so sorry if I offended you. You're too sweet to suffer beasts like me."

"I wouldn't be sweet if I thought you were a beast."

"How sweet of you."

They watched as Jessica left the room.

"Tell me more of your arrangement, Angelo."

Angelo had a sudden feeling that maybe he could take this screwy mogul for some travel money.

"There's a guy named Grew," Angelo said, pouring himself another drink.

Last Feather Rye Whiskey. Top shelf. Sal had a top ten list of brown and white whiskies taped behind the bar. Angelo had been studying them since he dropped out of high school.

"Dr. Ralph Goodsen Grew. Director of Ravine Farm Sanitarium. About 120 inmates. Patients. Suckers. He's got them all on an expensive line of meds. I mean there's no Fed money in here. It's all strictly private. Everybody pays through the nose for a la carte designer service. Like if you pay a grand for a pill it makes you happier than if you paid a buck for the same pill."

"A chocolate on the pillow is very heartwarming, Angelo. What's the revenue?"

"It varies. At the bottom, Grew gets 120 large per annum per patient but he kicks it up if he sees a soft spot…"

"A soft spot?"

"A chance to bilk the family for more. Grew comes up with new treatments and new drugs that are gonna make a world of difference in the quality of grandpa's life but now Grew's got to raise the freight charge. Like that. It's an open line of profit. Death's a threat you can hold off with cash."

"What's your connection to this Dr. Grew?"

"Grew's a con artist. Well known. He was running his scam on Alice. He's got his hands on her money."

Robert's attention immediately sparked.

"I intervened," Angelo told him.

"How so?"

"I got Alice back in control of her own money. I got enough evidence to show that Grew was mishandling her funds. He's her court appointed something. I couldn't pass muster anything like that. Yeah, he knows how to play the game. He'll go along with a laundering operation."

"I'm sure you can keep him in line, Mr. Bari. I have both confidence in you and gratitude. For what you've done for our dear Alice. This may be a winning conniver proposal, one in which good money replaces bad and bad people go to jail. I believe you and Alice are giving me a chance to redeem the illicit dealings which birthed and at the same time blighted the wealth I have inherited."

Angelo nodded. Whatever this guy needed to feel he wasn't bad and mad. Was he dangerous? Could this guy read that Alice didn't have any money and that when he, Angelo, the honest guy, thought she did, he was willing to rip some of that off for himself? Did his warped brain go that deep?

Robert stood up and went over to the fire. He began to poke at the coals.

"How do you hide millions and billions and gazillions, Mr. Bari?"

"I put my gazillions in my sock drawer."

"In the Cayman Islands?" Bellator asked. "Cyprus is good too. But the truth is, I don't have to rely totally on laundering. It's vital, Mr. Bari, to recognize that the Federal government is a predator and you need to defend yourself. You do so by putting your money into untouchable off-shore accounts. But you obstruct the "Wealth Squad," which is what the government calls those who are seeking to appropriate your money for tax purposes. You confound them by transferring money from one company to another until you develop a labyrinth without a center. No heart. It's the shell game where you put your money under the shell that's not there."

"I played that when I was a child," Alice told them. "There was a pea under one of the shells but which one?"

"I'm not fond of the government myself," Angelo said, thinking he was in the same relationship with the government as with the carpets and walls in the room. No relationship.

"Money, like truth, is always buried under layers and layers of … What would you call it, Angelo? Drama? Half dozen states are tax havens, so I don't have to go to the Cayman Islands. I'm here in Delaware, for instance. I like to support American business and American workers. But I do look for laundering opportunities where I can find them so that my own dirty money can be washed clean and returned to the honest but poor people who work hard and earn nothing."

"Okay."

"I inherited controlling stock in a number of pharmaceutical companies who could supply your sanitarium with its daily meds. At fair prices. And it seems at first glance that this sanitarium could expand its laboratories to create highly profitable product, kept far below a 1000% price hike that thieves think they can get away with."

"Yeah, no deep drama there."

"I've arranged for both of you to stay the night and in the morning, you'll be driven back to the city. Is that agreeable, Angelo?"

"Okay," Angelo said, putting an arm around Alice's waist.

"She's barely awake," Robert said. "I'd like to help you with her.'

"Not needed. But thanks."

"As you wish. I seek no profit or reward in what I do."

"Okay. Where we sleeping? She's tired. I'm tired."

When he and Alice were in what looked like one of those historical rooms laid out in a museum, he wondered what kind of communicating he was having with Robert. That was easy. He was communicating with him the way he was communicating with Alice. Too much fucking drama he told himself. And he still couldn't see any of the corners of the game board.

CHAPTER SIXTEEN

DANGEROUS TO KNOW

"What the fuck gives here, Jessica?" Angelo said, the next night when Jessica walked into *The New Pompey*.

She walked to a booth, sat down and lit a cigarette.

Sal was on her in a matter of seconds.

"Nice seeing you again, beautiful. Rye?"

"God no, A Martini. Very dry."

Angelo sat down across from her. He was going to trim her sails.

"I think Sal must have been #MeTooed," she said, smiling.

"What am I into here? I want it straight. No bullshit."

"Feel like you're over your head?"

" I don't know who to fear. You or Bellator. Thing is, I kind of like him and you, not so much. Maybe not at all. You're a bad lady, Jessica. He's just fucked up."

Sal returned with the drinks.

"I'm not dangerous to know," she said, smiling at Sal who took the words as an encouragement.

"That's me. I get off at 2AM."

"I'll be here waiting."

"Get lost, Sal."

"Part of me doesn't want to get me or Alice mixed up with whatever rift is going down. I don't even know who's running who."

"It's a long grift. And you wanted in. And you walked into it. And she walked into it. We are all, my dear, inside it now. The belly of the whale. The mouth of the shark. You could take off with Alice but where's your traveling money. You could just stay here in these lovely surroundings. She'd love that."

"Look, I don't feel like I'm on the inside. I feel like I'm on the outside. From what I see, there's as much a chance that I'm the mark as Bellator is. And I don't like it."

"Calm down. It's all playing nicely."

"What? You bring me in and then you throw me out the door."

"I told you before that Bellator would be suspicious if I were sponsoring you or Alice in this. Now he sees that you and I are not friends at all. That places both of us above suspicion. It's the kind of mind he has. We're not tag teaming him."

"Okay. So, explain how making Alice look like she forgot to take her meds is part of the grift?"

She seemed to be enjoying his frustration.

"Don't do your strong thing with me," he told her sharply. "Or whatever it is that you do that Bellator likes. I don't like it and I've got no patience."

"Did you ever think that what you know about human nature is just short of what's required here?"

"Oh, yeah? Educate me."

"Bellator has a strong streak of masochism in him. He needs people to feed it And he hates them for being that for him. Thus, the sadistic that's in there too. He wants to hurt people that are already dead, like his father. Oh, he's twisted in so many ways."

"I ain't seeing it. Being told by you that it's there doesn't put it there."

"And you don't trust me, of course."

"Fuck no."

"He doesn't need the petite laundering operation you offer. He doesn't launder money. He was telling you the truth when he said his money is legit. But he does need to play the game, to be the Reynard who outwits everyone. It's an Achilles heel of an otherwise honest man. He's a real do-gooder. A philanthropist with wide open arms. All that being there, makes it difficult for you to see how much he hates himself for loving his money so much.

"You got it all figured out," Angelo said, shaking his head. "What are you some kind of psychiatrist?"

"Just a student of human nature, aka, a grifter, like you who studies closely the mark."

"So, what's this got to do with you taking Alice apart so we can see she's ... what? ... apart?"

"Alice brought you to him. He was fascinated with her before he even laid eyes on her. Maybe she doesn't feed his masochism or his sadism. Don't ask me what the fascination is. You are obviously under her spell. I don't care. She's the one who brings us to him."

Angelo closed his eyes. He saw where it was now.

"Alice is your roper?"

"Ours. Our lure. Yes. When I was pushing Alice's crazy buttons, I was just kicking up her attraction to Bellator level. It's a kind of magnetizing thing that you ignite. The more helpless, bemused and childishly innocent she looks, the more he's drawn to her. Beautiful, innocent and crazy is so far out of the box that Bellator can't resist it. He wants to be the prince in her life."

She paused.

"That's why the end game for him might not be beating you or me or Grew but getting you out of her life."

"He's gonna kill me?"

"I told you. He's not bad or dangerous. Just fixed and fixated. Weirdly."

"Those are the scariest guys."

"He wants to beat the Devil at the Devil's own game. And of course, he now has irrepressible desire to own our Alice. He needs to show her he's the better man. The real prince in her life. Oh, you are so key to it all, Angelo."

Sal interrupted then and whispered to Angelo that Summer Arpeggio called for him and he told her he was there. She was coming over.

"We have to get out of here," Angelo said getting up. He expected that Summer would be fired up about the Dr. Grew money not coming through. And Jessica, sitting there in her designer clothes and botoxed face, would be for Summer like a red cape to a bull. He knew her better than she knew herself.

"He'll find Alice wherever she might go" Jessica said, not moving. "You can't run from him. You've got to stay in place and beat him."

"Is this the bitch?" Summer, who had come in and seeing Ange, marched over to the booth.

"I prefer Jessica. But I can be a bitch. And you are?"

Summer squeezed in next to Angelo.

"Take it easy, Summer. She's on our side."

"Oh yeah, well I'm on the side that sues people who promise to pay and then don't."

"Oh, you're the attorney. Dr. Grew told me about you. You didn't expect to get all that money, did you? Some thirty thousand dollars a month in perpetuity for just showing up and being you. Whatever you are."

"I did. And I do. And I'll tell you who I am. I'm the one who made a binding deal … "

"That deal has nothing to do with me," Jessica said, looking over at Sal and pointing to her glass.

"She's lying. Picco told me before he left that this bitch was running a game on us through Dr. Grew. We're pigeons."

"Alice is your connection to Grew. Not me. Talk to her."

"Leave Alice out of it."

"Oh, I forgot," Jessica said, smiling at Angelo. "Alice is just an innocent who fell from the stars and went down a rabbit hole and doesn't know a thing about what's going on here on planet Earth. And certainly not Brooklyn. This last relic of a dying Brooklyn. She must get the shivers every time she comes into this place."

Sal came over and put another Martini in front of Jessica.

"Rye, Summer?"

"No. And fuck off."

"And we were sweethearts in the 5th grade," he told Jessica and then made a quick escape.

"Okay, so tell me what's going on?" Summer said to Jessica. "Alls I know is that we had a short con going and it worked, and somebody fucked it up. And I think that somebody is you."

"Is "alls" a word lawyers in Brooklyn use?"

Summer reached out and grabbed Jessica by the throat. Angelo grabbed her arm.

"Let her go, Summer. Let … let her go. Come on."

He slowly pulled Summer away from Jessica who rubbed her throat and then calmly sipped her drink.

"There's a long grift going here," Angelo said to Summer. "For big money."

He felt he had to say that to calm Summer, but he had only a vague idea that there was a long con operating and no idea what kind of payoff was involved. That feeling he had that he was a mark had shown up the first time he heard Alice speak.

"Twenty grand a month is big enough for me," Summer said. "I want that money or I'll blow a hole in your game. How's that sound?"

"It sounds like money is your huckleberry. As it is mine. And everyone involved. But we don't need any attention placed on Grew. So, to keep you happy, let's say, Angelo here gives you a percentage of his when we get what we're after."

"I have a percentage? News to me. Anyway, that's not going to happen because I don't want anything and I'm not doing anything to get anything. I finally decided that. I'm out."

"He's afraid Alice will get hurt," Jessica said to Summer. "She has a gift for enchanting men does our Alice. And Mr. Bari here is totally enchanted. No pot of gold is big enough to break that enchantment."

"I'm not enchanted. I should let Summer strangle you."

"What's the pot?"

"It's a coffin is what it is Summer," Angelo snapped. "Coffins. Plural. Forget about all of it, Summer. Go home."

Summer nodded her head, too many times Angelo thought. Too many yes nods meant a negative.

"Okay, first off. I'm not going home. Second is, I want the money Grew was going to shuffle our way or I bring charges against Grew and close that nut farm of his down and whatever grift you think you're running."

Jessica sipped her Martini..

"You know what kind of mind a dog has when it comes to a bone?" she asked Summer. "Well, you have that kind of mind."

"You snotty bitch!" Summer said, reaching for Jessica a second time but Angelo was prepared and had his arm out pushing her back in her seat.

"I'm going to introduce some facts now," Jessica said. "One is this."

She brought one hand to the table. She was holding a small pistol.

"Taurus G2S Slim," Summer said, whistling.

"And it will send a bullet into you if you try to throttle me again."

"No throttling," Summer said, stretching both hands out.

"Okay, Ms. Arpeggio, see if you can absorb this. There is no money to give you. Dr. Grew ... "

"That Alice trust has millions..."

"No. It has nothing. Zero. Grew promised you a payment just to buy time."

"Time for what?"

Jessica closed her eyes and it looked as if she were meditating.

"Time," she said, opening her eyes. "For you to either be brought in or not. Or now it looks like, shot."

"Maybe you should put the gun away," Angelo told her. "Sal keeps a Glock behind the bar."

"Time for you also," she said to Angelo.

"I told you. I'm out of the running. I'm out."

Jessica shook her head.

"Alice is in. She can't get out. Where are you?"

Angelo felt like reaching across and grabbing her throat. As Summer had. Maybe it was a Brooklyn thing? You stop the shit you're hearing by strangling them or punching them in the face. Old Brooklyn, he reminded himself. Not gentrified Brooklyn. They left you to die outside the gate. Sal had told him that he wasn't Woke. And Picco was less Woke. Whatever that meant. He also didn't want to get shot close range.

"I'm going to get her out of here," he said, in a voice that lacked confidence.

"Oh? Where are you going to take her? Are you going to take her non-existent daughter also?"

Angelo felt his whole body tense up.

"You know if it were someone who has ever gotten any place threatening to run off with Alice, I'd be worried. Where Alice is, that's no place anyone can go to. You might say she's already taken."

Angelo didn't know what to say. She was pressing all his buttons, the ones he pressed himself every time he came into *The New Pompey* and sat at the bar.

Summer wasn't so transfixed in her own mind.

"Fuck you. I don't give a fuck about what you do to Alice or where she goes. If you don't find some of that money you say Grew doesn't have, I'll break your grift wide open. I don't know how Grew or that sanitarium fits in what you're up to but if it is a long con working here and it's an important piece, you don't want to see it explode."

"I wouldn't advise trying to do that," Jessica said, calmly.

"Oh, you wouldn't? Then you better shoot me now."

Summer turned to Angelo.

"Picco told me this condescending bitch is married to Wall Street mogul. Is that right?"

"Robert Bellator," Angelo said, trying to get out of the fuck he found himself in.

"We're not married."

"But he pays the bills? Well, tell him you bought a 50K fur and send that 50K to a lady named Summer Arpeggio. We'll start with that."

Jessica looked at Angelo.

"She does want her money now."

"Money's her bone," Angelo admitted.

"Unlike you, Mr. Bari. Fortyish and smitten with a psychotic."

"She's not psychotic."

"Admittedly an alluring, quixotic one," Jessica said.

"Can it, bitch. Am I getting my money or not?"

"Yes, I think it's very possible. I'll do what I can, and I'll let Angelo know."

"Do that," Summer said, getting up.

She gave Angelo a disgusted look and walked out of the bar. Sal called to her about a drink he had waiting for her, but she gave him the finger and kept on walking.

"Well," Jessica said, lighting a cigarette. "That was interesting. Like so many people whose lives are small ... hardly a lawyer with any clients, is she? Well, she thinks small. She wants one golden egg when the goose is within reach. I feel kind of sorry for her. Alice has all the magnetic draw. And all our friend Summer is left with is ... "

"I didn't like the threat you made."

"I didn't threaten her."

"Alice. I don't want her to be any part of this. Whatever the fuck it is."

"She's in. Once again. She's already in. He wants her."

"I could kill the guy. Make him vanish. I don't have to keep myself and Alice in your hustle."

"I suppose you could do that. You know or be killed yourself. Or go to jail. Or blah blah. And leave poor Alice out in the cold. What makes more sense is helping us and walking away with money that should have been Alice's in the first place."

Angelo was trying to figure out what made sense.

"What is going on over there?" Jessica said, looking over at the bar.

Angelo looked and saw a boom microphone being held over the heads of two men standing at the corner of the bar. A tiny woman with a high head of multi-colored hair was slouched mostly on the bar.

"That's Eve Solly and Bratter. They been doing their radio show in here. Getting the chat from citizens on the street. Which for those two is the bar."

"I know the show," Jessica said as if it were a Eureka moment. "My employer loves it. He says she's a mean interviewer when sober and meaner when drunk."

"Solly? I've never seen her what you would call sober."

Just then four uniformed NYC police came into the bar, saw the tiny woman, went over to her, talked, she shouted some obscenities, they pulled her off the bar, handcuffed her and pulled her to the door, still shouting this time, at her co-host, who followed along, cuffed and meek.

"Now that was amusing," Jessica said, motioning to Sal to bring her another Martini. "Is this a regular floor show?"

"I don't pay attention," Angel told her. "I'm topped off with this kind of stuff. I'm confused enough with what you're telling me. Eve's a mean drunk, too smart for her own good, and Bratter killed his girl friend and let his twin brother take the rap."

"My goodness! How exciting. I need to hear more. What really was going on there, Sal?"

Sal set their drinks down.

"Long story short. Somebody calls into Eve's show, dares her to use the seven words you can't use on the airwaves in one sentence. So, as Eve's got the kind of mind that skipped all of junior high school and went straight to the senior year high school … "

"This is the short, Sal?"

"Yeah, Ange. Back story the lady here needs."

"I do. I just love it. Go on."

"Thusly, in ten seconds Eve comes up with this. I got it taped behind the bar. One sentence with what she called an absolution ablation. Or something like that. She puts the sentence on the air cause you can't tell Evangeline Solly what not to do. Now, as you see, they come in here and arrests her."

"I'd love to meet her."

"You wouldn't love it believe me. Back to reality. When Alice takes my place in Bellator's psycho-drama, I'm gone. His perverted psyche will no longer need me around."

"And so, Angelo, you need to stay to see that he doesn't do what he wants to do with her. Is it possible for you to call me a cab, Sal?"

"I thought you were hanging around till I get off."

She smiled.

"You look like someone who's used to getting off on his own."

"Oh, that's low. You're hurting my image."

Those at the bar who had heard were in hysterics. "But I forgive you. I gotta improve on my game is what it is."

"Angelo is in the same fix."

"I'll get the cab," Sal told them, winking at Angelo.

CHAPTER SEVENTEEN

THE CACKLE-BLADDER SCAM

"Angelo isn't here, Mr. Bellator," was the first thing Alice told Bellator when he showed up at her Coney Island apartment the next morning.

"That's okay. I wanted to talk to you. You must call me Robert."

"I'd like you to meet Gloria, my daughter but she's out for the day. With friends."

"Well, I'd love to meet her someday."

He moved past Alice and into the living room where he took a seat. He noticed an easel by the window. A large easel, not a French portable one. There was a cover over the canvas she was working on.

"Have you given up writing children's stories? And taken up painting?"

She looked nervously at the easel.

"My mother taught me to paint. She told me that it was a way to bring to life everything we see in our minds but can't...can't see in the world."

"Action is the last resource of those who know not how to dream. I'm quoting our friend Warwick. Sadly, I'm not a man of action either. But I am fascinated by artists and dreamers. 'To see the world in a grain of sand and a heaven in a wild flower hold infinity in the palm of your hand and eternity in an hour.'

"'A robin breast in a cage puts all heaven in a rage.' Oh, you love such words too?"

"I would have preferred to be a poor poet than what I was

destined to be."

She hesitated. He seemed so sad.

"I saw your Hitler paintings. They made me shiver."

"I didn't buy them. They came with the house, as so much of the furnishings did. My grandfather bought them. My ancestry is unspeakably evil.. I keep those awful paintings to remind me the dark affinities of my ancestry. And who is this little fellow?"

She saw that Sailor, her turtle, had ambled close to Bellator's feet and she bent down and picked him up.

"This is Sailor. He's a boxie. Tortoise. I named him after Sailor Kerplowski. He's Thomas's first cousin. He was in The Sands. Not Coney Island, I think. And he wants me to know he's alive. Don't you, Sailor?"

"I thank you for your recommendation of Mr. Kerplowski. I intend to proceed with his project."

"That is so good of you," Alice said, sitting down across from Bellator on a sofa strewn with drawings. "My mother's paintings. I don't know where they are? Was your mother a wonderful mother like mine was?"

"My biological mother mysteriously disappeared when I was just a tot. I don't remember her. My father went through a series of, in the contemporary parlance, trophy wives. I believe my mother must have been also. None of my ancestors could establish an equitable relationship with women. All of my male ancestors violated the #MeToo wokeness. None of my relatives had any interest in me. Neither did my father. I was virtually an orphan living in a big house."

"Angelo is an orphan. Oedipus came to Corinth as an orphan. I remember Jessica telling the class that. He had a terrible fate."

Robert was focused on a strand of hair that had come loose and now lay across her forehead. She swept it back or tried to ineffectually. Her awareness was elsewhere. But where he didn't know.

"You know after I met you," he said, watching her hand move to her forehead and then down. "I bought all the Little Pearl in Foxler Holl'er stories and read them. Wonderful stories. Your daughter is the Little Pearl in your stories. I know that."

He had Alice's complete attention. "You've read my stories?"

"I like the one about the two squirrels who live in a tree house. Seeley Circles and Soley Only."

Alice leaned forward and whispered:

"You know I would like Pearl to meet Angelo and Picco in one of my stories. And Sailor the boxie needs to be in the story too. Can I do that? And the big, tall, Swirling Wind that blows everything down when he comes into the room..."

"I don't see why not. I take it he is Warwick, the larger than life stentorian voiced actor?"

Alice stopped and laughed, holding a hand to her mouth.

"Yes! He would pop right out of the page and then he shouts: I take my vorpal sword in hand! "

Alice jumped up and raised an arm.

He took his vorpal sword in hand:
Long time the manxome foe he sought --
So rested he by the Tumtum tree,
And stood a while in thought.

She looked at Bellator, ablaze with excitement.

"That sounds like Warwick," Bellator said, laughing.

"I had him in mind."

"I love Aperitivo, the Giant who sucks everyone into his cave and makes them waffles," Bellator told her.

Alice's eyes lit up

"Guess who?"

"I'm afraid I don't know him.".

"That's The Lutheran. But he's in jail now. I hadn't met him when I wrote the story, but I think I imagined him into existence. I'm sorry. That sounds terrible. I think I just imagined him before I saw him. Do you think we first have to imagine everything we then see?"

"Our friend Blake did. What is now proved was once only imagined."

To Robert, at that moment, she seemed more amazing than what he himself had imagined. A mind like this so far from his own twisted roots could lead him to something that it would take the world a hundred years to bring into existence. No, not the world. A destruction and then new creation of himself. Like gold from base metal. She was magical. Pure magic.

"And Foolery and Foolerah, the silly chipmunks, who live in Tent Town. They are so funny. One just repeats what the other says."

Alice clapped her hands.

Alice found herself speechless. She had no idea that Robert had been reading these stories. He had them by heart.

"*Pearl in Foxler Hollow*, the first one, is my favorite. And *Pearl and the Secret Society*. I liked that one too.

Did your daughter like being Pearl?"

"Pearl is very important," Alice told him seriously. "My emissary. She finds out what I don't know. Or tries to. I learn a great deal through Pearl. She helps me see clearly what I don't on my own see very clearly."

"Your daughter does?"

"Yes, sometimes. Not always. Sometimes she avoids me."

She fell into a kind of instant depression and then she popped right out.

"But do you know who's Retort Rethought and Banana Cannon and Native Wing and Little Shimmy Townie and Flask Freddie Five and Reddy Words ... "

Alice stopped, out of breath.

"So many!" she cried out. "So much fun. Did you ever live in a tree house like Feral Franny and Circle Sally and Silent Lester? Oh, they are so much fun!"

"Yes, they are. They are timeless. Immortal characters. You know, I wonder if you could put me in one of your stories?"

Alice frowned. She didn't do that anymore.

"I can't. I can't bring the words to where I want them. I paint now. Could I paint you?"

"Of course. I'd be honored."

"I mean the way I see you."

"I wouldn't have it done any other way."

Two days later, Robert was in Alice's apartment sitting for the painting. Alice wore a smock covered with dried paint and her long,. disheveled hair was shoved under a large, floppy hat.

Robert had been speaking about Angelo, but Alice was reluctant to speak about him.

"I know he's trying to become part of your life."

"He is that," she told him, dabbing at the painting and not looking at him.

"And more. That you don't know about. You need to know that he's become part of a scheme to take some money from me. He's gotten to me through you. He's used you."

"I don't think so."

"You don't know it, but Angelo blackmailed Dr. Grew into giving him and two of his accomplices a percentage of your trust money."

Alice froze, her brush still in hand.

"Dr. Grew told me this. He's frightened of Angelo. And his accomplices. You know, Alice, sometimes we imagine people we love to be better than they are. I know. I've done that with my own father. I made a hero of him. And he wasn't that at all. But for a long time, I needed him to be. I need him to be different than the horrible thieves who were my ancestors. But he wasn't different."

"We sometimes fall," she said, in a voice he could hardly hear.

Fall or fail?

"I suppose it wasn't all my father's fault as to what he became. He had to find a reason as to why he could have everything he wanted when all around him people hadn't that power. He decided he was godlike."

"That is so sad. Was he sad?"

"Sad? Sadness is reserved for the weak. He was proud. Of himself. He gave himself talents he didn't have. A superiority unearned. He wasn't better in anything or than anyone. I came to see that. He never did. His mirror was covered with wads of money."

"I'd like to see his face."

"There are a few portraits. You know, Alice, it's very difficult to break through the mold within which our lives are cast. And we sometimes do very awful things to do so."

"Angelo?" she said in a faint voice.

"He was destined to be no more than a pair of hands to swing a sledge hammer or drive a jack hammer before his mind could be cultivated. It's a sad destiny shared by so many in his world. I have placed a great deal of money into a foundation designed to alter that sad destiny for many in the future."

"Thomas. Trip and Angelo grew up together. It is so sad, but I don't know their world. But I know it's not bad."

"What do you think my connection with Angelo is?"

"He doesn't like you and you don't like him? Is that a connection?"

"He wants to launder my money, so I don't pay taxes. I told him I have legal, safe havens for my money and therefore do not need his criminal services. My dear Alice, I don't need Angelo. I don't need the petty laundering. And I don't need someone around who will kill me given the chance."

The word frightened her.

"Angelo wouldn't do that. Why would he kill you?"

"He won't. He's not a killer but he's become associated with people who do kill to get what they want. I've offered to track down his biological parents, but he wasn't interested. He's probably right. The roots of my being darken my life. I wish I had never known any of them, yet their vileness courses through my veins."

"Those associates are not the kind of people Angelo knows."

"He's with them for you. I think he's making a desperate effort to bring himself to the level where he can be with you. Right now, he's a lost man pinned to a barstool."

"You can't see what people think. No one can. But maybe what they have thought is in their faces. If the light is right."

"I need to see what's clearly in front of me. I need to do that for my own self-protection. You need to do that. In Angelo's mind, my life is all about possessing, possessing everything I desire. When the truth is, I've spent my life separating myself from what my ancestors have tried to make of me. I want to possess nothing but the rightness of my own soul."

She started to paint again.

"Don't move your head. Is it so difficult for you to stop moving your head?"

"Sorry. I flutter when I'm upset."

"You need to stop talking. I can't paint you talking. I can't paint you fluttering."

"Listen. If Thomas is alive, I can find him."

That news startled her.

"You can?"

"For you I would. But I need you to tell me in the smallest detail everything about your life before, during and after Thomas. I need to find a thread in there that will lead me to him. If he's alive, and I think he most likely is."

"Why do you think that? Can't I know?"

"Didn't he call himself Trip? And isn't it true that when someone says "trip" it implies a return. Otherwise, it wouldn't be a trip. It would be an end. His was *au revoir*."

"Yes, you're right. It wouldn't be a trip if you don't ever return. It would be more like death. Is that why he doesn't return? He's dead."

"Perhaps. And perhaps something or someone prevents him."

"Perhaps he's running as fast as he can but is still in the same place?"

"That could be," Robert answered, totally magnetized by Alice's conjecture.

"Gangsters could have him. Or it could be a grift. Don't move your head."

"What do you know of grifts?"

"I know a great deal," she said, standing back from her easel and admiring her work. "I know the blessing grift. The mark thinks something bad is going to happen to him and a blessing ritual is needed but the mark must value its power by putting something of value into a big bag. Money or jewels. If the mark doesn't do that, he remains in danger. The bag with the money is swapped for a bag of baubles."

She had stopped painting and froze in place, reciting as if she were on a stage.

"That's not a mark, I believe. That's an idiot."

"I also know the sunken treasure grift, which is when there's evidence that a box with as much as four tons of treasured metal inside can be found in a sunken ship that a grifter will sell you a map to."

"Nevertheless, Alice, ships laden with treasure have been discovered. What you need to discover first is a plausible history as to why, how and where that ship was sunk. For example, Mr. Kerplowski was left a chart locating the wreck and with the help of GPS, he tells us he can put us right on top of the gold. All he needs is some financing, which I was prepared to provide."

"Why is that ship sunken?"

"Why? Oh, yes, well, a Mr. Paul Limone had an arrangement with an Argentinean gold mine to ship gold into this country illegally. He could do that because he had both ILA and ship owner connections. On February 10th, 2003, a ship, The *Merchant Queen*, sunk off Montauk Point. You see, I did my research."

"You know that's the Paul Limone who left me money but there never was any money. He's Thomas's father. Summer said he was a gangster like Don Coralloni but only in the neighborhood."

"I challenge the corrupt and their schemes."

"Oh, yes. Your foundation will alter them."

"You're right to be skeptical. Foundations are fronts or shells or sops to the conscience of people like me. I deceive myself, Alice. You make it impossible for me to continue doing that."

"I don't know if any of that would be in your face if I painted you. Every face my mother painted was hers. I think I was the only one who saw that."

Talking to her was like holding a burning match in your fingers that sparked and died, sparked and died. You could get the flame, but you couldn't get it to hold.

"Don't move your head. I also like the Cackle-bladder scam.

What the grifter does is fake someone's death through the use of a rubber bladder filled with fake blood, which is usually chicken blood. Chickens do cackle. The mark shoots the shill and thinks he killed him because there is so much blood but the gun has vacant bullets in it. Then the mark pays the grifters a lot of money to keep the murder quiet. He pays and pays his whole life just to stay out of jail."

Robert couldn't help moving his head to watch her. Her mass of hair, swept this way and that way as if there was a breeze passing through the room, was now like a tousled field of gold, a good part of it hanging down across one eye.

"But my favorite," Alice told him, laughing, pointing her paint brush straight up into the air, "is when a swindler who has swindled a lot of money goes to an honest man to mix the swindler's bad money with the honest man's money but the honest man really doesn't have any money at all!"

Here Alice spread her arms wide and, in the process, flicked some red pigment on Robert's face.

"So, you're talking about two swindlers?" Robert said, taking out a handkerchief and wiping his cheek.

"So, the honest man wasn't honest at all. And he runs away with the swindler's money! The swindler gets swindled. Dr. Grew told me that one. He studies confidence games. The games of trust in a world that has no trust. That's what he said."

"You know, Alice there is no trust, no faith, no honesty in men; all perjured; all forsworn, all naught, all dissemblers. Their blood taints you at birth and you spend your whole life trying to get clean."

"I think I will some day put you in a story. Timble Tumble Tewks. Warwick told me that was your real name."

"Yes, not a heroic name so it had to be changed. We became bellators. Warriors. Anyway, they're all dead, their fight with worms over."

"Don't you think it's odd that so many people we know have mysteriously disappeared?" she asked him, as she suddenly put her brush down and went to the door. She opened it. He followed her.

"You mean Thomas?"

There was no one at the door.

"Thomas and his mother and your mother and Angelo's mother and my mother."

"Some are dead, aren't they? Your mother, for instance."

"Yes, she was there and then she died, and she wasn't there

anymore but I think that is a mystery, don't you?"

He nodded.

"Yes, a mystery."

CHAPTER EIGHTEEN

ON BOARD *THE BABY CHEEKS*

They were just off Jacob Riis Park on Jamaica Bay, the wind holding steady, filling all sails.

Alice watched her two new friends, Sonny and Touchon -- one at the wheel and the other now climbing the main mast. Picco's replacements, Angelo had told her. She wondered where Picco had gone.

Angelo came up from below, holding two mugs of coffee.

"Where has Picco gone?" she asked, as she took the mug he handed her.

"He's out of town for a while. He's got business elsewhere."

"You're missing him."

"I'm used to missing. I grew up on it. Head her out and then turn her along the coastline!

"Aye, aye, Capitano!" Touchon called back.

"We've got to counter the flood tide heading from the Atlantic into the bay and at the same time resist the pull of an ebb tide drawing us into a lee shore."

"It sounds dangerous. They won't get hurt?"

"Sonny and Touchon? Those guys have sailed in every body of water on the planet. I'm a landlubber compared to them. They're never happier when they're sailing in blue water. They jumped at the chance to come out today. And I needed them. I can't handle *Baby Cheeks* by myself."

"This is the first time I've seen them on the water. I always see them at *The New Pompey*."

"Yeah, well, they're waiting for a ship. The work isn't regular anymore for merchant seamen. They're all queued up to get a ship. It's been taking longer and longer for them to get a berth. Too many of our ships flying under foreign flags with foreign crews."

She watched both sailors at their work.

"Don't be angry. On the blue water you said all fears and anger vanish."

She pulled at his jacket. He laughed.

"I wonder why they don't do something else," she asked.

"They probably will once they grow up. They'll have to. They'll get stuck like the rest of us. No more sailing off into the sunset to far off places. Dream worlds. Women will bring 'em to port one of these days. Anchor them on land. Or they'll get too slow or arrive too late to go to sea."

"I'm so sorry this isn't the world we dream."

"Well, you can make up stuff for just so long. It's kind of like your roots. I mean where you began pulls you back so you can go just so far. Touchon was brought up to Brooklyn by an uncle. He says. From some place near New Orleans. Escaping some shit. He says his father was a pirate and his mother a gypsy but Touchon makes a lot of stuff up. I don't know what brought him here, but I think it was a girl in the neighborhood. Sonny was left on the same doorstep I was."

"And that's how you know him? You were friends on the same doorstep?"

"Some years separating us but the same deal. I mean his parents dumped him like mine did me. Brought up in an orphanage. He went to sea before anyone ever fostered or adopted him. He and Touchon. The seas call to them, but Brooklyn pulls them back. Summer Arpeggio thinks Gigi is Sonny's father. Could be. I don't see Gee claiming a burden. Probably what my old man figured."

There was some chop now and the ocean spray came up and slapped them in the face. Alice shouted happily. They saw Sonny hastily swing down from the mast.

"The white whale!" he shouted, laughing. "The white whale!"

"Oh, I'd love to see him!"

"We better go below."

"They won't need your help? With the whale?"

"Don't embarrass them."

Down below, Ange started to prepare some sandwiches and Alice watched him as if he were doing something she had never seen before.

"Is Robert going to help you leave? I mean go where you want to go?"

"You mean Bellator? How's he going to do that?"

"He has placed a great deal of money into a foundation designed to alter the sad destiny for many in the future. I read that on-line."

"What? I don't know about that guy. And I'm not about to ask him for anything."

"He says he can find your biological parents. He can also find Thomas."

Angelo stopped with the mayonnaise. This was more important.

"I told him I wasn't interested in knowing people who dumped me. And I'm wondering why you want to find the guy who dumped you."

"Did he do that? Dump me. And no dumpster?"

"Look, I'm sorry for saying that. But, really, why try to find Trip?"

"For Cathy. My daughter. She needs to meet her father."

He stopped from saying what he wanted to say.

"Dr. Grew says that we are what we choose to do."

"He's selling you a line. I don't know for sure what it is but it's not going to turn out good for you. Or for me. I mean whatever Jessica is making up for us."

"I think I'm already made," she told him.

He handed her a sandwich.

"Like the sandwich," she said and laughed.

"Hey, Allie, you think you've been making choices. But you haven't. I don't know where you are, but I do know you don't ask to be there."

She was suddenly on the verge of tears.

"I don't want to hurt you, but you've been in an out of …. this place and that place and this shrink … "

'Life coaches."

"Life coaches. You've had more of them filling your head than the whole NFL has coaches. And meds. You got them in there too."

"When I was with Thomas, I didn't know I was really with Trip. So, I can't say anything about then. But when Dr. Grew showed me that I was Alice, I became Alice. I wrote and illustrated all those books about my daughter. I … "

"And what's her name?"

"Pearl."

"Not Cathy like you just said? And your daughter has the same name as the Pearl in your stories?"

"What? No. She changes her name when she wants. Pearl is always Pearl."

At that point, the cabin pitched back on itself.

"We crossed the bar!" Sonny screamed down to them. "Calm waters ahead!"

Angelo looked at Alice who was biting at the tips of her fingers.

"Look, Alice. You know if the person doing the choosing is kind of like us right now. Wobbly seas. Nothing on a smooth, steady course but rocking this way and that. I'm saying there's no space or time to set a right compass reading. And when you can't, somebody else does it for you. That's all I'm saying. These people. They want to use you. And it's crazy but I'm helping them. You want them to do something for me. And that's the hook they got set in you."

She had her head down and he didn't know if she were listening. She finally looked up.

"I'm not the Alice who went down a rabbit hole. I know that I am on a steady course I set myself."

He dropped to a seat at the small galley table. He heard Picco's voice in his ear. Okay, get out of my head. But he listened. Get it out in the open. Get ready, Alice. It's time to make it real!

"Then show me your daughter. Let me meet her. Show me that she's real. Or that you know you made her up and she's not real and you know why she was in your life in the first place."

He went over to her and tried to put his arm around her, but she pushed him away.

"I need to get some air," she mumbled.

He watched her go up the gangway. Why confront her with the kid? What did it matter whether the daughter was in her head or some place in the world? She'd either work her way to the other side of that or she wouldn't. Either way, he was, as Summer put it, smitten.

He was on his second shot of Jim Beam when he heard some commotion on deck.

He was on deck just in time to see Sonny take a dive from the head mast into the water. Touchon was by the gunwale holding a life preserver.

"She fucking jumped in!" he shouted. "We told her the water is too rough, but she just fucking jumped in!"

Ange kicked his dockers off and dove in, heading to where he saw Sonny's arms stroking out of the water.

There was no grace to his swimming, but he could swim long and fast. Picco was the fish in water, like a little penguin Paul would say.

By the time he reached where he had last seen Sonny, he wasn't there. Ange jackknifed out of the water and dove, only a few feet down and then flipped and back stroked, looking all around him. The water was churned up the way it gets when big fish were by. He saw a flash of light and dove to it, only to discover it was a mess of plastic wrapped around something. Not Alice. And then he saw Johnny Picco. Arms and legs spread out. Eyes closed. His hair floating high off his head. And then nothing was there. It had been an illusion. And even if it wasn't he had to find Alice first.

His lungs began to ache. He shot up to the light. When he broke the surface, he looked around. No Sonny. And then he heard a shout from the *Sweet Cheeks* and saw Touchon waving and pointing.

There, ahead of him fifty yards was Sonny. And he had Alice in tow.

On deck, she sputtered back to life after a few very anxious moments.

She looked up at Ange and then looked away.

Sonny helped her down to the galley.

"We told her there was too much chop to swim.," Touchon told him. "But she said she'd rather be in the water than in the boat. Me and Sonny were trying to figure that out. And then she went over. Swam some and then, man, she went down. Went out of sight. That's when Sonny dove in."

"I said some stupid shit," Angelo said, mostly to himself, looking out at the water and then at the cabin hatch.

"Hey, we all do, Ange. Sonny more than me, of course. You know how he is. Sometimes he says some stuff to ladies that just ain't ready for it. I mean he doesn't understand the fragile ones. You know what I mean?"

"Let's take her in," Ange said, pointing to the wheel.

CHAPTER NINETEEN

THE LEGENDARY COMMANDER

"I would like to have all the money my mother left me," Alice told Robert Bellator.

They were in that part of Bellator's mansion that she had been living in.

A bedroom for her and one for her daughter, as well as a sitting room and a studio where she had been working on Bellator's portrait for the last three weeks.

A rush of break-ins around her Coney Island apartment had frightened her. She imagined they were lenders, gangsters and grifters, burly men who broke down your door with sledge hammers and jack hammers, and threatened harm to you and your daughter.

When Robert had come to her rescue with the invitation to live and paint at his Compound, she had accepted.

She had met Angelo at *The New Pompey* a few times after the boating incident, but their relationship seemed to be in ruins. Angelo never mentioned her daughter again. But he couldn't help telling her he was troubled by the way she transferred her hope in him to Bellator, who he felt was deceiving her into thinking he could find Thomas. Trip was on a trip and would return. That was ridiculous Angelo had told Alice who had responded the way she had when he questioned her daughter's existence. But she hadn't jumped in the ocean or out a window.

She didn't jump into the Atlantic, but she did move into Bellator's compound.

"I want what my mother left me," she repeated now. "I want to be free of everyone."

"You most certainly are, my dear. I'm sure Dr. Grew can give you an account of that," Robert Bellator said, glancing at Dr. Grew whom he had summoned. "How much is in her account Dr Grew?"

"All told from various streams of investments, including offshore accounts, shell company accounts, various trusts and foundations approximately 1.8 billion."

"Mr. Bari quoted a considerably smaller sum."

Dr. Grew glanced at Alice who showed wide eyed interest.

"Go on," Bellator instructed him.

"Well, as Mr. Bari was demanding a certain percentage of the only trust he knew about, the Darden Trust, I did what fiduciary responsibility required of me, I deliberately withheld the amount I have just revealed to you and Ms. Darden."

He hesitated.

"Mr. Bari had not the qualifications to dispute what I told him."

"Help me make something you said clear. For Alice's sake. Mr. Bari was taking a percentage of her money? For what reason?"

"He claimed he would make a case that I was not properly handling Ms. Darden's money nor her health. In short, he wanted me ousted from my position as guardian and conservator and arrested. My incompetence and corrupt behavior were causing her mental anguish. There was more but I forget, none of it being true. One seldom has reasons to remember falsehoods."

Bellator nodded. The phony Oxbridge accent was very good. His people radar was telling him that Dr. Grew was an authentic swindler, exactly what Bellator had expected. A phony shrink, a self-taught fiduciary, and a scam artist who had managed to get control of what he claimed was a 1.8-billion-dollar trust. It seemed to Robert that his entire ancestry was here in front of him encapsulated in this fraud. It was so wonderful to meet two such catalytic figures as Grew and Alice.

"Did you feel that Dr. Grew was corrupt, incompetent? Causing you mental anguish?"

Alice looked at Dr. Grew, who removed his glasses as if his honesty was there in his eyes and it was the eyeglasses that were corrupt and incompetent. He winked at her with the brown eye.

"When I knew him long ago as The Commander, he was very kind to me, though Thomas thought he was a confidence man."

That testimony was what neither Bellator nor Dr. Grew expected. Bellator studied Grew's face. He had the look of someone insulted, not surprised, as if something clever he had done had not been clever at all but quite transparent. He had thought he was hidden but a blind girl had found him. It was thrilling to see a naïve, slightly cockeyed innocence make a corrupt man cringe.

"Dr Grew?"

"I'm not sure if that memory is a real one. Alice is an extremely fascinating individual. She blends ordinary reality with what her imagination conceives. I did not choose, as her psychiatrist, to blunt any of that with psycho-medicinals. I firmly believe that Alice possesses those rare qualities that only a very few possess. She remains utterly herself. Magnetizing I would say. And I am proud of not sullying that charisma."

"And yet I know that your name is on all of her meds. We'll let that go. Tell me, when was it that Alice knew you as a Commander?"

"I have a twin brother whom I'm sorry to say is not as honest as he should be. He often presents himself in a fraudulent manner. I'm sure it was he that Alice met on that boat."

"Somewhat far-fetched, I think. Was that your honest twin? Apologies. What do you say to that, Alice?"

"I've had troubling experiences on boats. I don't know when a boat is a ship. I do like voyages but not if they become journeys."

"You are firmly on land now. And safe here. I suspect the money Dr. Grew reports was money your mother left you."

"Yes, she did."

"Shall we talk some business in my den, Dr. Grew?"

"I should apologize to Alice for my brother's behavior."

"Spare me your fabrications. All I want to know is whether the 1.8 billion is real and if it is, why haven't you run off with it? Waiting to grab a little more, this time from me? Of course, it's not 1.8 billion or anything like it. Why such an extraordinary number? Not even millions is what I'm thinking. Your ante up, get in the game money? A half million, perhaps? Waiting to greet my millions and then goodbye, as Alice says when you least expect it."

"Truth is, I was hoping to launder some money through your enterprises."

"I don't mix dirty money with my clean clothes."

"I'm offering ten million. All illegal. Not really mine. Or Alice's. I'm in a long grift with very nasty drug lords. There's a dwarf that's running the show. Evangeline Solly. Perhaps you've seen her at the dive bar Alice too often frequents. It's Bari's hangout."

"I haven't had the pleasure. Either meeting the dwarf drug lord or the dive bar. You seem to plot the preposterous, Commander."

"Well, they're real and anxious for their money to be cleaned. The ten million is a trial run."

"So, you come to me? And I know your game."

"Sometimes one needs to share."

"You don't mind if I ferret this out? After all, I'm talking to a man who doesn't stop with his con. I'm only interested in getting back Alice's inheritance. You understand?"

"Of course. But Alice's inheritance was always imaginary. Her father left her with nothing, and her mother's money went for Alice's care all these years. Can I also point out that if I hand over ten million to you to launder, I can't see the con in that? I'm trusting you, not the other way around."

"I could bring you to the police and get that money from you that way."

Grew shook his head.

"It's the kind of money that the Feds would claim. Forfeiture. You'd get nothing. And you'd make those drug lords very unhappy. To the point of killing you."

"Telling reason for me not to get involved. Alice would never hurt for money as long as I'm alive."

"Then you are clearly not for the game. I thank you for seeing me."

"Well, I'll be candid with you, Commander. You admit there's no money of Alice's for me to retrieve. And there's no reason for me to be involved at all in this illegality. I don't want to associate with drug dealers or with grifters such as yourself. I'm neither my father's nor my grandfather's nor my great-grandfather's offspring. I'm not a thief but merely the unfortunate heir of thieves."

"I shall also be candid, Mr. Bellator. I know that you believe there are no drug lords at my back. I assure you, they exist. But I'm hoping to take them and you along with them. You, of course, enjoy odds that are clearly against you. Your confidence in your success regardless compels you to join the game. That in short is the game we're in. If you prefer to think that we're working a sort of reparatory confidence game on your ancestors, that's your business. Are you in or out?"

"Do you drink, Commander? I'm having something."

"Not while working, thank you."

Soundlessly, Ret came into the room with a tray, holding a bottle and glasses. He made a drink for Robert and handed it to him.

"Leave the bottle."

Ret placed the bottle on a lamp table .

"Hate to disturb the fun, Mr. Bellator but that crazy lady and the old man are still living above the pool house. She pulled a gun on me. Should I call the police?"

"Where did they come from, for God's sake?"

"She calls herself Aunt Rita. She says that big guy, Bari, told them they could live here. "

"They were at the sanitarium," Grew said. "She shot one of the ground keepers. I would leave her be for now."

"She says she needs a TV to watch her show."

"Alright, alright. For God's sake, accommodate her until we can evict her without bloodshed. That's all, Rettin. Tell me, Doctor, Jessica give you your notes on my psych profile?"

"She did. It's rather complex. On one hand, you're a magister ludi, who never loses. At anything. It's beyond narcissism. On the other hand, you feel that all that is on polluted ground. The thievery of your ancestors. You need to launder that."

"She's impressive, isn't she?"

"Jessica or Alice?"

"Both in vastly different ways. Do you know why Jesus Christ kept Judas around, although he knew that man's deceit? You could say, he used him. A useful idiot in the grand plan to redeem the world. Nevertheless, it seems to me a poor start for a resurrection story. I mean it seems rather odd behavior for a man who, quoting Matthew, tells us: *'If a man has a hundred sheep, and one of them has gone astray, does he not leave the ninety-nine on the mountains and go in search of the one that went astray.'*"

"So, I take it, you don't keep Jessica around to use her but to somehow save her? I see that a man so full of beatitudes would have led poor Judas to confession and redemption. And may I point out that you seem to be placing yourself in the Jesus role. Way beyond simple narcissism."

"Well, I guess that supports one aspect of Jessica's profile of me. But I keep Jessica in my employ because for me she is the true offspring of my ancestors. She's out to deceive and rob me the way every one of my ancestors lay in wait to suck the blood of others. And I've inherited all that. It's all laid at my feet."

He flung his glass across the room, hitting nothing and rolling on the Persian carpet.

"I'm not them. Not any of them. Not anything like them. She sees that. She can't win. She tries. Now with you. All of you."

"We do our best," the Commander said, smiling.

"I amuse you? Well, I won't be drawn in. You get nothing from me. This is not the game I'm playing. I'm not going to try to cleanse all of this."

He gestured wildly with both arms, looking up at the ceiling.

"Get out," he said, turning to the Commander. "Doctor, Commander or whatever the hell you call yourself."

The Commander remained seated.

"I did think our friend Jessica's read of you was just too much of a tangled twisting sort of thing to fit a single fellow creature. But she has a background in Greek tragedy. Very contorted and curling in an out of itself. Prophecies, Fate, abandonment, incest, self-mutilation, suicide. Choruses echoing your guilt in your ear. Hubris and all that. Running from dire prophecies. Ending in tragedy. Not my style at all, though I've found it's foolish to ignore close accounts of our marks."

"I told you to get out. You won't like it if I call McCord."

"Captain McCord works for us. You are, in fact, surrounded by a cast of my choosing. Here's what it is, as our friend Sailor would say. We've used various enterprises under Alice's name., the Sanitarium I run and which she frequents being one, to launder our assets. The Feds are now onto us and an infusion of about ten million of healthy funds from reputable sources is needed. Or Alice goes to jail."

"What? Listen, my family has had the best lawyers on retainer. We could easily extricate Alice's from your dealings. She's no more than an innocent front. Not difficult to prove at all. This is nothing. In fact, I'll go to the Attorney General myself. Put you out of business faster. "

"Two points I will make, Robert. One, you don't really know how deep Alice may be in our operations. She may not be as transparently whatever you think she is. And two, if she is what she seems to be, she won't survive this ordeal. You've taken her protector, Mr. Bari, from her. I've helped you dethrone him from that princely place in her mind. Now, she has only you. But a mere ten million will rescue her. Or save her, if that's your narrative. And remember, your inherited wealth is not clean at all. You know that and I know that. What better use for it than keeping our dear Alice intact."

"She's stronger than you think. When it's all explained."

"She won't put her daughter through the trials and all the nasty publicity. I can reveal to you that a great deal of very dirty money from very nasty operations of mine are in any number of washing machines owned by Cecily Darden Limone. Our Alice."

"What are you talking about? Her daughter doesn't exist."

The Commander now stood up. He went for the bottle of vodka and poured himself a drink.

"Precisely," he said, raising his glass to Robert. "Heartlessly put, but our Alice is cracked but not yet broken."

Robert watched him leave the room. It was a redemption plan, he told himself. And bad in all the same ways.

CHAPTER TWENTY

BRINGING SOME CLASS INTO THIS PLACE

"I'm not moving off this bar stool. You want to talk to me, you talk here. Sal only repeats what he hears to our friends."

"Truth is, Miss Lovely, I take the liberty of joining in the conversation of anybody sitting at my bar."

"Fine. I'd love to hear what you have to say, Sal. Can you make a super dry Martini for me also?"

"Spill it, Jessica but I'm telling you, think before you open your mouth. You're not any kind of untouchable in my world."

"Okay. Understood. But you need to stop trying to hurt Bellator."

"Oh, yeah? How am I doing that?"

"Dry enough?"

"Superb. Captain McCord knows you have people following Bellator wherever he goes. You've got your aunt squatting at the compound. She's armed. She shoots at the peacocks from a window."

"I don't know anything about that. Wait. Calls herself Aunt Rita?"

"Precisely. Bellator is afraid she might be a relative. He starts to shake when he thinks someone carrying the family blood is around."

"I've got nothing to do with that. Summer is just trying to fuck up the game. What game I don't know. She's hell's fury when she thinks she's been fucked over so I'd be careful."

"Whatever. Bellator gets the feeling that you're ready to strike.

I know you think you're protecting Alice. I get it. But we don't need him hurt or worse. We need him fleeced."

"Do you now? Well, I need her away from that guy. I can't see myself trusting him with her."

"We can't do that. We need her."

"Then bring me close enough so I can protect her."

"I don't think you or yours can be of any use to us. You're not ready. No, it's not that. Yes, it's that but the truth is that there are degrees of separation. Levels. Like floors in a building. Basement to penthouse. That's the house of the game we're in and you, Mr. Bari, are not in the basement but you aren't totally out of it either. And we're close to the penthouse and what they've got there. We can play on a level that will take us there. The long con. We can work it. And it will take us there. You are not near what we need. Robert is a complex man. You're right when you say you can't see him. All you would have to do is listen when he talks. He's a man with all kinds of handles spouting out of him that can be grabbed. But you haven't been listening."

"So, I'm in the basement and I can't listen. So why are you even talking to me?"

"I think Miss Lovely here is drawn to the hidden prince in you, Ange."

"Shut up, Sal.

"Of course, there is that. I'm very susceptible to princes, especially the moneyed ones. But the better reason is Alice is talking to you and we need Alice."

"You're full of shit. She's barely talking to me. So, I'm useless there. And Alice is not ready to cross the street by herself. So, she's also useless to you."

"No, she's not what you'd call fully volitional, but she can get anyone she wants to follow her. Even if the light is red. You're an illustration of that, Angelo. Alice has a natural gift and that is to draw, like the moon draws the tides, the moth to the flame. Diabetics to sweets. She's done it to you, so you know what I'm talking about."

"She's not in on whatever you're doing. You're conning her. She's not inside this. I don't believe it. She's lost inside her own head."

"She's not. And she is. You know what I mean about her. She's here and then she's not. She can't stay real. You've seen it. And that makes her real to you. You came on the scene accidentally. She wandered into you. We couldn't stop it. We've used it.

But understand we can't use you."

"Too low for you, right? You know, I don't know why you're here spinning me. Alice has dumped me. Maybe she belongs with Bellator. He comes from her world."

"That's a world I like to break into. And so do you, if I'm not mistaken. We have deep grievances, you and I. The money is just the sword."

"I don't know what twists you, lady. But I do know you can uproot moguls like you can move the Earth on its axis."

"You know, as I listen to you it becomes clear that you're stunned. I recognize the reveals. So many are stunned now. Cyberspace enclosure, I suppose. Smart phone enchantments. Who can resist multi-colored apps? But that's not your case."

"And what am I stunned by, whatever the fuck that means?"

"You're stunned, she's stunning."

"Why thank you, Sal. The stunned, Mr. Bari, cannot identify the cause of their stunness. Is that a word? Of course, there are societal reasons why people are stunned. But they can't see them. Thus, the state they are in."

"And Ange here is stunned?"

"Shut up, Sal."

"Absolutely. Stunned. Like a butterfly pinned to a postcard never sent. I don't know if I prefer it to what poor Warwick is."

"And where's that?"

"Our Warwick is on a very small stage in a very small theatre playing a great role. All in his own mind. He's the lead in every performance."

"I know several people like that and they ain't actors."

"I'm sure you do, Sal."

"He's happy wherever the fuck he is. Is that bad?"

"Well, Angelo, it might be so much better if he were in the world as it is. Don't you think so?"

"I don't. The world's fucked."

"I'm asking this, Miss Lovely, is this guy functional? Can he come in here, order a drink, get into the flow of the conversation and so on?"

"When he does come in, if he does, ask him, Sal, who the president of the United States is."

"I'm asking you what are you after with Alice? She one of the stunned like me you gonna use?"

"I don't like to see the innocent getting chewed up. The con is an avenger's play."

"Give me a break. It's the money you want. You'll chew up Alice quicker than … You're chewing her up right now. Roping Bellator for you."

She finished the Martini Sal had placed in front of her.

"Please heed what I'm saying, Angelo. Don't hurt Bellator before our game is done. And make up with Alice. Okay? Her goodbyes have no closure. Good bye."

"Hey, goodbye and thanks for bringing some class into this mausoleum."

"You're welcome, Sal."

They watched her all the way to the door and then out.

"Do you think she was packing?"

"I don't know, Sal. I don't care. Somebody needs to shoot me. It's one of the better ways to die. Straight to the head. Or somebody needs to get shot. Give me a drink."

"Yeah, she was, I think she was packing that Taurus G2S Slim she pulled on Summer. She better not try that with Summer again. You know, Ange, I still think she was drawn to the prince in you. Comb your hair."

"Good of you, Ange, to let me in on the shit after everything has already gone to shit," Summer said, standing by her liquor closet in her own office and pouring.

"Maybe nothing has happened. I don't know. I'm closed out. I can't get anywhere near that compound to pull Alice out."

"Oh, yeah, the princely rescue of the fair. Wait. No, let me say, totally bells in the belfry damsel in distress. Why don't you wake up? Alice is knee deep in that con. You got played."

"So, what was my part, Smarts?"

She handed him a drink and they clicked glasses.

"That takes some research as we lawyers say," Summer said, settling behind her desk. "What are you wearing? Pajamas? You look like you're doing ten to life at Rikers and you haven't taken your monthly shower yet."

"Have you run into Picco?"

"Piccolino? Little Johnny what's his face? Who's he? Look, here's what you were good for. You're not gonna like it."

"I can take it. Shoot."

"You're the fall guy. You're the guy the mark is coming after. They set you up to throw you to the wolves. The cops come after Bellator summons them after the fleece. He points them to you. And between you and me, it's probably the best destiny you'll ever have."

"Naw. That don't work. I'm not in the basement but I'm not on the first floor of this house either. He'd put the finger on Jessica and Grew."

"Yeah, but they're already in a country where you can't extradite. And, where are you? Sitting on a goddamn barstool. Over at the Pompey. And, what house? What the fuck are you talking about?"

"It's got a penthouse. That's where Bellator is. Jessica and Grew can play in the penthouse. I can't. Bellator knows that too. He won't see me as the guy working this. I mean if it works. And I have my doubts. That guy is wrapped six ways from screwy."

"You need to face it, big boy. Your Alice will turn you over. She outed every player right in front of Bellator? Degrees of separation? She knew Grew as The Commander. She knew what's his face? His bodyguard as … "

"McCord? The Captain. And she knew the other one too. Retch or Wreck or something like that."

"Another one of Bellator's people. People close to him, protecting him. Alice knows them from some shit in the past. And she knows Jessica. That bitch who thinks she's so tight with this mogul he'd never think she'd fuck him over. Alice is in the penthouse on this. It's where all the evidence points."

Angelo got up and went over to grab the bottle. Summer held out her empty glass. He poured for her and then himself and sat back down, the bottle on her desk.

"They got inside this guy. Found his jones and then sent Alice in to bring him to the stupid point. You know, like where you're at when it comes to her."

"You're wrong there, Summer. Jessica says he's been knowing for years that she's prepping a big game to raid his loot and that's why he keeps her around. It's exciting for him. He's nuts like that."

"Yeah, it's like me keeping Picco around in the 8th grade when I knew all he wanted to do was get in my pants. Don't ask me how that turned out. I think we had a baby and they called it rock 'n roll. The way I see it the moguls run out of the whatever that floats their yachts. The risks don't kick anymore. They need to get bigger and bigger. It's like a guy hanging himself, jerking off and snorting coke – all at the same time -- for the biggest rush."

"You don't give that kind of example to a jury, do you?"

"What jury? When have I faced a jury? Somebody would have to hire me first. I say 'youse' guys.'"

"Alice knew Warwick, Jessica's ex, too."

"There you go. The mogul knows he's surrounded by a pack of wolves. And he knows crazy, innocent Alice might at any moment finger all of them. She told you she knows them. She'll tell Bellator. What we also know is that snotty Jessica … "

"She's not so bad. I mean besides that. Stealing from the stealers is like her noble mission. Alice told me that Jessica was a poor kid that won a Bellator Junior Achiever Foundation flight out of the basement."

"Fuck that and get your head out of the basement. Okay, that, whatever that is, being admitted as whatever. Evidence. This noble person knows that the mogul could very likely have the names and addresses of everybody who might rob him. So, Jessica? She's going ahead with this the way Danielle walked into the Lion's Club bra-less? So, I ask you, in summation. What the fuck? I mean what the fuck is going on?"

"Right off, I'd say Jessica's a high-risk junkie but I'm in the basement on this. But yeah, it's a WTF moment. Let me try a third. See the light."

He reached for the bottle, poured himself another drink, waited until Summer finished hers, and then poured. They clicked glasses.

They both sat with their eyes closed.

"You know I should have gone for you in the 8th grade. Or any grade thereafter. Now, I don't know. You need to clean up."

"Yeah, I'll do that."

"You never know. Alice may show up back in your life. Reappear like one of those lost damsels in the story books who get lost and then show up. And then throw up."

"Bellator has reasons not to trust anyone. Anyone but Alice. She's proven to him that she's totally innocent."

"You're right. Son of a bitch. She's the … the what do you call it?"

"The Roper. The one person the mark thinks is totally honest with him. Everything she says rings true."

"I see you know all about the roping allure of Miss Alice? Yeah, he's looking at your noble Jessica setting up to thieve and meanwhile it's our lovely, sweet Alice. So totally real and true because she's so totally whacked out. He'd never suspect her. Might put her back into the looney bin but, hey, it's a better destiny than winding up with you. Can you imagine?"

"I try not to. Imagine anything. I have a hard time imagining myself not left on a doorstep. You know, I'm sure Jessica's got an escape plan. She won't hang around."

"Maybe she's expecting a prince to come and rescue her. Then you can run off with both of them."

"Oh, yeah, what's with stashing your old man at Bellator's?"

"The lenders are still looking for him."

"You put them on to Alice and now your old man? They're all too stupid to know you swindled Paul's money?"

"They think I'm looking for it just like they are. Yeah, they're stupid, otherwise who would lend any money to anybody we know?"

"But Aunt Rita? I heard she shot somebody over at the Sanitarium. What the fuck was she doing there?"

"She was safekeeping my old man out there. So, she shot a guy. It's all Texas stand your ground. I got her off on the charge."

"Then you shuffle them off to Bellator's compound? Why don't you send them to the White House so Aunt Rita can shoot off some rounds there. "

"Well, big guy, did Grew ever fork over that money we were supposed to get? No, because they haven't taken Bellator for a dime. I figure I'll get room and board for my old man and that's probably all I'll get."

"That's a shit of a reason. What else is going on there?"

"Aunt Rita is bagging merchandise. She can sneak into a room and pull out a sleeping man's teeth. She's that good."

"She's that crazy is what she is."

"That too."

CHAPTER TWENTY-ONE

A CAST OF SUSPICION

Robert found Alice putting the final touches on his portrait. She allowed him to look at it now.

"Which one is me?" he asked as he looked at not his face alone, if any of these faces was indeed his, but a grouping of faces that seemed to float in mid-air.

They didn't look all pig fat or stretched out like rubber and none had more than one face, two eyes, two ears, one nose, and one mouth. They didn't look frightening or comical, dark or mysterious, disgusting or appetizing. He didn't have the words to describe them, but he was frightened. He recognized features, expressions of the mouths and eyes. They were familiar. His ancestors. All packaged into one portrait.

"It looks like the portrait Dorian Gray kept hidden."

"I read that, Robert. I remember: `*Behind every exquisite thing that existed, there was something tragic.'*"

"Do you know if Jessica is planning a trip?"

"Oh, when will she be coming back? Will she be bringing Thomas back?"

"Maybe she's not coming back."

"But you said a trip … "

"People intend to come back from a trip. Just like we intend to wake up in the morning. That doesn't mean you don't come back, or you don't wake up. Intentions do not sway opposing power."

Alice's face began to move downward like fresh paint on a canvas.

"She's dead?"

"Don't think of her like that. She may return to us. But she may be running away, as Thomas did. She may have done a bad thing she's trying to run from."

"I wait for so many people to return.'

The more he scanned her with his truth and reality detection sonar, the more he felt that with Alice the sonar didn't work. She always blipped as true. And if she wasn't true, then she was the greatest actress the world had ever seen. She could play Ophelia to a standing ovation.

"You knew right away that Grew was a con artist called The Commander," he said to her. "How did you know that?"

"Thomas and I sailed with him years ago. A wonderful voyage to Iceland. Although Thomas had *mal de mer*."

"And this Commander ran a con game on that voyage?"

"Yes, he did. Thomas told me all about it afterward. Of course, Thomas wouldn't know about such things, but Trip did. He told me that Captain Wolf and the steward, Ret, were The Commander's accomplices. They got a lot of money out of a mogul named Griffen."

"I have a Ret working for me. Odd name. But obviously a different man."

"Oh, no. He's the same Ret. He winks at me a lot. And Captain also works for you. You call him McCord."

He didn't need this confirmation of what Grew had already told him but there it was. For the second time in a matter of a few days, Bellator felt like the sand had run out of him. He fell back on a chair and looked at his feet to see sand flowing onto the carpet. They had wrapped him totally in a false reality, made a total dupe of him. Grew had told the truth. He was surrounded by thieves. Why hadn't he believed them? There seemed to be no escape.

He looked at Alice. No, she couldn't be involved. Otherwise, she'd have to be that unbelievable actress. Otherwise, she would not have spilled the beans like this. Why would anything other than her almost total distancing from reality prompt her to tell him all this?

And yet, they had all been good in their parts. And the one who had plotted the whole grift? The Commander. Doctor Grew. Not Alice.

As he looked at her, his gut instincts and all his experience dealing with his fellow humans told him that the person behind all this could not be Alice. Let his venal ancestors think that. And they would. He wouldn't.

"You don't look well, Robert," Alice told him, with a look of fright in her eyes.

He stood up. His legs felt wobbly. He looked at her. If she were The Prime Mover in all this, she would be so enjoying what she was looking at right now as she looked at him. She would be feeling the satisfaction of making a fool of him, the sort of satisfaction his great grand-father must have felt the first time he swindled a hapless fool.

That realization made his blood boil at the very same time that he felt that this distracted soul, so magnetically off-key, was guilty of nothing.

And it was that state of knowing and not knowing, a cast of suspicion he could not dissolve that prompted him suddenly to turn to this portraiture of all his dark ancestry, the wicked blood that coursed in his veins and punch one fist into it and then another, a rich tattoo of blows, sending the canvas off the easel and on to the floor where he thrashed it over and over again with his feet.

Paint was like blood. It flowed.

At that very moment, Aunt Rita barged into the room.

"Lydia just wandered outside the gates again!" she shouted and then left as suddenly as she had entered.

Bellator was frozen. He looked at Alice.

"She's watching her show," Alice said. "I let her use my TV. I don't use it much.

CHAPTER TWENTY-TWO

IN THE WIND

"How's the leg, Mister Bellatori? Just a small bullet graze, right?"

"Call me Mister Bellator, as that is my name. My leg is fine. I've been shot before and more competently. Give me your report."

"Captain McCord and his associate, Mr. Ret, are sailing somewhere in blue water, Mr. Bellatori. Without GPS. A small vessel under sail somewhere north of the Equator heading possibly for the south Equator. Maybe not. Anyway, that escape is a … what is it? Buddy?"

"A prophylactic defense against digital pursuit. A condom on GPS detection is the way I'd put it, Buddy."

"They're in the wind, literally."

"And the Federal investigators?"

"They're working through what was left behind on site. Not much. Not anything, really. Right, Buddy?"

"Copy that, Buddy."

"And a trace on where my funds were wired?"

"Parceled and rewired all over until untraceable."

"And Alice Darden. Have you found her?"

"We're still looking. We have some leads."

"You're concentrating on finding her and not the thieves or the money?"

"Those may lead to her, sir. It can't be a coincidence that Ms. Darden has disappeared at the same time this gang vanishes."

"Dogs search. They don't give me their opinions. Report immediately to me when you find her.

Or where your leads take you."

"Buddy and me are thinking you should have ID'ed the shooter.to the cops. What's his name, Buddy?"

His partner looked at his phone.

"Warwick Marune. Got a lot of selfies from *Facebook* of the guy. Looks like he'd stick out in a crowd."

"He's confused. And hurting, His ex-wife isn't ex. She just left him a couple feet away. It's confusing. Let him be."

"Well, Buddy and me … "

"You both have the same name? Buddy? Or is that a term of endearment?"

"It ain't that. We use it to confuse a guy when we got him in the Box. We retain all our practices when we're working off-duty, private cases like this one."

"So, Buddy and me, based on a combined 43 years of experience, believe the shooter, this guy Warfield, will come after you again."

"Probably with a bigger gun."

"So, Buddy and me want to stay on him. It will increase our billable hours."

"I don't care about that. Find Alice."

"Whatever you can tell us about Jessica Moroney would be a great help, sir."

"I'm trying not to think about her, thank you. Her name, by the way, is Marune. Maiden name Vivash. A terrible name. It might help you find her if you have the correct name."

When they left Robert recalled a thought that had often come to him: the minds of dogs do not benefit by being treated as though they were the minds of men. He had read that long ago. A cynic. It was a dark thought and he realized it was a genetic visitation.

Robert thought about Jessica as he slept. A conversation.

"You had a scholarship to … I forget. Ivy league. Your mother was a hair fixer … "

"Dresser."

"Your father. Well, vanished. And then you. A doctorate. The Greeks. The ones who could persuade."

"Orators. Rhetoricians. Sophists."

"Yes, those. I remember you saying that these bullshit artists could convince a crowd in daylight that it was nighttime. And you had a doctorate, specializing in all their tricks. I was intimidated. So dangerous."

"You wanted to see me whip out that bag of tricks on you and see who would win."

"You were a challenge, Jessica. I woke up every morning excited. I couldn't wait to see you and hear whether I should think it was daytime or nighttime."

"I'm flattered."

"Tell me, Jessica, what do you really think of our Alice?"

"It's simple. She's insane."

"I'd say she's an interesting departure from the norm."

"You would. You've never experienced the norm. You have a gate."

The two investigator Buddies appeared the next morning.

"Grew mentioned an evil dwarf. Evangeline something. She frequents a bar on New Utrecht Avenue in Brooklyn. She's a drug lord. Coming after him. He needed to move faster. I understood that."

"We checked that out, sir. That's a fantasy story he sold you. Evil dwarf and all. She's not even a Little Person. She's your height give or take some several meters. And she's a mean drunk who insults people on the radio. But she ain't no drug dealer. Am I right on this, Buddy?"

"Copy that. She's got a foul mouth on the radio but she's clean. And there were no seized assets by the police. Not any Federal forfeiture funds either. No investigation going on of the Ravine Farm Sanitarium. We couldn't trace any of the names you gave us to any holdings or enterprises. We couldn't find no records on any level tied to any living person. All of them were names of deceased individuals."

"The Maroney guy is in the wind. But we're looking."

"Who? Marune?"

"What I said. Yeah."

Weeks later, Robert thought of Marune. Warwick Marune. He remembered what Jessica had told him once: *"You do know that Warwick is all things foolish, but he's devoted to me, like Adonis to Aphrodite. He'll give his life to protect me. Revenge me."*

CHAPTER TWENTY-THREE

"WHERE'S ALICE?"

"That place is a fortress," Touchon told Angelo.

"What place is that?" Sal asked, laying two shots in front of them.

"Bellator's. And I don't ever see her coming out. Not even to walk the dog."

"Who's that? Alice? She's got a dog now?"

"Shut up, Sal," Angelo told him. "I'm not in the mood for questions."

"I got answers," Sal said. "Or more like information. Summer Arpeggio's been arrested. Something to do with her setting her old man up with an off-shore account in … Cyprus. FBI confiscated what she was bringing into the country. Swooped her up."

"Jessica," Angelo mumbled.

"Jessica? You mean that lovely dish I'm hooking up with?"

"In your dreams, Sal," Sonny, at the bar alongside Torchon, told him. "What are you gonna do? Take her on your row boat around Jamaica Bay."

"That's an idea," Sal said, just as two men wearing suits that looked like they had slept in them for months and neckties with coffee and whanot stains, came into the bar. Ex-cops, Sal mumbled.

Sonny and Touchon got off their bar stools and moved across the bar and into one of the booths.

The Buddies walked up to the bar and faced Sal.

"We work for Mr. Bellatori. He's hired us to find Alice Jardin."

"Darden. Alice Darden, Buddy."

"Copy that, Buddy. Mr. B thinks you can help us with that."

"Also, somebody tried to shoot Mr. B. A guy named Maroney. No, Maroon. Like the color."

"We think you can help with that also."

"If anyone here got a gun, you better show it to us. Mister B was shot with a Raven .25 caliber. In the leg."

"They tickle him with that?" somebody at the bar said and then some laughs.

"You wanna a shot and a beer, Buddy?"

"Copy that, Buddy."

"Did your boss get taken for ten mil like we heard? "Sal asked, putting two shot glasses on the bar in front of the Buddies.

"We're also looking for a guy named Barry. Barry Angelo."

"Angelo Barry, Buddy."

"Yeah, that guy. Mr. B wants to talk to him personally."

"Mr. B wants to talk to him so maybe he can help us find what he's looking for."

"You know, Buddy, this guy right here fits the description we got. Right, Buddy?"

"Built like an outhouse, Buddy. Just like this guy right here."

"I didn't shoot Bellator, " Angelo told them, dryly. "And I didn't take him for ten million. I'm been here at the bar for the last eighty thousand hours."

"Mr. B still wants to talk to you personally, Barry."

"Why don't you come along with us after we have our drinks. Okay, Barry?"

"You don't have to go anywhere with this guy if you don't want to," somebody yelled out. "Cause I don't think these guys know that most everybody in here is packing something. We've been known to shoot people in here. Right, Sal?"

"It's not the kind of reputation we like to have," Sal said, loudly. "But, sure, we shoot people who some big shot sends over to push a good friend around."

"Ease up," Angelo said. "I want to talk to Bellator. I need to know where Alice is."

"Yeah, me and Buddy are looking for her too."

"Like we said."

"That fool Marune shot me," was the first thing Robert told Angelo as Angelo entered Bellator's capacious Louis XIV bedroom. He was propped up on pillows and one leg was elevated.

"Marune's an actor. He probably only shot a gun probably on

stage. I'd say he was trying for a vital and got you in the leg."

"Kill me? Why the hell would … "

"Jessica. Where is she? Where's Alice."

"Jessica ran off with my money. I have no idea why Alice left me."

"Didn't even say goodbye?"

"You seem to think this is all funny. That poor girl was probably abducted. She could be brainwashed. The Commander is one hell of a piece of … ."

"Mindfuck? Did you ever think Alice was part of the whole game?"

"I need a drink. You?"

"Rye."

"Once or twice. Well, more than that. I think she just ran off. Nothing to do with the scam for my money."

"I heard you handed it over to make Grew's operation whole again. Truth?"

"Do you mind if we drink out of the bottle?"

"Pass it on."

"The Commander … Grew. That man probably has more names than you can find in the Begats. He said every bit of his shit operation was in Alice's name and the Feds were closing in on that."

"So, you gave up ten mil to keep her out of jail? And now she's in the wind."

"I was there for her. Where were you? Oh, yes. You were safe in your little scummy, greasy digs. The old neighborhood and all that chumminess. You know what Jessica told me? A toothless wolf pack of losers. Or more precisely, some soon to be extinct species., private equity burying them. She said I should just develop your whole neighborhood. High end. No low lives. Nobody who talks like you and your friends. Replace you with gentrified folk who know how to speak educated Indiana. She could be quite the snob, our Jessica. My ancestry is loaded with the type. By the way. It wasn't ten million. One million is the correct amount."

"The actor thinks you killed Jessica. She was kind of what you call a soul mate. I don't. But you probably do."

"Ridiculous. She ran off with the money and left him behind. He wasn't at all worthy of her."

Angelo shook his head.

"Alice once told me that Jessica thought Warwick was the better part of her soul, as much as he annoyed her. She wouldn't leave him. Anyway, he believes that. So, she's gone means she's dead.

You're the one who would have killed her. That's the way he's thinking. Proof? He already shot you. He'll try to do it again."

Bellator sighed.

"I didn't think that silly man could act. On stage or off stage."

"I don't care if he shoots you or you shoot him or Jessica shoots both of you. Where's Alice?"

"You're the prince in her life. You tell me where she is."

"We're going around in circles."

"Look, do me a favor. Tell Marune when you see him that the thought of suicide suddenly came upon Jessica and she shot herself. It's the way I feel right now."

"And Alice too? She suddenly had an urge to kill herself? I feel like punching your lights out for pulling Alice away from me."

"Well, the punch is obsolete. Old school. You know, I believe you when you say you don't know where Alice is. You wouldn't have come along so willingly if she was with you. No, you would be with her. Perhaps you would be making plans to run off with her on your boat. No. I can see it in your eyes. You yearn for her which means she's gone. You have great fear that something terrible has happened to her. As I do."

"You? Hate and love twists inside you like an oil rig in mud."

"I would be as likely to harm Alice as you would," Bellator cried out angrily. "You're a threat to her soul, Mr. Bari. A clog of rootless appetite whose sense of what Alice possesses in a solar lunar manner is beyond you. You can't conceive of what pleasure I get in just being in her presence, limited as you are to the pleasures of your own bowel movements."

"You're bat shit crazy, Bellator, is what I'm hearing. You are for sure, mister, gonna have to let her go."

"Now why would I do that?" Bellator said, wincing. "Forgive me for being a bit slow but I'm on some strong painkillers. Pass that bottle back. And really, I don't think she'd come back to either one of us. I think she's looking for her Thomas."

"Trip?"

"I told her I could find him. And I guess I did. I did, didn't I? I mean I may have. I gave away ten million dollars. I mean one million. To save a young woman whose lost lover I found for her. None of my ancestors could have done such goodness. Is that a word? It sounds awful."

For some reason, Angelo wasn't surprised when he was leaving to see Aunt Rita coming out of a room. She had a small pistol in her hand, didn't see him and went back into the room.

He didn't make anything of it. It meant nothing.
"She's with Trip?"is what he was asking himself.

CHAPTER TWENTY-FOUR

THING IS

"She's gone," Angelo said, flatly.

"Who? Alice. Yeah, well, we know that. It don't matter. She's Alice."

"She's taken off, Sal. Nobody knows where. She's not wandering. She's taken off."

"Yeah, but I still say a wandering mind likes to wander."

"Thanks for that, Sal. I'm out of here."

He realized Sailor was standing there, behind him, like he materialized out of nothing.

He had a stank to him, that preceded his entrance. Sand, salt water, sea shells, horse shoe crabs, and sea weed. If they could put it in a spray bottle, they could market it as "Artisanal Brooklyn Sailor Fragrance."

Sal had this theory that if you put the name Brooklyn in front of anything, claim it was artisanal and curated by the Woke Vegan Gluten Free Society, charge a bundle, you'd make a bundle.

"I've been looking all over for you Ange," Sailor said, hoisting himself into a barstool. "Thing is … "

"Thing is," Sailor repeated.

"Fuck off, Sailor. You're already making no sense. I'm not in the mood for it. What do you want, Sailor? And don't use the word thing. Thing doesn't get us anywhere. Okay. Go."

"I heard about Bellator being shot but he ain't dead. And the truth is … "

"I saw him. He got shot with a pea shooter. And don't say 'the truth is.' Every time I hear that I want to throw up. And don't say you want to make things clear. Go."

"Yeah, it's like 'Let me be perfectly clear here,'" Sal said. "Words to run from. "Like, 'The People.' What people? And, the next idiot who comes in here and starts off with a 'So' ... "

"I'm not in the mood for you either, Sal."

"Okay, here's what it is, Ange. He's hired goons. He's looking for people. People that know people that maybe know people ...

"That's enough," Angelo told him, raising a hand. "Get out of here. Unless you can tell me where Alice is."

"Wait," Sal said. "And what is it that they know? These people."

"The guy who shot him. ... And Alice. He's looking for her."

"You know where Alice is?"

"That's why I'm here. That's the thing of it."

"What did I tell you about thing?"

"See, Bellator gave me 10k to pull up that gold from the bottom."

"He gave you the money for what?"

"That's the thing. I got money to hire your boat. To pull up that gold from the bottom."

"What the fuck are you talking about?

"My uncle's gold that he sunk so the lenders wouldn't get it. You know gold doesn't get messed up in salt water. On the bottom."

"But brains do," Sal told him. "And you're a case in point. You been sleeping on the waters too long."

"Okay, so what does this look like?"

He pulled a small packet out of his pocket, opened it up and spilled the contents in an ash tray on the bar.

"And what's that?" Angelo said, peering at it.

"Gold. From the sunken ship. From the bottom. The one coming from Argentina, but Paul had it sunk. It went right to the bottom."

"Looks like tooth filling is what you've got there," Sal said. "So, you're saying Bellator gave you money to bring gold dust up from a sunken ship?"

"It's in boxes. In bags and then in boxes ... "

"I'll shoot you if you say bottom again? Okay?"

"And one of the boxes washed up on shore and it was empty except for this stuff was scraped out. Box had the name of the ship on it is what it is. Some name in Argentinean. Name of the ship. The one Paul had sunk. It's kind of like leaving it there until he needed it. Like an underwater bank account but then he died."

"Is that it?" Angelo said. "Okay, Paul Limone wouldn't have done something so cock brained as that. And if he did, he couldn't arrange the sinking of that ship. And lastly, did you ever hear of salting? I mean the grift. Guy salts a mine or a sunken ship or in this case, a broken fucking box with some gold dust and convinces an idiot that there's tons of it. In this case, the idiot is you Sailor."

"Bellator went for it."

"I'll bet what's left of your brain that so far Bellator hasn't given you a dime."

Sailor gave Angelo an unsettled look, like a driver at a crossroads.

"He's in is what it is. Soon as we bring up one or two boxes from the ... he'll come up with money."

"We?"

"You guys got the boat. You and Picco."

"Leave Picco out of it. He's moved on."

"Mines too small to get out in blue water. We could do it. You and me."

"There's no you and me, Sailor. We're just two fucked up guys in our own corners."

Sailor thought about that.

"What about the gold?" he said, emptying the gold dust back into an envelope.

"Want I should throw the sailor out?" Sal said.

"Why? You think he's crazy, Sal?"

"There's that and that he stinks up the place."

"I'll smell better when I got all that gold."

"Did I mention that if there was a sunken horde of gold, you'd be the last person anybody in their right mind would pay to retrieve it."

"The thing is, Ange, I'm first cousin," Sailor told them, tears in his eyes. "I was Paul's nephew. I got a right to that gold."

"Sure," Sal said. "You're entitled. We're all fucking entitled."

"But I can't work this out legit by myself. Thing is I don't know how to work this. You're the operator, Ange. You can manage this."

"Yeah, you need Ange," Sal said. "Bring him one of those boxes of gold dust and he'll show you what to do with it."

"Okay," Sailor said. "I got other friends. Relatives."

He pulled up off the bar stool and walked out.

"He's got relatives? I mean living?"

Before Angelo could reply, Sailor came back into the bar and stood in front of Ange.

"I plan to sail through the water gap into Chesapeake Bay and then into the Atlantic, up to the *la Voie Maritime du Saint-Laurent* access, into the Great Lakes waterway on to the Illinois waterway and then the Mississippi River system straight down to the Gulf. Navigable channels with some off locks bypassing rapids and dams. From the gulf through the Panama Canal and then sail straight across the Equator."

"Okay. Send us a postcard."

Sailor's jaw dropped and he riveted Angelo with a hard gaze.

"I was in The Stands. All of them. Afghanistan, Pakistan, Iraq, Syria."

"The Stands? I thought you were saying The Sands. Iraq is a stand?"

"You should tell Mr. Bellator that I was in the Sands."

Sailor turned around and headed for the door.

"I guess he's gonna do it," Sal said, amazed, shaking his head in disbelief. At everything. "Do you think there's a pot of gold he's going to bring up? I mean with Bellator's money? You think we should tell Bellator that Sailor was in the Stands and the Sands?"

"Either. Doing a lot of killing is what I think. That guy smells but he's dangerous."

"Damn! I thought he was just off his rocker. But you know I like the guy. He never starts off with a `So.' He's got a thing about the bottom though. "

"It's what his mind doesn't have," Ange said.

CHAPTER TWENTY-FIVE

HEY, BUDDY

Summer Arpeggio sat behind her desk in her office looking at she didn't know what.

Yeah, Alice. Looking like she was still down the rabbit hole. And Polock Kerplowski's son. Tim. He called himself or they called him Sailor. His friends. Did he have any friends? She remembered him from grade school. He did smell of seaweed rotting on the shore.

He was sitting right alongside Alice. They looked like they were a circus act. She wanted to aim her cell at them and take a picture, but she was afraid of scaring them off, like not getting too close to something come out of the water, resting, but you didn't know what it was.

"Do you remember when you said I should give back what I owed to Mr. Limone's lenders?"

"Yeah, I remember, Alice. So, the ones that are gangsters, which is all of them really, would spare your life. Yeah, I remember. But what I know now is that you never had any money to give anybody. I mean it was just a line of bull. It was all part of the con you and your friends were working. I was supposed to get a monthly taste. But you know what? I got nothing. Oh, wait. I got set up and went to jail for money laundering and now I'm on bail. What was that all about? So, where's your sweetheart of a friend, Jessica?"

"Money laundering. *The concealment of the origins of illegally obtained money, typically by means of transfers involving foreign banks or legitimate businesses.*

"So, I'm gonna make you eat that thing if you pull it out again.

Gimme that fucking thing or get out of my office. I don't need this. I guess I got in the way of the Big Con. I threatened that stuck up bitch if she didn't get me what was promised."

"Jessica. Robert gave her two million dollars and she went."

"What? Two million? Went where exactly?"

"The thing is, we didn't come here for this is what it is. We need the lenders to lend us what we need is why we're here."

"Shut up, Tim. Where did Jessica go? With the two million."

"Ten million I think."

"Eight-million-dollar difference. Which I see means nothing to you, Alice my lovely."

"Here's what it is … "

"What? Look, don't talk. You smell more when you talk. So, Jessica Rabbit has. … I need a drink. Anybody … forget it. Just me."

Summer went over to her liquor cabinet and poured herself a Mister Jim Beam She knocked it back quickly then returned to sitting behind her desk.

"So, okay, here's what I knew before you two walked in. Besides knowing I was set up and spent a couple of days in jail and now I'm on bail and I'm representing myself, which means I'm fucked. Jessica managed the whole grift is what I'm thinking. And you, Miss Went Down the Rabbit Hole, was in on it."

"None of which is what we came here for."

"Shut up, Tim.. I will shoot you if you interrupt again. To continue. Nevertheless, and notwithstanding and fucking unbelievably, she's skipped with the money and you're here sitting in my office with smelly here and …. you want what?"

"Warwick shot Robert in the leg with a small gun."

"Who the fuck is Warwick? A warwick shot Bellator? Sounds like a video game. Or Aunt Rita's second favorite soap: *One Life to Kill*."

"Warwick. Jessica's ex-husband. He wanted to kill Robert because he thinks he killed Jessica."

Summer shook her head.

"So, allow me to summate. Is that a word? Robert gives ten million, maybe eight million, maybe one million, to Jessica who runs off with it but maybe she didn't and maybe she's dead and maybe the one million is gone or maybe she's alive and she's got it."

"We have to go. Trip is waiting for me."

"Thing is we need seed money."

"Think about a bullet in your head, Tim. Say that again, Alice. You heard from Trip?"

"Sailor did."

"He called and the thing is he needs money and I told him where we could get it. It's on the bottom. So, he's in on our deal."

"The millions?"

"More than that. Gold dust at the bottom."

"The bottom of what?"

"We get a boat and what we need, and we can get it."

"And you say Trip likes that idea?"

"It's what his father wanted me to have. Trip wants us both to have it. He told us to come here because you and your Dad are connected with lenders."

"I see. You come to me to get some of the people who loaned Paul money and never got repaid to give you guys more money so you can find gold dust at the bottom. And then you two along with Trip give the gold to the lenders. Is that it?"

"We'll give'em twenty per cent above the loan."

"Very generous of you, Tim. Before I sum up once again in the light of this new evidence has either one of you seen Trip Limone alive since, say, nobody's seen him in a decade?"

"I see him sometimes but then he goes away."

"Of course, Alice. What about you, Tim?"

"I talked to him."

"Where? On your cell phone that you don't have?"

"I got a house phone."

"You have a house?"

"A boat. A rowboat phone."

"I need just one or two more drinks. If you'll excuse me."

She stood at her liquor cabinet and drank.

"My counsel? Alice, get back on your meds. Get back with Angelo. You'll need him. Better yet, go back to Bellator. Nurse his leg back to health and live off his gazillions for the next fifty years. I say this because you both are certified auditors of voices and faces that ain't there. So, there's that."

"I can't. Angelo doesn't believe Sally is real and Robert is a murderer. He murdered Jessica."

"Who's Sally? Oh, wait. Your daughter. But is she really real, Alice? Say like this Glock in my hand. Think about it. Has anyone seen Sally alive since ... say, ever?"

"She doesn't go out much."

"She doesn't ... you mean, into the real world? Look, I'm going to use an expression we big shot attorneys use a lot to make it clear to a client exactly where they are. You, Alice Darden ... "

"Thomas Trip would want me to use Limone."

"Whatever the fuck. You are in between a fucking rock and a fucking hard place. The guy sitting next to you has more rocks in his head than Reagan on Rushmore."

"Here's what it is!" Sailor screamed. "Are you gonna get that lender money for us or not? The sun's going astern."

"The sun's … what the fuck does …. astern of what? The bottom?"

Summer got interrupted. A knock and then a woman's face.

"Yeah, you can go to lunch, Aunt Rita. Bring me back a veal parm. By the way, you didn't get kicked out of Bellator's? My old man all nice and snug?"

"Mr. Bellatori got shot. I'm protecting him now. Your father is sleeping."

"Veal parm."

"But these gentlemen … "

Aunt Rita got pulled out of the room and the two burly ex-cops who had taken Angelo to see Robert came in.

"Hullo, Alice. We been looking for you."

"We been watching this place for … how long, Buddy?"

"Too long, Buddy. Come on. Mr. Bellatori wants to see you."

"Who the hell are you clowns, barging into an attorney's office? You can't drag my client out of here under duress."

"How about over my shoulder?" Buddy said, lifting Alice easily out of her chair.

"Whatya you guys think?" Sailor said to the ceiling. "She saw something. She didn't see nothing. The thing is, we got to go."

"Who are you, jackwad?"

"Hey, Buddy, that's the guy been hanging around pestering Mr. Bellatori."

"I think you're right, Buddy. Same fat ass."

"Hey, you two fucking buddies. Look over here. And get your paws off the lady. She's fragile."

When they looked, they saw that Summer had a big, black gun in her hand.

"9 milli," one Buddy said.

"Sig Sauer P226," Sailor told them, looking at the gun. "Navy Seal's gun of choice. 12 rounds in 9mm."

"How come you know so much, fat boy?'

"We need to find the gold," Sailor said, smashing one hand into Buddy's nose. Blood spurted. Alice fell out of his grip to the floor.

"You can't take her right now," Sailor said, punching into the other Buddy's throat. He fell to his knees.

The first Buddy pulled out a small gun. Sailor looked at it.

"Double Tap. Smallest .45. Two in the chamber. Two in the handle."

"Drop to the floor, jerk," Buddy ordered.

"Shoe ... him," the Buddy on the floor blubbered.

Sailor picked up the chair he had been sitting in and holding it as a shield, he charged the standing Buddy. Two shots went into the chair. Sailor smashed the chair over Buddy's head, grabbed him in a choke hold and held till Buddy fell to the floor, alongside Buddy.

"Mother fucker!" Summer shouted, coming from around the desk and kicking at the collapsed Buddies. "What am I going to do with these guys?"

"I think I once put them in my stories," Alice whispered.

"Here's the thing. I think you should tell the lenders how good this deal is," Sailor said to Summer. "I'm leaving you with a sample of the gold dust. We'll be back."

"Wait. Alice, don't go with this guy. I'll get Angelo over here. He can protect you. This guy ... "

She looked at the crumpled buddies.

"Yeah, well this guy can protect you but ... think of your daughter. Can he protect her too? I mean on a ... on a huge body of water. In a ... he doesn't have a ship. Just a rowboat."

"Trip is waiting for me. Thomas too."

Before Summer could say anything else, Sailor and Alice were gone.

Aunt Rita stood in the doorway.

"Should I have them put out in the dumpster?"

"No. Go see if my father is still sleeping. Wait. Bring me back a veal parm first."

CHAPTER TWENTY-SIX

THE GREASY GOAT

The bar phone rang. Sal answered then handed it to Angelo.

"We've got to talk."

"Who is this?"

"Warwick Marune."

"I thought you'd be in jail for shooting Bellator."

"He told the police he didn't know who shot him. But I think he's got somebody following me. I'm in disguise and have thus far eluded them. Can you meet me at the *Greasy Goat*? You know, the place when we were with Alice. Near the Medicine Show?"

"Listen, where's Alice?"

"Be here and I'll tell you."

As soon as Angelo came into the café, he remembered it. The smell of grease. He saw someone wearing a cowboy hat and handle bar mustachios wave to him from a rear booth.

"Something from *Oklahoma*?" Angelo asked, as he sat across from the actor. "The hat is good. It adds another foot to your six foot six. Be hard to spot. Where's Alice?"

"Menu, sir?"

"Just coffee."

"You should try the special. The meatloaf here is good."

"Just coffee. Don't jerk me around, Marune. I'm not in the mood. If you don't know where Alice is ... "

"I need to know stuff first and then I'll tell you what I know.

Okay? Did Bellator confess?"

"For what? Being shot?"

"Killing Jessica."

"Two questions: Why would he do that? And how do you know she's dead?"

"She beat him at his game. Got his money. And I don't know where she is. I always know where she is. When alive."

"He's got some ex-cops looking for you."

"Fine. I'm looking for him. I've got more bullets."

"But the same aim. And get a higher caliber bullet. My advice is … "

"I don't want advice. I don't need it. I'm in an end game. No exit. You are your life. And nothing else. And my life was Jessica. And he killed her."

"You don't buy that she got the ten mill and ran off? Or committed suicide? She seemed manic depressive to me. More manic than depressive really."

"That scenario wouldn't even work in a TV soap opera. She had grandiose plans. She didn't know what depression was. Truth is, Jessica would more easily kill everyone in the room rather than shoot herself. I'm not saying she was heartless. But she would leave suicide to lesser lives."

He paused and poked at the meatloaf on his plate.

"Myself included."

The waitress placed a cup of coffee in front of Angelo. Marune reached in his jacket pocket and took out a half pint flask. He handed it to Angelo.

"Brandy."

Angelo unscrewed the cap and poured some out in his coffee then handed it back to Marune who ran some on his meatloaf.

"To cut the grease."

"You know, chances are that you won't get a chance to put another bullet in Bellator but a good chance the goons he hired will put one in you. How did you ever get close enough to him to plug him?"

"You forget, I've lived on that compound of his as long as Jessica has. Had. Her presence kept him in a daily battle with his thieving genetics. She played the part of a thief with his father's genes. It was an act and it was also real. She was there to bilk him, and he knew it. I was there because she was there. I knew his daily routine. I knew where and when to put a bullet in him. I'm only sorry I botched it."

Marune pulled out his flask again and took a long pull.

"She didn't fly away. They grabbed her. Somewhere. I wasn't there."

"Where's Alice?"

The actor didn't hear him or just ignored him.

"Jessica was a classicist, believe it or not. She taught the Greek tragedies. *'Have I not seen two tyrants thrown? The third, who now is king, I shall yet live to see him fall, of all three most suddenly, most dishonored.'* Aeschylus. She wanted to be there to see him fall, the fall she had arranged. She called it a grift but it was more to her. I think she stayed around too long, and he found her and killed her."

"I'm sorry but I don't see that in this guy. Bellator ... "

"He inherited that name. The family name was originally Tewk or Toke or something like that. Too much a loser's name. Bellator. Warrior. He didn't like it, but he couldn't change it because an empire was built on that name."

"That's what I mean. Maybe his father would have killed Jessica but not the son."

The actor took another pull. He poked at his meatloaf.

"No. That wouldn't have happened. You see his father was also Jessica's father. She was the daughter conceived in an upstairs maid's bed. Or maybe downstairs. Anyway, she wasn't given the family name. The old man did put her through all the best schools."

"Did Robert know?"

"He thought she was a distant cousin, six times removed. She never told him. She didn't want the money really. She wanted what he had. The legitimacy."

Angelo wasn't ready for the revelation.

"She was the female Edmund. *Wherefore should I Stand in the plague of custom, and permit The curiosity of nations to deprive me, For that I am some twelve or fourteen moon-shines Lag of a sister? Why bastard? wherefore base?* I always knew it. That was the secret deep bond between us. I loved her way beyond that."

Warwick swigged at the brandy once again.

"You gotta have a plan. You can't just be walking around, Marune. I got friends who could help you get out of the city."

"You wanted to know about Alice? All I know is that Thomas is back and she's with him."

"Trip is back?"

Angelo felt a collision of emotions hitting him from all directions.

"How do you know that?"

"She called me and told me. She heard that Jessica was dead, and she knew I would be devastated. She wanted me to live for Jessica's sake. I told her I didn't understand that. I did live for her sake and she died. I need a new part to play. And I'm too old for that. You know a director once told me that I was a very tall man, imposing figure, yet too small for great tragedy."

"Where is she?"

"I don't know. She wouldn't tell me except to say she was safe, and I was to tell you that she was sorry things had not gone the way you wanted them. She loved the times you both had on your boat. And then she said she was on a boat and something about her cousin who had been in the Sands. I didn't understand."

"Sailor. And Trip. I guess she's got what she was looking for. Who."

"It's not for you to name its end. *'Love, like fire, goes out without fuel.'*"

Angelo felt stunned. He needed more than a shot of brandy.

"Did you ever think she was part of the Bellator con? I mean Jessica was inside it. She told me Alice was a roper, but she wasn't in on it. Just an innocent."

"I couldn't tell you. I thought she was a wonderful Ophelia, innocent in that way. But it's not a part she ever played in any of our productions. What I recall is that she was an excellent Rosalind. *As You Like It.*"

"What was she like?"

"She could pretend to be what she was not. *'Beauty provoketh thieves sooner than gold.'* Our Alice was the most gifted student I ever had in my acting classes."

Angelo stood up. He remembered something.

"Who's the president of the United States?"

"Black man. No. An orange man. A very old man?"

Angelo looked around and then out the window at people passing in the street. He saw the burly figures of the ex-cops. They were coming in.

"We gotta run," he said, reaching out and grabbing the actor's arm. "Or we are going to die right now."

"*'What of it? If I die, I die. It will be no great loss to the world, and I am thoroughly bored with life. I am like a man yawning at a ball; the only reason he does not go home to bed is that his carriage has not arrived yet.'* My day to quote Lermontov."

Before he finished his lines, Warwick stood up and shouted.

"Are you Bellator's emissaries of death?"

"Whatever, cowboy. Just calm down and come with us."

"Mr. Bellator holds no hard feelings. Am I right here, Buddy?"

"Right as rain, Buddy."

When Angelo saw two guns suddenly in the actor's hands, he ducked deep down in the booth, his legs stretched out into the aisle.

"They're gonna kill you, man. Drop those "…""

The guns looked like props in Western movies, but they fired. Warwick was pulling both triggers like he was Clint Eastwood. He was aiming at the ceiling. When he dropped both guns and slumped forward, his head hitting Angelo's shoulder, blood coming from his neck, Angelo knew all shots hadn't been fired at the ceiling.

CHAPTER TWENTY-SEVEN

SAILOR VICTORIOUS

"What's he say?" Sal said, setting a rye shot and a beer in front of Angelo.

"Alice is with Trip."

"Damn! She's with him where? I mean if he's dead … You're saying she's dead too?"

"Apparently Trip's not dead. Wherever they are, they're both alive. I think the two of them are on that boat with Sailor Kerplowski, looking for the sunken gold dust, bars, coins. On the bottom. Whatever the fuck."

Angelo shot down his drink and then held it forward. Sal repoured.

"Your face is telling me dark things, Ange. What happened?"

"The two Buddies working for Bellator came into the greasy spoon. There was a shootout. Marune lost. Fatally."

"Jeez. You were there?"

"Under the table. Being the prince that I am."

"I forgot to tell you, Summer called, and she says Sailor and Alice came by to get her to arrange for the lenders to back them on their treasure hunt."

"Alice is with Summer?"

"She took off with Sailor. Summer's got other problems. She wants you to meet her at Dino Kim's."

Summer was in Parlor A without a casket. Still the parlor looked like the Grim Reaper's parlor. The fragrance of flowers filled the room, a decayed fragrance.

Summer was seated on a couch in the back.

"Where did she go?" Ange said, first thing.

"Hullo to you too. You want my advice … "

"No. Just tell me what happened."

"The two come in. She's looking like, well, she spent some time behind the looking glass and Cousin Tim? Do you believe I went steady with that guy in the 4th grade? I thought he smelled like wild oats."

"You're plucking on my last nerve end, Summer."

"So, they come in, give me the spiel. There's gold dust at the bottom. What bottom where or what he doesn't say. I tell him everything's got a bottom, so I need more than that. Even a black hole has a bottom, although I don't know fuck all about black holes. Anyway, it's at the bottom. When they vacuum up the dust, Trip shows up or he's already there or he's someplace but he's not then in my office. By the way, she hasn't seen him, and Cousin Tim hasn't seen him. Not since eons ago. They just hear his voice. So, personally, I don't think he's above ground. But Cousin Tim has this idea that Alice can come into my office and I hand over bags of money because the gangsters trust me to … "

"They don't. Did Sailor say where he was going to look?"

"One of the oceans, I think. Somewhere north or south of the Equator. Or maybe Ecuador. I tell Alice to ditch this guy, and just imagine that Trip is nothing more than a lure for Sailor to get money through her."

"Is he that smart?"

"He didn't have to be. You know she thinks Sailor is her last living relative. She thinks she needs that. A relative. Of course, he's only an in-law cousin. What is that? Once or twice removed? I've told her she could have Aunt Rita, to which Aunt Rita got very mad with me and told he she wasn't promiscuous."

She gave Angelo a pitying look.

"Okay, now, comes the exciting part because it turns out Bellator has had my office staked out."

"I don't understand. She was here. In your office. With that lunatic and you couldn't get her to come to me?"

"No, big boy. You don't see daughters that are not there. Tragic flaw. Or, put it this way. You point out like the kid and the Emperor without clothes that there ain't no daughter. Did I say ain't your honor? I meant there ain't ever been a daughter. There is not a daughter. I mean, I ask you, Angelo, how can you take care of her daughter if you don't think she's real?"

"I listened to Picco on that one. Confront her, he says. It will bring her back to reality."

"Reality? So, I always advise my clients: Do the opposite of what Johnny Piccolino tells you to do. And run when someone says he's a witness to reality."

"I'm not hearing anything exciting here, Summer."

"So, the guys staking out my place, see her come in and they barge in. The two buddies. Come with us. No, she ain't going. Doesn't she want to talk to Mr. Bellatori? No, she doesn't. Back and forth like that for all of fifteen seconds."

"And then they took her?" Angelo asked, jumping up. "Back to Bellator's?"

"Naw, what's exciting about that? Our Cousin Tim, Sailor Kerplowski, son of Pollock Kerplowski, stands up, smashes this one Buddy in the nose, then in the neck. No, wait. I'm out of sequence. When Buddy picks up Alice, I pull out my Glock and tell the two Buddies to drop their pants. They start discussing the Glock and Sailor gives them the specs on it and one says you must be a Navy Seal and Sailor then throttles the guy. The second Buddy."

"Alice?"

"Safe. And on the floor. The other Buddy pulls out a small gun, which Sailor gives us the specs on while picking up a chair, charging this Buddy with the small gun, gets him in a choke hold and chokes him unconscious. I'm standing there just muttering what the fuck what the fuck."

"Amazing."

"You know I thought Cousin Tim, smell and all was a clown. Now I'm thinking, fuck this guy is real. Really real. Which gets you wondering? Was I, an attorney with a southern bumfuck nowhere law degree, witnessing a bit of the real? I'm beginning to think his gold dust bullshit is real. It may be on the bottom. Fuck, there may even be a bottom."

"And she wasn't hurt?"

"Alice and Sailor took off. Nothing on where to reach them. Cousin Tim said they would be in touch. But I don't think so."

"Where are the two guys now?"

"The Buddies? Dino Kim picked them up and deposited them in local dumpsters. Although, they are not dead. They'll wake up smelly. I had to send Aunt Rita back to Bellator's. My father is sleeping. Maybe dead. Anyway, Aunt Rita doesn't like violence she's not involved in."

"They must have rushed over here after shooting Marune. He's dead."

"There's an injustice right there. Guy's ex-wife tries to run off with a half a million and he gets left behind and killed. You know, Ange, I think justice gets prosecuted every time."

"Have you heard from Picco?"

"No, and it's a continued blessing. I'm looking for him the way I'm looking for one of those malaria mosquitoes."

CHAPTER TWENTY-EIGHT

BODIES DON'T ALWAYS WASH UP ON SHORE

"Bodies don't always wash up on shore. Sometimes they sink or the sharks get them. Then, sometimes they go off on a ship to where they want to go. And they get there safely."

"You know, Sal, I should have paid more attention to where Sailor said he was going."

"Sail through the water gap into Chesapeake Bay and then into the Atlantic then something French to the Great Lakes waterway on to the Illinois waterway and then the Mississippi River system straight down to the Gulf. Navigable channels with some off locks bypassing rapids and dams. From the gulf through the Panama Canal and then sail straight across the Equator. It doesn't make any sense. That ship would have gone down not too far from the Brooklyn piers. Off Fire Island maybe. If it's blue water, you need a chart."

"How do you remember all that, Sal?"

"I don't. I copied it off the bathroom wall. Sailor put it up there few years ago and I left it. Look, Ange. They never got a ship. There's been no reports of a ship lost. I've told you before … "

"Summer doesn't think Trip is real. I mean, anymore. Sailor wants Alice to get him the money he needs for his treasure hunt. So, he says, Trip's in on it and that brings Alice aboard."

"Maybe, Sailor is after Bellator's five mil and figures Alice is the one who can take him to it. Five mil and the gold dust."

"His idea of the good life is living in a fucken rowboat, Sal, how greedy can he be? Anyway, Bellator claims they only got him for one mill. Summer thinks it's half a mill. Jeez, Sal, I don't know half of what's going on and that half is fake."

"Half a mill will still buy a bigger boat. Look, how do we know anybody got any money and made any kind of escape? Grew could be enjoying the grab somewhere and Alice and Trip could be offloading gold dust somewhere and Sailor could be buried in The Sands. Or, they could all be drowned. Rich or poor."

"I'm having a hard time getting Alice out of my mind. Marune told me that love dies when you don't fuel it but I'm still fueling it. It's like good whiskey I can't water."

"That's the way I feel about Jennifer."

"Who's Jennifer? You mean Jessica?"

"Yeah, we didn't even have a first date but I'm fueling it."

"Marune figured she was dead. That Robert Bellator killed her. But that doesn't figure any way you figure. I think he knew she was his illegitimate sister."

"Damn. You know, she kinda of did have that incest look."

"Summer said that Jessica was trying to get away. Like, she was still trying."

"And never succeeded," Sal said, nodding. "Or, maybe she did."

Angelo found Gee in the back where he was, as he had been for weeks now, supervising the remodeling of his restaurant.

"Sal said you wanted to see me, Gee."

"Yeah. I'm millenializing the menu. Is that a word? What do you think of a c-rated meatball sandwich?"

"You mean curated? By who?"

"By me. I got a Woke Up Frittata and Uber pizza. Here. Try some of this. I got a call from Dino Kim. Summer Arpeggio brought him a body to be incinerated."

"What?"

"He did it in his crematorium. He called me because I own that operation. Not the funeral parlor but just the incinerating services. What I'd like you to do as you were her steady in the 8th grade ... "

"Not me. Johnny Picco. 4th grade."

"Is to find out where did the body come from, whether anyone will miss it, and whether it can be traced to her and thus to the incinerator and to me. Okay?"

Angelo felt dazed.

"I'd speak to her myself but I'm busy here with this menu. I got enough trouble turning Sal into a Master Somalieri. Wine guy."

"Why me?"

"Johnny Picco? He can't attend."

"Where is he?"

"Somewhere where he can't come back is what I heard unless you believe in the After Life. What do you think of that Q-rated eggplant?"

"I would have had to run" was the first thing Summer told Angelo right at the door that Aunt Rita had opened for him. Summer was behind her desk. An open bottle in front of her.

"Go to lunch, Aunt Rita."

"I already been."

"Then go fuck yourself. Just get out of here."

"Not a way to talk to your aunt," Aunt Rita said, slamming the door behind her.

"You're a bit hard on your aunt, aren't you Summer?" Angelo said, sitting down and grabbing the bottle. He took a swig.

"Glasses behind you. She's not my aunt. She's nobody's aunt. That's her birth name. Aunt Rita. Can you believe it? She said her mother expected that after she died Aunt Rita would be lonely. No family left. So, now strangers have to call her Aunt Rita. Makes her feel good. I inherited her from my father. Along with other shit. Most in my head."

"Gee wants to know whose body you want Dino Kim to incinerate?"

"Don't worry. It wasn't Alice. That bitch Jessica. She was running. I caught up. She didn't have any of that thirty million. It was all computer transfer. Where? She wouldn't say. Then she goes for that Raven .25 caliber. You remember the BB shooter she pulled on me? I was willing to take one of those in the arm and then I got mad. You know, I got my old man's temper. I sucker punched her, pulled out my Glock and put one in the temple. I brought the body over to Dino's. I got an arrangement with Gee. He owns that place. So, I got a dead body and no money. I thought I'd get it from that stuck up bitch. That's the whole story."

Angelo took another swig at the bottle.

"Glasses behind you. You know I should be running now but I'm also thinking what if I don't run? Manslaughter. Womanslaughter I get sent up but I'm safe. The lenders will leave me alone. Whatever. But I ain't running."

"Did Jessica tell you Alice was in on the grift?"

She ignored the question.

"You know, Ange, you're the hero of the neighborhood. Truth is, my prince, I stole that money from Paul Limone. My father didn't. He was too stupid and also too stupid. Did I mention that he was too stupid to skim off all that illegal money of Paul's?"

"And you set Alice up. You let the lenders believe she had the money or knew where it was."

"Yeah. I went through it over the years. I invested in different enterprises that sucked in my money but didn't pay out. So, yeah, I'm the thief and I put everybody following her scent. The inheritor. You gonna hate me forever for that, aren't you? You still looking for her?"

"Not physically. And I'm trying not to think about her. I had my shot. She lost interest. I'm not fueling that fire anymore."

"I had to put the rush on Jessica. I needed … or need … money fast. The intellects you and I are surrounded with figured out I was the thief. I got signs, like when they ate part of my old man, that they were losing patience. As much as I would like to shoot my old man myself, I don't want anybody else to do it."

"How did you know where to find Jessica? Warwick couldn't. And he thought Robert had killed her. He shoots Robert and then he dies in a shootout. He was shooting at the ceiling. They weren't. The Buddies."

"I met them. Cousin Tim ripped them a few new ones. I told you about that."

Angelo took another swig and then stood up.

"How did you know where to find Jessica?"

"You mean smarter people than me were looking? I jacked that crazy phone of Alice's when she was in the office. I pulled an Alice. I said: 'Safe House for Grifters.'"

"And that got you an address?"

"I copied it to my phone. Listen:

"*A safe house (also known as safehouse) is, in a generic sense, a secret place for sanctuary or suitable to hide persons from the law, such as grifters. Find a vacant warehouse in the Flatlands section of Canarsie.*"

"And you found her?"

"Found her. Talked to her. Traded bullets with her. Nothing left but the body in the trunk of my car."

"I'll tell Gee the body pulled first."

He paused at the door.

"You're not suicide prone, are you?"

"You know, my prince, we let the people around us kill us when they find the time."

CHAPTER TWENTY-NINE

WORD LIMIT

'Shot her in the head while she was sleeping.," Gee said as they stood beside the casket

"Close range. Kind of a message shot. I'm thinking revenge. Our Summer killed a couple of people. Over the years. A real Annie Soakley."

"I thought she was a lawyer," Angelo said, without thinking.

"Tough lady. She could crook and she could shoot. Wasn't much of a lawyer though. Let's go to the bar I got something to tell you. I already said my farewells at the casket."

"Yeah. Dino made her look … kind of … "

"Stunned. Summer didn't expect to die. I'm that way myself and I'm on the wrong side of seventy."

"Leave the bottle."

"I can't do that, sir. I do the pouring."

"Just put a bottle of Jim Beam rye in front of us and take off."

"Gee, Are you saying you don't think the loan sharks had Summer killed?"

"You wanna hear what I got to say or you wanna ask questions? One or the other. I'm at my word limit for the day."

"I'm listening."

"I don't have to tell you anything, kid. Sal gets himself webbed in other people's lives. I don't have the patience and the what do you call it? Compassion? With Sal it's just a hard-on."

He paused and poured them a drink.

"Salud."

"I see you, Angelo, I'm reminded. I was just past drinking age. She was a knock out. I go for her like we're both dogs in heat. She gets pregnant. She goes off and has the kid. I don't know where. I never see him or her. Or her again."

"So, you're my father?" Angelo asks, smiling.

"Yeah, that's it. I'm finished. Am I gonna tell this because now I'm thinking fuck this kid and I'm telling him nothing?"

Angelo put one finger across his lips. Gee studied him, poured, drank and began again.

"It's raining sleet and all kind of miserable shit like a son of a bitch. Like late November. Paul had just died. Your girl Alice hadn't popped up out of wherever she was. I don't judge. Sal has already closed, but he comes back and tells me Summer Arpeggio called. She's got to talk to me. It's all emergency and hot flashes Sal says, totally Summer's style. She comes over. He brings her back where I'm doing the count. She's wetter than a seal in water. I give her a drink. Two. Three. Then I cut her off. She's upset. She's in pain. She's having a heart attack. A baby. A brain hemorrhage. I don't know. I'm thinking if she don't settle down, I'm gonna shoot her. This is not a scene for me. I yell for Sal, but he's already gone. Then she says, 'I shot Trip Limone.' And I say, 'When did you do that?' That's what I say. Not how, why, or where but when? I mean I already know the why. Trip. He was the kind of kid that should have been shot out of the chute. Then I say, 'Was it a lethal shooting?' 'Yeah,' she says. 'I need you to get Dino Kim to pick him up and put him in the incinerator.' I mean she didn't say that right out but that's what she wanted from me. So, I go back to asking why did you kill him and she says, 'He said I stole his old man's money.'

I didn't ask if she did because I already figured she had clipped Paul. Everybody knew it. But I did ask how much? And she says, 'Trip thinks it was about a half a million.' I know Trip wouldn't believe that because I didn't. More like two mil, maybe three, most probably ten. Paul wasn't a small-time thief. He went large. He went from auctioning off damaged cargo to lifting entire boxes and putting them up on what he called auction. That's when only the chosen few get a bid. He also borrowed big time and just paid the vig. He didn't need to borrow but why not if the lenders wanted to lend? He Ponzi schemed the big banks on collateral loans. So, I say to Summer, 'So, you told him you ran through it all and there wasn't a dime left? And she nods. 'I told him there was a couple of thousand' That he doesn't believe. She's living a piss ant's life so how could she have gone through all that money? So, she says that's why I'm living this piss ant's life because I only scammed thousands. But he ain't buying that. She's got it and she stole it and it's his so hand it over. She then says, `At that point, he made the mistake of putting his hands on me and I told him this wasn't the 8th grade and so I took my Glock out of the desk drawer and he looked at me and laughed and I shot him.' She says so she shot him a couple more times."

"The way she shot Jessica Marune."

"I don't know her. I don't care about anybody with that kind of name. Summer. She's a ... "

"A shooter?"

"Poor self-image. She spent too much time with Piccolino when she was supposed to be growing up. Besides Carmine brought her up wrong. I mean he was around when she was growing up. That ruined her. That's why I tell you you're lucky your father didn't hang around. "

"Did Picco know she killed Trip? And she had the money? Paul's?"

"You're running out of story time. I told you I'm flagged in interest on all this. From when he was a kid, I thought your friend Picco had a short life thread. Trip, too. You're the only one ... "

"Yeah, the prince. Keep going. The story."

"So, our shooter, she wants the favor. You know with Dino. At that time, Dino's funereal enterprise is going into the toilet and stupid me, I got a big stake in it, and I'm going in the toilet with the bar, so I make Summer a business proposition. She salvages the funeral home and the bar, and she gets a stake in both. Dino takes care of the body. Cremates and as a ... what is it? Compassionate thing he puts Trip's ashes underneath Paul's body."

"You're kidding me. You mean, when Alice was at the Wake?"

"Yeah, he was right up there in the casket. Spread of ashes under his old man."

He poured for them.

"End of story. I'd give you a lift, but I ran out of my word limit and you're full of questions. You want to yap more, go on *Spacebook*."

"Just one. Why tell me? I mean, besides you being my father?"

"You got a choice between me and not knowing, I'd go with not knowing. Besides, I found my kid. He too had a short life thread. That's on me. Yours is this: You can get your sweetheart, Alice doing something hot and nasty with Trip out of your mind.

The guy is dead and buried. That's what my story did for you. Capisce?"

CHAPTER THIRTY

TAKING THE BOAT OUT TOMORROW

"Aunt Rita is in the back. She wants to talk to you. You know, Ange, if she was your aunt … "

"Can it, Sal. Anything new since I've been gone?"

"You heard about Sailor being seen back there in the Bay living on his boat? Let's see, I also heard there's a new Cecily Darden Pearl book just out. *Pearl Goes to Brooklyn.* A guy who can't read told me that and I never seen the book. I usually wait for the movie. You think I might be in it? Tanya looked into the future and she saw someone like Alice eating at *The Red Lobster.* Could or could not have been her. Mr. Mensch doesn't believe there will be any more lobsters in the future. We will have exterminated them. Tanya … you know Lady Aquavilla, says she didn't see a scary little white girl look like the mother anywhere in the future and that the mother was enough for her. So, I guess that settles it regarding the existence of the daughter. Tanya's going around saying Alice put a spell on Angelo Bari. You apparently ain't ever gonna be the same, to which I disagreed. I never seen you change, Ange. Not even the shirt. It's Connolly's opinion that Alice, Trip and Sailor went for the gold. Couldn't find it and Sailor twisted their necks, like he did those guys in Summer's office, and dropped them in the Atlantic. Or, they did find it and he twisted their necks. Anyway, lots of neck twisting."

"Is that all of it?"

"I'm thinking. Oh, Balsio says Sailor is back because he figured Alice was nuts and he ran. Or she figured he was nuts and she ran.

You know, sailed away or whatever. Eve Solly, who is out of jail on the profanity rap, doesn't think Trip was with them. Ever. Because he's been dead a long time. Oh, yeah. That mogul Bellator? Some kind of blood clot …. He got shot, didn't he? Went to his brain."

"He's dead?"

"Yeah, I think so. Maybe. It's hard to say when they got so much money. They put pockets in the shroud. He may buy his way out of it. Oh, yeah, we did a poll here at the bar last week. Strongly in favor: Alice came out of the rabbit hole for a time and then she went back in."

"Next time I ask you to tell me anything, don't tell me a fucking thing, Sal."

"Just trying to keep you updated. Oh, Ange. Your aunt in the back. She's packing. That's just an FYI."

"Of course, I saw her. Alice in Wonderland? Whatya think? I let her in. Brought her right up to the bed. Put a gun in her hand. Told her to pull the trigger. Summer was mumbling all her sins. Drunk. Bang! But you couldn't hear it. Right through. Then she was bleeding. I got my niece out of there, put her in a cab, called the cops told them a bunch of gangsters had come in and put a few bullets in Summer. I'm protecting Alice. I'm a true aunt to my niece. Alice loves me."

Angelo felt frozen. Words can freeze you he thought. He looked at Aunt Rita for the first time. She was packing. This woman was dangerous? She killed Summer that was for sure. Alice wouldn't step on a roach.

"She didn't want to leave everything to me. But I got it. It's in the will. She signed it. But I got nothing. Gee took it all."

"Before I hear any more of this crap Aunt Rita, I want you to put your gun on the table where I can see it."

"My niece with the eyes. She did the shooting. Revenge shooting. For Trip. My nephew. She found out Summer killed Trip. Thomas was what Alice called him."

Angelo lost track of the square he was squaring. It all went screwy.

But Aunt Rita was still talking.

"Flow of bodies. In and out. Hard to miss. She was a bad lawyer. Bad bookkeeper. I shuffled the money to the safe zones. She wasn't a good niece. And I went out for veal parm just to make her happy. But she wasn't grateful. Nothing worse than an ungrateful relative.

Then, I figured, I'd rather she be dead, and I'd inherit. Summer. She wasn't a good niece."

"The gun. I'm not going to ask again."

Summer's Glock suddenly appeared in her hand.

"Here's where you can help your Aunt Rita. Gee took all the money. I want that money. It's mine."

"Why tell me? Putting a gun in my face is a help here?"

"Alice is happy now with her Aunt Rita. She's warm and cozy but I got her."

"Where?"

"Her fingerprints are on the gun. I'll turn her in."

"You killed Summer."

"All you have to do, nephew, is that when Gee dies, and everything goes to you ... "

"What the hell are you talking about?"

"Summer made out the will. Gee left everything to you. You have it. Your Aunt Rita has it. It will make you and Alice very happy. You want to be happy with Alice, don't you, Trip?"

Angelo shuffled in his chair. It felt like he had reached his tolerance level for craziness.

"You gonna kill Gee, is that it? By the way, I'm Angelo."

"He fell off a barstool. Down the stairs. Hit his head. On the stairs. In the shower. He slipped. A tree fell on him. He had to run too long, and his heart stopped. A car hit him. He took the wrong meds. Ice made his brain freeze. Who cares? Your father is a thief."

"Shut up with the crazy. I want to see Alice. I don't think you have her. I don't think she was even there. I don't think she ever came back."

"There's a gun with her fingerprints. Maybe she's gone now. The gun isn't."

She giggled, or what Angelo thought was a giggle, but it could have been something else.

Angelo sat there looking at crazy Aunt Rita. Then at the gun. It didn't really matter if Crazy here had Alice or didn't. have her. Wherever Alice was now or had been, the cops would find her, match the prints and send her up for Summer's murder. Then it could be Crazy here didn't have a gun with Alice's fingerprints on it. Maybe nothing she was telling him was the truth. Maybe Aunt Rita was talking the kind of talk that hadn't an ounce of real in it. The thing is, as Sailor would say, there are no things here. Just a mind gone off its reel. Just a sad lady that lost her niece who wasn't really her niece and she got tired of going out for sandwiches.

Why wasn't that reason enough when there was never any reason in the room? Whatever mess went on in people's heads just sometimes let reason visit for a while, like a visit from something fantastical or lunatic. Or Aunt Rita here. Everything that made any sense in Aunt Rita's head had fragged and couldn't be defragged. Like Alice's head. Picco, Trip, Summer, Gee, Jessica, Marune, Bellator, Grew. And Alice. Everybody he knew. An endless fucking list. He wasn't good at finding any meaning in any of that. He was a short grift low return player. And there wasn't anything that made sense in being that. He didn't know what sense Dr. Grew, the Commander, made but if he had walked off with even one million grifting had been a good answer for him. And whether it was for Alice also. …

"I like this place," Aunt Rita told him, looking around.

He did too. He saw Sal in the shadows. He wondered if she had seen him too.

"I'm going home. Good night, Aunt Rita."

He got up, ready to feel the bullet but he gave that thought, and the bullet, a fuck you and walked back to the bar.

"How am I gonna get home?" she called after him.

Sounded like she was crying.

"Sal, get Aunt Rita a cab."

"Right away, Ange. I got a shot poured."

What seemed like hours later, Sal was escorting Aunt Rita to the door. When he came back, he pulled her gun out of his pocket.

"Custom compact .45," Sal said. "Damn, Ange, I couldn't believe what I was hearing. She was gonna shoot you. How did you know she wasn't gonna shoot you? I wonder if she was gonna kill Gee. I wonder if she does have Alice locked up somewhere?"

"Taking the boat out tomorrow, Sal. Early. If you wanna come."

ABOUT THE AUTHOR

Joseph Phillip Natoli was born and graduated in egg creams, the Dodgers, Steeplechase boardwalk and stickball Brooklyn, now has a website www.josephnatoli.com, is a contributing writer for *Counterpunch*, oil paints on self-stretched canvas boats or houses. *Between Dog & Wolf and On a Lee Shore* complete a trilogy, the *New Utrecht Avenue trilogy*, begun with *Get Ready to Run*. Some characters die, some reappear.

www.ingramcontent.com/pod-product-compliance
Lightning Source LLC
Chambersburg PA
CBHW030737110726
47900CB00008B/2342